KERRY CRISLEY

Summer of Georgie

Dear Reader—

This book is a thinly-veiled retelling
of the way many women were fired
by Bill cummings ("Frank") from both
cummings Foundation and cummings
properties. I know because I, too,
watched female colleagues get fired
left and right before his sights were set
on me, by the woman doing his
dirty work, "vera". Enjoy.

LAZY
SUNDAY
BOOKS

For John, the cream in my coffee, the bubbles in my seltzer.

Acknowledgment

Publishing a novel has been a dream of mine for decades, long before the seed of *Summer of Georgie* planted itself. I'm forever grateful to the supportive and talented people who were with me for all or part of this journey.

To my mom, for being my longest-serving and fiercest cheerleader, and for her unwavering conviction that I could, in fact, write a novel, even when – or *especially* when – I didn't believe it myself.

To my dad, for showing me how writing a novel while working full-time was done, and for bringing me into his writer's group. *Summer of Georgie* is far better with his input – and that of fellow group members Henry Dane, Rose Cummings, Janet Fantasia and Maura Greene – than it would be on its own.

To my editor, Alyssa Matesic, who challenged me to grow my story when I was utterly and completely convinced I couldn't write another word.

At its core, this book is about women supporting women. I am blessed to have so many strong, talented, kind, and witty women in my life. To my beta readers, Deirdre, Julie, Kelly, Lisa and Sara. Thank you for your insight, your encouragement, your endless supply of hilarious texts, and your decades of friendship. I am not me without you! To my beloved book club – Dawn, Debbie, Kate, Kim, Michelle, Rachel and Sara – reading, running, and road-tripping wouldn't be nearly as much fun without all of you, my Vixens!

Finally, thank you to John, Ben and Erin, who let me sit (mostly uninterrupted) at the dining room table as I made my dream a reality, one keystroke at a time. There's no one I'd rather share my life with than you.

Chapter 1

Prologue

"To new adventures!" Jules proposes, raising her martini. Tess, Nora, Natalie, and I do the same, clinking our glasses and causing tiny ripples of cosmopolitan to surge precariously close to the rim.

"To happy children," adds Tess, smiling at me.

"Happ*ier*, at least," I say. "I'll settle for not riddled with anxiety. Not failing any subjects would be a nice little bonus, too." Next to me, Jules presses her shoulder gently against mine for a moment in support.

I take a sip of the cocktail and shudder. "Oh my God, that's strong."

"We're in a sports bar," Jules reminds me. "If it isn't on tap, it's too complicated."

"How are you, Georgie?" Nora asks, leaning forward. Her eyes are sharp and interested, searching mine with concern. "Was it hard leaving today?"

Leaving. As in my job. The lovely and serene museum where I've been working for well over a decade. Had. Where I *had* been working until today. I consider Nora's question.

1

Was it hard? Am I sad? If I am, is it sadness for me or for my son, struggling with autism and the trifecta of a new school, growing pains, and little assholes for classmates?

For months now, Max's panic attacks over his first year of middle school had become so acute that they had consumed our family's morning routine, making my and Dan's train commute into Boston impossible to maintain. It didn't help that the museum required weekly late nights for board meetings and member events: nights when I came home to a tearful son with a stack of unfinished homework, an aggravated husband, and a daughter retreating into YouTube.

After spending the bulk of my working life in relative contentment, I came to understand the term "rat race." I was exhausted, worried, and easily triggered. Dan and I were snapping too quickly and too often at each other, and taking our daughter Shannon's good grades and calm nature for granted. Dan had the higher salary and better health benefits, so it made more sense for me to look for something closer to home that afforded me quicker access to Max's school when needed, far fewer late nights, and a commute not wedded to a train schedule. The solution presented itself as an opening in Hudson Hotel's Communications and Foundation Department, located within its flagship hotel and conference center a short drive from my house.

I know Nora is asking if I'm still confident in my decision to take a new job with less responsibility (and pay); if I'm making my own happiness a priority. The truth is, I have no idea. Was it hard to leave the museum? Meh. I'll miss the people, sure. And the setting. But did I love the work? Did I bound out of bed on Monday mornings, ready to take on the world? No. I never have. In any job, actually.

What does *my* happiness have to do with it right now, anyway?

I shrug and smile at Nora. "I'm fine, Nor. A little excited for the change, actually."

"What will you be doing at Hudson?" Natalie asks.

"Your typical communications stuff mostly," I say. "Newsletters, press releases, social media, that kind of thing. The part I'm excited about is working on their annual charity event, the bike ride."

Jules turns to me. "Wait. Didn't you tell me about this job like a year ago? When that head hunter called you?"

I nod. "Yes. I never applied, though."

"So it's been open for a year?"

I shake my head. "No, they filled it, but I guess the guy left."

Nora raises her perfect eyebrows. "Already? That's a bit of a red flag."

I shrug again. "There's a hundred different reasons to leave a job after a short time. I'm not worried." I neglect to mention that the job I'm stepping into was posted *again* just a few months ago. *That* hire apparently didn't last long, either.

The opening bars to Right Said Fred's "I'm Too Sexy" float above the din of the happy hour crowd. Jules squeals and gets up. "Dance, Georgie!"

"There's no dance floor," I point out, sliding off my stool anyway.

"We'll improvise."

We clink glasses again and groove right at the table. I *am* happy about the new job, I decide.

And anyway, how bad could it be?

∞∞∞

Eighteen months later

All I'm trying to do is dial a damn phone.

When I attempt to hit five, my finger presses seven. I start over in frustration. Six, six, five – *fuck.* Seven again. And the next time. Furious, I smash my phone on the concrete sidewalk and move to grind it to dust under my shoe. I miss – of course – and my foot leaves the curb. The sense of falling jolts me awake.

I'm in bed, on my right side and facing the window. I lie there, sensing, listening, remembering. My pulse is fast, throbbing in my chest, my ears, and my throat.

That was the saddest anxiety dream ever. Girl, even your dreams *need work.*

The clock on my dresser reads 5:36. I could try to doze off again, but these days it's unlikely. Instead, I get up and pad to the bathroom, careful not to wake Dan. Cupping my hands under the faucet I take in a few sips of water, flooding the desert determined to take up residence in my mouth. In the mirror above the sink, my reflection is glum. Her mascara's smudged and her dark blonde hair needs a trim.

Lookin' good, my internal judge and jury whispers.

"What's up with you?" I whisper back at the mirror. "You never used to be this mean."

Well, you *used to actually remove your makeup before bed*, she reasons.

I give her the finger and stalk away, pausing in front of Max's door. I ease it open and survey the room. Yesterday's clothes are strewn inside out across the blue carpet. His hamper is overflowing. On the desk, however, his orange camouflage backpack is neatly zipped, filled with completed homework

4

and ready for school. Max himself is an unmoving hump in the center of the bed, dark brown hair peeking out from under his comforter, his breathing even. He'll wake rested and calm, as he usually does now. The opposite of me.

I push the last thought away and tiptoe downstairs to the kitchen. The coffeemaker isn't programmed to start brewing for another 20 minutes. I press "start," reassured by its familiar clicks and gurgles, and wander into the family room. I sit crosslegged on the sofa, staring at nothing.

Fine, my inner bully sighs. *If you* must *sulk, do it now. Then suck it up and get on with your day.*

On the sofa next to me is a pink hooded sweatshirt of Shannon's. I grab it and press the soft cotton to my face, stifling my hiccuping sobs. I cry for five minutes, then wipe my eyes, smearing tears and day-old mascara onto the cloth.

"Right. Now coffee," I say out loud, then stare down at Shannon's sweatshirt. "And maybe a load of laundry."

Upstairs there are footsteps. A toilet flushes. The day is on.

I get up, arrange my face into the mask I've been wearing for months, and head for the kitchen.

Half an hour later I'm back in Max's room. He's still in bed. "Max, get *up*," I say. "There's 25 minutes 'til the bus."

No response. I grab the corner of his comforter and slide it off his face. His eyes are closed. He is curled up on his side, the quintessential picture of the angelic-looking sleeping child. And it's all B.S.

"Ooooo," I whisper, leaning in and pushing a lock of brown hair off his forehead. "I have an idea." I trace my finger along his forehead and pause. "I think I'll give him a little tattoo right….here." He smiles, turning his face into the pillow to hide it.

"Come on," I say, giving him a few slaps on his hip. "Up, up, up."

He sits up and yawns extravagantly. "What's for breakfast?"

"Eggs."

"No," he says, a little too quickly. "Grilled cheese."

"OK."

Max looks up. "Really?"

"Sure," I say as I walk out of his room. "Grilled cheese. With egg and a little bacon."

"With bacon and A LITTLE EGG," he shouts down the stairs.

"Get today's clothes from your drawer, NOT THE FLOOR," I call back. I stop, causing a family of dust bunnies to skitter over the step. "Not the hamper, either!"

Downstairs, Shannon is sitting at the small breakfast bar munching on cereal and taking an online quiz with my phone. Where Max is an immature 12, Shannon is a wiser than her years 10.

I refill my coffee cup, and retrieve the provolone and butter from the fridge. "Are you a Miranda or a Charlotte?" I ask her.

"Huh?"

"Never mind."

She looks back at my phone, nearly dipping a chunk of her long blonde hair into the cereal milk. "No. I'm going to find out where we should go on vacation this summer based on how I decorate my apartment."

"Awesome. Keep me posted." I start to butter two slices of sourdough bread and turn to Dan, who is scrambling the eggs. "He's up. Bacon, egg, and cheese sandwich."

Dan plops a spatula full of egg onto the bread. "I'm a short order cook."

6

"You're just noticing this now?" I ask, winking at him as I place Max's sandwich on the heated pan.

"Paris!" Shannon announces triumphantly, holding up my phone. "We're going to Paris, guys."

Max leaps into view from the dining room, clad in a (relatively) clean t-shirt and shorts. "G-Fest!"

Dan pauses. "G what?"

"G-Fest. Godzilla Fest in Chicago. *That's* where we should go."

"Sit, King Ghidorah," I tell Max and slide his sandwich onto a plate. I grab his prescription bottle and shake it at him, the pills clattering inside like maracas. "Take your pill, too, OK?"

"Hey mom, if we won the lottery, could we go to G-Fest?" Max asks, starting one of our favorite mealtime conversations.

"Yes," I say definitively. "We'd fly first class, and stay in the largest, nicest room in the whole hotel, and you would get any figure you wanted, no matter how much it cost."

"And then," Shannon picks up the thread. "We'd go to Paris and ride to the top of the–" she pauses to consult my phone. "Eiffel Tower!"

I turn back to the stove as Dan joins the kids at the breakfast bar to make plans for our imaginary future. *Right*, I think. *Chicago and Paris. With my 22 hours of vacation.*

At the thought of work, a small knot forms in my gut. *My sizable gut*, the criticism comes before I can stop it. It'd been coming a lot since discovering early on that my job move was a profoundly bad one. *How much have you gained this year, Georgie? Ten pounds? Twelve? Is it worth it? The weight? The pay cut? Lena? The complete and utter misery?*

"Oh, shut up," I mutter quietly to my inner commentator, shifting the pan on the stovetop so Dan can't hear me. *At least it's Friday. And yes, you asshole. As a matter of fact, it* is *worth it.*

I give my head a small shake and turn around, smiling. "And then, we would find a beautiful house on a lake and spend the rest of the summer in it. Nothing but swimming, kayaking, and paddle boarding all day." I pause. "Except if it rains. Then we'd have movie marathons or read on the porch. Because there would definitely be a screened porch."

Shannon gets up from her stool and puts her empty bowl in the sink. "Would we invite Nana and Bop Bop?"

I place my hands on her small shoulders and plant a kiss on the top of her head. "Well, *duh*," I say. "Of *course* we invite Nana and Bop Bop!"

"Better stock up on gin," Dan offers, goading me.

"Helpful," I say, swatting him on the shoulder.

Dan turns back to Max. "Ready for your science test?"

He nods, chewing a bite of his sandwich. "Mom helped me study last night."

His confidence buoys me. A scrap of goodness I can hang on to until five o'clock.

The next few minutes are a blur. Locating socks (Max's), signing a field trip form (Shannon's), arguing over who gets the last snack size bag of popcorn (Shannon), and triple-checking the presence of the homework folder in the backpack (Max's).

"I'll be back in a few minutes," I call to Dan, as I gather my too-long hair into a ponytail. "Can we take a quick look at the summer camp schedule then?" He gives me the thumbs up on his way upstairs to shower.

Max, Shannon, and I step out the front door into the late spring sunshine. The morning is gorgeous, nudging my dark mood aside a little. The patch of phlox in the front yard is peppered with pink flowers. Along the front walk, the coreopsis buds haven't revealed their cheerful yellow blooms yet. *See?* I tell my inner critic. *That's another thing to look forward to, right?*

Meh. She sniffs, unimpressed.

When we reach his bus stop, Max is three minutes into his latest monologue, summarizing the plot of *Godzilla Destroy All Monsters* with the laser focus and precision that his particular place on the autism spectrum affords him.

I wave to him as he crosses to the other side of our street, then Shannon and I continue on for the quarter mile walk to her elementary school.

"I don't *want* to go to summer camp," she mumbles, head down. Clearly she'd caught Dan's reference to the camp schedule.

"I thought you liked the horse riding camp," I say, lamely. A weak attempt at dodging the real issue.

"That's just one week," she clarifies. "Then I'm in that stupid camp at school. I *hate* spending the whole summer at my school."

"It's not the whole summer," I reason. "We have the week in Vermont, and you'll be at Nana and Bop Bop's during the day during the first few days of summer *and* week of the fourth of July."

She shrugs as we turn the corner onto her school's street. Ahead of us, two backpack-laden kids wobble as they propel towards the school on scooters.

I look up at the sky and took a deep breath. "How many more days of school are there?"

Shannon perks up. "Twenty!"

"That's it? I can't believe you have just 20 days left of fourth grade. These are your last 20 days at Greenwood, *ever*. In

September you'll be on the bus with Max. It'll be fun. Aren't you excited?"

Shannon looks up at me, and I'm struck – as I always am – by the beautiful pale blue of her eyes. Dan's eyes. "It wasn't fun for Max."

My heart constricts. "No," I say lightly, waving a thank you to the crossing guard as we step off the curb. "It wasn't. But it's better now. And it doesn't mean that you will have the same experiences that Max did. You and Max are different."

She nods as we arrive at school, and are buzzed in to join the other students at before-school care. Quiet giggling drifts from the library door, while deeper into the building the thundering sound of feet and basketballs emanates from the gym.

"Who's picking me up?"

"Nana," I say. "We're having dinner at their house tonight."

"Can I skip before-school for the rest of the year? Can you just bring me at the regular time?"

I wink at her. "So you can sneak some more TV?"

She hides a smile. Busted.

I gaze down at my daughter, feeling the fierceness of my love for her, and give her a hug. "I think we can arrange that. Have fun today. I love you."

"Love you, too," she replies. "But I still don't want to go to camp all summer." She walks to meet her classmates in the library, her backpack suddenly seeming enormous on her 10-year old shoulders.

∞∞∞∞

Dan is upstairs in the home office when I get back. The room is small, painted a pale salmon color with a muted gray striped rug covering most of the hardwood floor. On the walls hang a vintage, black and white photograph of a Tour de France mountain stage, and a framed *Rushmore* film poster, which until last summer had hung in my previous office on Boston's Beacon Hill.

Along most of one wall is a two-person workstation. The theory behind the idea (Dan's) was for it to be a place where Max and Shannon could do homework. In reality, the surface is perpetually covered in paper. Junk mail, bills, those endlessly annoying four-page "Explanation of Benefits" forms that follow every physical, sick visit, and dentist appointment. ATM and grocery receipts are stuffed inside a short cylinder which is supposed to be for pens. The pens, instead, are…I don't really know, actually.

Dan is on the opposite side of the room, at an intricate roll-top desk made of honey-colored oak he inherited from his dad. The ornate piece should conflict with the sleek workstation, but it doesn't. Or if it does, no one has had the nerve to tell me. And I probably wouldn't care if they did. This desk is where we keep our laptop, our printer, and our checkbook. Dan sits on one of the office's hard plastic wheeled office chairs from Ikea. These chairs, in fact, *do* contrast with the rest of the office. Life is flawed.

I have a love-hate relationship with the office. After years of watching much younger couples on TV purchase enormous homes with luxuries completely foreign to me – like guest bathrooms and man caves – I love being able to say phrases like "my home office" and "it's up in the office." It feels grown-up, like I've made it. Which, at 46, is a long time coming.

But I quietly hate the clutter. The tsunami of paper screams "Fraud! Fake adult!" Dan claims to despise the mess as much as I do, but not for a moment do I believe that he links it in any way to his adult credentials.

"Hey," Dan says, standing up and swiveling the chair in my direction. He's freshly showered, and dressed in his boxer briefs and dress shirt. His dark brown hair is still air drying, causing the ends to flip up slightly. "I queued up the summer spreadsheet."

"There's a spreadsheet? No way," I say. Dan is one of a team of accounting managers sorting through billable hours at a law firm in Boston. There's always a spreadsheet.

He pauses, not sure if my teasing is good natured or annoyed, and appears to go with good natured. Which it is, this time. "I've got to be on the 8:20 train, but take a look. I have it laid out in chronological order by week, with the deposits paid and the balance owed, and the start and end times for both kids."

I walk over to take his place in front of the computer, and step on a plastic binder clip on the rug with my bare foot. "Fuck!" I yelp, hopping onto my other foot. I spot the offending clip and kick it under the workstation. "God damn binder clips are the Legos of the office world. This room, Dan. Seriously."

"Just sit down, will you? We only have a few minutes."

A surge of irritation courses through me, sharp and hot. *Is an "are you OK?" too much to ask?* I swallow it and sit down. I'm not looking for a fight.

I take a look at the spreadsheet.

"How the hell are we supposed to get Shannon to the stable and Max to zombie apocalypse camp?" I say, peering closer

12

to the screen. "They start at the same time and are 15 miles apart. What is it with camps starting at nine and ending at three? That's enormously convenient for working parents." The pit in my stomach creeps back. *Fraud! Fake adult!*

"I know," agrees Dan. "Shuttling to and from is going to be…interesting. Let's talk to your parents tonight. They can probably help. And we'll hire a sitter."

"Or," I reason. "I could drop Max off at the Hudson Hotels. He can do my job and I'll take his place at zombie camp. I would *rock* zombie camp. I know exactly how to survive the apocalypse. I'd –"

"Focus." Dan nods to the screen.

I turn back to the computer. "So these summer camps are costing us, what, four thousand bucks? Ish?"

He nods. "About that, yeah. Plus the cost of the sitter we'll have to hire to bring them."

I roll my head in a slow circle to ease the tension out of my neck. "Huh. An extra couple of hundred a week to hire a sitter to bring my children to camps they hate while I get flagellated at work. Yeah, that tracks."

Dan's eyes crinkle in empathy, and I secretly forgive him for the binder clip mishap. "I know, Georgie. It sucks. But it's helped. It's really helped." He searches my face for another few seconds, then stands up. "I gotta finish getting ready."

"But you look fine," I say, staring pointedly at his bare legs. "I like the black socks. Wear them with your Tevas."

I close down the laptop and head to the bathroom to shower. An upside of my current job is the added time I have in the morning to get ready. With just a 10-minute drive, I can focus on the kids first and then relish the quiet of the house during the half hour grace period between dropping Shannon off and leaving for the hotel.

I lather my hair, thinking about what I have to do at the hotel's Communications Department today. It's Friday, so the weekly newspapers will have run the most recent round of press releases. There will be media tracking logs to update, stories to share in our social media outlets, and one or two to include in the newsletter, which I also have to finish today. There's also a meeting today on logistics for our annual charity bike ride in September.

And reporting on any new book sales for your fearless leader, Frank. That comes before everything else!

"Are you going to be with me all day, Grouchy Gilda?" I ask the voice out loud.

That's up to you, she says.

"What?" Dan's head appears through the slightly open door.

"Nothing. I'm talking to myself."

"Oh. Anything good?"

"Porn monologues. I'm just getting to the good part, too."

"Dang, just when I have to leave," he grins. "I'm heading out. Have fun smashing the patriarchy."

I laugh and blow him a kiss. "See you tonight."

Turning the water off, I slide the shower door open and grab two towels. I twist my hair up in one and use the other to dry off before wrapping it around me for the handful of steps to the bedroom. Robes are for Real Housewives. Dan has left my "getting ready coffee" on my dresser. Half and half, with a drop of maple syrup. I sip it and open my closet door, surveying the array of white and navy. My eyes fall on a pair of white capris.

It's going to be humid later; you won't want any buttons pinching at your waist. They've gotten a little snug.

14

"True. Good call, Gilda. And *thanks*," I mutter, and select a navy and white striped skirt with a comfortable elasticized waist. "And my favorite white sleeveless blouse is clean, too. Woo hoo!" I glance out the window to make sure none of my neighbors are outside to hear me.

You're nuts, Gilda says. *But in a good way.*

"Back atcha," I say, slipping into a pair of black low-heeled sandals.

I finish my coffee as I look into my jewelry box, finally deciding on the silver chain with the starfish and Nantucket basket charms that Dan gave me a few anniversaries back. I pair it with silver hoops and the fun, quirky, silver and green sea glass ring that I impulsively bought for myself on a weekend trip to Cape Cod.

I give myself a final glance in the mirror.

"T.G.I.F," I tell myself. "Thank God I'm Fabulous."

I almost buy it.

∞∞∞

As I'm about to pull out of my driveway, the sounds of "I'm Too Sexy" fill the front seat. Jules.

I pick up. "Hiya, Jules. Are you doing your 'little turn on the catwalk'?"

She laughs. "You haven't changed that yet?"

"Never." I tap the speaker icon and continue out of my driveway. "You were pretty insistent that night that it should be your assigned ringtone 'forever and ever'," I say, deliberately turning up my Northeast accent. *Fuh-evah and evah.*

"I still blame you."

"Not the martinis?"

15

"You gave them to me. And you know what they say about martinis."

"I don't," I say. "Enlighten me."

"They're like breasts."

"Are they?"

"Of course. One's not enough, and three's too many."

I laugh. "You're better than morning radio, my love. What's going on, Jules Martin-not-martini?"

"A couple of things. First, I'm hosting book club two weeks from today. Anytime after seven."

"Great. Is there anything special you want me to bring? Martinis?"

"Funny. Whatever strikes your fancy, dearest," Jules says. "Next topic: are you still trying to get in touch with that book blogger?"

"The Book Prophet? Yes." I sit up higher in my seat. "Wait. You didn't. Did you?"

"Bembé Jean-Baptiste," says Jules. The tapping of her keystrokes filters through the speaker. "I was right; one of the nurses here is friends with his wife. I have his contact info; I'm emailing it to you."

"Shut up! And it's OK if I reach out?"

"He's expecting you to."

I slap the steering wheel in my excitement. "Yes! Thank you! Thank you, thank you, thank you. You're the best, Jules."

"That's true," she replies. "How's everything else?"

I pause, weighing the pros and cons of being honest with my oldest friend versus sounding like a professional whiner. Jules and I have been friends since seventh grade, and have seen each other through layoffs (hers), miscarriages (mine), and the rest of the drama that comes with life between puberty and menopause. But this nugget of gold she's just given me has lifted my mood, and I feel almost optimistic.

"Pretty good. The kids have exactly 20 days left. Shannon's moaning a little about camp, but she'll be fine."

"And Max?"

"Still good. He's not constantly trying to get out of going to school. He might even make honor roll this quarter. *That* will be a first."

"Aww, that's great," says Jules. "Now tell me an 'Ebenezer Gates' story that I can share with my assistant. The stingy philanthropist details just kill her."

"OK," I instinctively look around, as if expecting to find a colleague riding quietly in the backseat. "This week I got in trouble for having the wrong kind of Post-it Note."

"There's a wrong kind of Post-it?"

"Of course," I explain. "We're only allowed to use those wicked small ones. Like, they're an inch and a half by two inches?"

"They're 1 ⅜ inches by 1 ⅞ inches," she says. "Shit. I said that out loud, didn't I? I can't believe I know that."

"Nerd. Anyway, I attached one that was bigger than that to Frank's book sales report, and he came over to my desk to ask where I got it. I thought he was talking about the numbers, so of course I start going into the process of how I pull from all the sites where we're selling his memoir, and then he pulls off the Post-it and waves it at me, saying, 'No, where did you get *this*?' Apparently Purchasing is only allowed to order the smallest size, because anything larger is a waste of money. And as Frank puts it, 'If you can't fit everything you need to say on it, then you should be having a conversation, not a correspondence.'"

17

Jules chuckles. "And how much in salary did the time he took to walk over and personally investigate this black market Post-it cost?"

"The thing is, I get his reasoning; a lot of the hotel's profits go to the foundation, yada yada yada. But he was just such a *tool* about it."

"Yeah," replies Jules. "Ebenezer Gates."

I laugh. "OK, love. I'm getting closer to work, so I need my final few minutes of zen. Thank you for the Bembé hook up. You've made my day so much more bearable."

"I'm glad. See you in two weeks, if not sooner."

I hang up and drive the last few minutes in silence, replaying the conversation with Frank. *What a strange place*, I think, as the navy and white double "H" logo comes into view.

Hudson Hotels. The New England chain was somewhat of a fixture of my childhood. When I was growing up, my parents were more cottage-renters than hotel-stayers, but one Hudson property or another always seemed to signify a milestone of sorts during long car rides, marking the home stretch in the journey to my grandparents' house on Cape Cod, or the halfway point in the ride north to a New Hampshire lake.

I'd been here nearly 18 months. At first, the relief was palpable. A shorter commute not dependent to train schedules, extra wiggle room in the morning and evening to manage Max's anxiety and schoolwork, and more time and mental energy to give to Shannon.

And it helped, I think. *Everyone's happier*.

Everyone but you, challenges Gilda. *Maybe now it's time to leave Crazytown?*

"We'll talk when Shannon hits fifth grade," I mumble, pulling

18

into the space in the lot that I'd come to think of as mine.

I see Lena's sky blue Mini Cooper a few rows in front of me and mentally ready myself for the day.

"Book sales, media hits, newsletter, and Bembé," I say, willing my light mood to return. "Bembé, Bembé, Bembé."

Leaving the peace and safety of my silver Honda, I turn to the hotel and make my way inside.

Let the micromanaging begin.

Chapter 2

"**A**hoy, thank you for calling Hudson Hotels, how may I direct your call?"

Mei, the seemingly effortlessly cheerful reception desk attendant, waves to me as I step through the glass front doors. Giving my skirt a pointed look, she stands up to model her own outfit. Having inadvertently worn identical dresses – like six-year-old twins – last fall, the morning once-over is our private joke. Spoiler alert: she wore it best.

While the hotel's housekeeping, maintenance, and catering/dining staff have branded uniforms, corporate colleagues do not. However, Frank decided (on a whim, not surprisingly) a few years back that everyone on his team should "look the part," and instituted a navy-and-white dress code for office staff. The palette is a nod to his love of sailing, and the theme is the anchor (see what I did there?) of the hotels' overall aesthetic. Vintage nautical charts and art deco travel posters adorn the lobby and common areas, accented here and there by large, clear vases filled with layers of sand, sea glass, and pebbles rubbed smooth by the ocean.

The walls are a soft white, drawing more attention to the colorful artwork, and the carpets are patterned in beachy shades of pale blues, greens, and gold. Instead of Muzak, a seaside soundtrack of gentle waves and bird life plays quietly over the din of employees and guests.

It's a pleasing setting – perhaps aiding in Mei's constant state of contentment – and one that I hate to leave behind as I open the frosted glass door to the offices. Where the lobby is airy and filled with sunshine, the offices are a landscape of beige. Way, way too much beige. It's on the walls, the cubicle partitions, and the carpet. Around me, as always, is the constant buzz of cheap overhead lighting. The visual and audial assault screams warehouse overstock discount. Which, of course, is exactly where it all comes from.

I weave through the Sales and Accounting departments, nodding and waving hello to various coworkers, and round the corner to Communications. The door to Lena's office is closed, a recognizable sign of a Foundation conference call. Kyle, Lena's assistant and the third member of the department, is standing near his desk looking dapper and fresh in his white shirt and navy tie, a lock of hair flopping above his right eye. At six-foot-two and very lean, Kyle is the Mutt to my Jeff. We may look odd side by side, but we're a good team.

I glance at the whiteboard that hangs outside my cubicle wall. The trivia quote I posted yesterday, "I'm familiar with the fact that you are going to ignore this particular problem until it swims up and bites you in the ass!" is unanswered.

I look at Kyle. "Seriously? You don't know it?"

Kyle glances up at me and shakes his head.

I give him a sidelong glance. "I don't believe you."

"Seriously. I don't know it."

"'You're gonna need a bigger boat?' Does that help?"

"Oh! Yeah, I've heard that one. What's that from?"

"It's *Jaws*, you cretin. How do you not know that?"

He smiles. "You know I was born in '97, right?"

"Birth year is irrelevant. Max and Shannon have seen it, like, a hundred times already."

"I'm sorry to disappoint you. Can we go over the book sales stuff real quick?"

"In a minute," I say dropping my purse into the bottom drawer of my desk and sliding into my chair. "I'm going to need some time to sit here and quietly judge your parents."

As my computer is booting up, I dial into voicemail, certain that there will be at least two messages from Lena, left either last night or early this morning.

"Hi Georgie, this is Lena," the first message begins. "I was just talking to Frank, and he'd like to get the names and towns – and states, too, if they're out of state – of everyone who's bought the book. So if you could include a list of all names with today's sales report, that would be great, thanks!" The last two words, as always, go up a few octaves. "And then, going forward, just add the new names to the same list each morning. Thanks."

I jot *include names of book buyers in sales report* into my day planner and delete the message. I add *call Bembé* to the planner before advancing to the next message.

"Hi, it's Lena again..."

Duh, says Gilda.

"I just wanted to let you know that Frank has a few more edits to the book."

Of course he does.

"So please check in with him this morning and then get those over to graphics, and then call the printer and let them know that we'll be sending a new file for the next print run. I already left them a message last night telling them to stop the presses on the current version until he hears from you."

There's a pause, and then a deep sigh. *Uh-oh.* "And in the future, Georgie, please remember to always triple check with Frank before the next books are printed in case he has edits. Thanks."

"Did you really just say 'stop the presses'?" I mutter. "And I *did* check with him. At 4:59 pm last night."

Get F's edits to Graphics, I write. *Call Tom @ printers re: new PDF. Kill self and make look like accident.*

I hang up the phone and glance at the large, framed poster above my and Kyle's cubicles – the front cover of Frank Hudson's book. In it, he's beaming at the camera, relaxed and happy. Below the photo, the title *The Business of Giving It Away* appears in white font on a navy blue background. Identical posters hang in every elevator of every hotel, with instructions on how to order copies online.

A five-year labor of love, *Giving It Away* is Frank's most recent – and by far his most beloved – baby. Since the first self-published copies came out a few months ago, the chronicle of his humble beginnings, first hotel purchase, his attainment of millionaire status, and launching of the Hudson Foundation has dominated his time, and that of numerous other departments. Everything – from proofreading and design to marketing and order fulfillment – has been kept within the Hudson Hotel corporate team.

Where he can micromanage it, whispers Gilda. *And keep tweaking the copy.*

I peer over the cubicle wall at Kyle, who is – I'm proud to see – Googling "Jaws quotes."

"Pardon the interruption," I say, resting my forearms on the

23

partition and placing my chin on my hands. "Have you heard about the newest addition to the book sales report?"

"Yeah," he responds. "I was able to get the list of the ones who bought directly from us, but I didn't get the list off of the other sales channels yet."

"I can do that," I say, sitting back down and logging in. "Did any orders come in last night when he was on that radio program talking up the book?"

Kyle's voice brightens. "Actually, yes. About 30. And maybe more on other sites."

"Nice," I reply, looking at the screen. "It looks like we have more from Amazon. More than 50 total during his radio interview. He'll like that. Did you listen last night?"

"I did. I thought he was good." Kyle stands up, checks to make sure Lena's door is still shut and lowers his voice. "Did you notice that the only people to call in to the show were the ones we planted? Is that weird?"

I make a seesaw gesture with my hand. "Maybe a little, but I think that right now people know the hotel brand more than they do its founder. Frank hasn't made himself the focal point of any hotel marketing before the book. It felt a little bit staged, but not too bad." I smile. "And planted callers are better than angry former guests."

Kyle grins back at me, and lowers his voice again. "Why does Frank want the names of everyone who's bought the book?"

I shrug. "To feed his ego. To make sure that the friends and neighbors who promised to buy it actually have. To see if anyone *other* than his friends and neighbors have bought it. Pick one."

"It's kinda creepy."

"There's a certain ick factor there, yes," I agree, as I copy the list of buyers into the spreadsheet. I consider saying more, but leave it at that. I try – sometimes successfully – to minimize venting in front of Kyle. He's just a few months in, and not quite ready to be my grousing partner. No need to rush things. "Right-o. Thanks for adding the other buyers in already. Let me take a few minutes to format this and then it'll be ready for him."

I scan the list. Most of the few hundred people are local, with the odd West coast or Southeastern US address mixed in. I recognize many of the names: staff, heads of organizations that have received grants from the Hudson Foundation, and a few people who have volunteered for the charity bike ride.

Clicking "print," I reach for my contraband Post-it Note pad and start to draft a note pointing out the uptick in sales occurring during the radio broadcast, then pause.

You should be having a conversation, not a correspondence.

I toss the pad aside, scratch the sales report item from my planner's to do list, and collect the report from the printer. "Kyle, I'm running this over to Frank's office, and then I'm going to grab a coffee. Want anything?"

"I'm good," he says. "I bought a stash of pods last night at the grocery store after Lena slapped my wrist for taking a cup from the lobby."

This rankles me. The idea of telling a 20-something assistant making a 20-something salary that the hotel's coffee is only free for its guests is ludicrous.

No, it's cheap, says Gilda. *This place is cheap.*

This place is ten minutes from my house, I counter. *Let's move on.*

I give him a wry smile. "You're not the first, and you won't be the last. I'll be back in a bit. Would you be able to find a link to the radio show and share it on social media? And include a note on how the host said the book makes a great gift for graduates."

"Of course," says Kyle. "'You all know me; know what I do for a livin.'"

I give him a thumbs up as I walk away. "Atta boy."

∞∞∞

I knock lightly on the frame of Frank's open door and walk in. He's on the phone, but he gestures for me to stay and wait.

Frank's office was designed to make visitors wish they were him. The drab beige wall to wall carpet that covers the corporate offices is hidden beneath a gorgeous oriental rug, warming the room with its deep maroon tones. His desk is a sumptuous mahogany, and perpetually neat. Two antique wooden Windsor guest chairs rest in front of his desk. In a corner, a dark brown leather Chesterfield sofa, matching armchair, and coffee table form a comfortable nook for longer conversations.

On display in a long wooden curio cabinet are hundreds of small glass jars filled with sand. The colors range from various shades of pink, white, and gold to vivid red, muddy brown, and shimmering volcanic black. Some of the sand is fine as powder; in other jars it appear pebbly and rough. On each jar is a tiny, handwritten label identifying the beach. Jekyll Island in Georgia. Boiling Lake in Dominica. Na Pali coast in Kauai. All places where Frank has sailed – with empty jars stored in a box below deck – and scooped up a handful of memories once on shore. Tucked in here and there around the jars are pieces of antique nautical equipment: a sextant rusted from years of

26

salty air, a bronze lantern, and a brass sundial compass.

His walls are covered in photographs. Some are black and white images from decades ago: his childhood home, his mother serving as his hotel's first front desk attendant, and family vacations on Cape Cod. Another series of photos – these ones in color – show Frank and his army of friends and family on numerous sailboats and in various seas: the Caribbean, the Mediterranean, the Bering. Still others have captured Frank's penchant for adventure travel. Bungee jumping in New Zealand, completing the Camino de Santiago in Spain, coming nearly face to face with a leopard seal in Antarctica. Peppered among the photos are award plaques, commendations for Frank's philanthropy as well as his business acumen.

On one wall is a different series of images. In these, Frank is standing with his bike in front of a hotel, having just cycled there from the Hudson Hotel headquarters. As the chain expanded outward across New England, Frank proudly pedaled to each new location. The habit evolved as the business – and then the foundation – grew. If he could have sailed, he likely would have, but since you can't sail a sloop on a highway, he went with his next-favorite sport. Now, the annual event celebrating each year's round of grant recipients – schools, libraries, police departments, food pantries, and other social services organizations – kicks off with a number of concurrent charity bike rides, which depart from hotels that are 25, 50, and 100 miles away from the headquarters. It's a complicated, yet hugely popular and well-attended, event to pull off each year.

Seated behind his desk is the man himself. At 70, Frank Hudson exudes vitality and strength. His six-foot frame is lean, and his face is weathered in a way only obtained through years of being outdoors. *I've got stories to tell*, it seems to say.

His full head of steel gray hair is closely cropped and – like his desk – perpetually neat. I run my hand over my own already disheveled mane and tuck one side behind my ear as Frank ends his call.

"What did you think?" He's referring to the radio program, I deduce. *Good morning to you, too.*

"I thought it went really well," I say. "The host clearly read – and liked – the book, and I loved his comment on it being a good gift for graduates. We're highlighting that on social media." I hand him the sales report. "We had an uptick in sales last night while you were on the air."

"Really? How much?" He looks up at me.

"About 50 new orders."

He pauses. "That's a lot?" He looks at me, a challenge in his dark brown eyes. *Black eyes*, Gilda starts channeling Quint before I can stop her. *Lifeless eyes, like a doll's eyes.*

"Yes," I say with a confidence that I don't quite feel. "More than 50 in a single hour *is* a lot."

He taps the copy that's resting on top of his desk. A copy that, I now see, is flagged with at least two dozen Post-its (extra small ones!). "I just would have thought that with all the media coverage these last few weeks there would have been more buyers *and* more callers." He looks at me pointedly. "Clearly you're not reaching the right audience."

I let that one pass. "Well, there will be a lot of promotion this summer leading up the grant event. We're planning on including references to the book in all of our emails, newsletters, and summer advertising." *Plus*, adds Gilda, *you're not, you know, Oprah. Just sayin'.*

Shut up, I tell her. *Let me focus.*

"Well, it isn't enough. We need reviews," he says, more to himself than to me. "We need newspapers to run a review of the book."

I pause, not wanting to bring up The Book Prophet just yet. "I'm pitching some reviewers now in order to have something in time for the grant event," I begin. "And some of our former grant winners who received the complimentary copies have posted online reviews."

"They should *all* post reviews online," Frank says. "Actually, they should all be promoting it to their own members. Start keeping track of which groups have already written reviews of *Giving it Away*. Add that to the sales report. I want 100% participation. Reach out to all grantee organizations – all of them – and tell them to post a review, and then share the book with all of their members. They should be emailing their members directly, not just posting to their websites or social media pages. Though they should do that, too."

"I...I'll talk to Lena about that," I say, jotting notes down onto the pad I've learned to have handy when I enter Frank's office. *That's gross*, whispers Gilda. *Asking – no, telling – charities to pimp your memoir? That's just gross.*

I should *tell* him that I think it's gross. That by keeping tabs on who's promoting his memoir and who's not could be looked at as an abuse of the grantor/grantee relationship.

"Speaking of, I can bring those edits to Design and get a new PDF to the printer," I point to the marked up book.

Frank pushes the book toward me. "So when will we have the new copies?"

"We'll get the proof on Tuesday, and-"

"Monday," Frank says. "Tell Tom Monday. And tell him to

wait here while I look it over and he can take it back with him."

How fun for Tom. "Then we'll have the new inventory 10 days after that."

He nods curtly, and looks over my shoulder to beckon someone in. I turn to see Angela Jimenez, Hudson's graphic designer. Frank points at me.

"Georgia has the changes," he tells her. Frank is the only person I know who insists on calling me Georgia, despite – or perhaps because of – my request to go by Georgie. "The two of you get together now to make them and then get it over to the printer."

My vision of a fresh cup of coffee bursts with an audible *pop!* Angela waits until we're safely tucked into her cubicle before letting loose.

"Mother *fucker,*" she spits. "I couldn't believe it when I heard he made more changes. Like I don't have enough to do with the creative for the event, the foundation report, the newsletter. Speaking of the newsletter," She pauses and looks at me. I hold up my palms.

"The newsletter's with Lena," I say. "I'm waiting for her final edits."

Angela inhales deeply. "Let's just blow through these." She queues up the book in her design software. "Go."

I turn to the first flagged page. "Page 14, second paragraph. Change 'seemed'...." I stop.

She looks at me. "What?"

"Change 'seemed' to 'appeared to be.'"

Angela looks from her screen to me. "No."

"For real."

Angela brings her hands to her head and rolls her chair back.

"Be honest," she says, looking around. "Does this cubicle make me look dead inside?"

∞∞∞

Thirty minutes later, with the edits made and my delayed cup of caffeine in hand, I return to my desk. On my chair is a stack of papers: the marked up copy for the newsletter. A Post-it – the small kind, of course – reads "ask me" in Lena's writing.

I cringe, as possibilities start scrolling through my head like cherries in a slot machine. Working for Lena is rocky. As the first (and so far only) director of communications for the hotel chain, Lena had developed the official "Hudson Language," a hybrid of Associated Press style combined with Frank's own quirky preferences. My early slip-ups – referring to customers as "guests" and not the preferred phrase "clients and friends" – were called out and filed away in Lena's uncanny steel trap of a mind. Nothing ever went out without her eyes on it, and nothing was ever good enough.

"I can't figure her out," I had confided in Angela after my six-month review. At the time, I felt on surer ground, but Lena quickly and firmly dispelled those notions, informing me that she had "concerns" I wasn't working at a "high enough level." Yet when I pressed, she couldn't tell me what that level was.

"She said she wanted to start sending out news releases every week, so I did," I explained. "Now she's criticizing me for 'only' sending out a release a week. And she did a complete 180 on my article about staff reaching their 25th work anniversary. First she says that the story should be 'heaping praise' on them, and then I get comments back telling me that I need to scale it back. I feel like I can't do a single goddamn thing right." I

31

stopped, hating the way I sounded.

Angela nodded. "Yeah. I'm sorry to be the one to tell you, but 'not good enough' is kind of her M.O." She glanced around the diner we were eating at to make sure no other Hudson colleagues were within earshot. "Don't expect a raise, by the way. Hudson's thing is merit-only increases, which means they are free to give you zip if they feel like it. They sell it like they're doing staff this huge favor by offering increases based on performance instead of cost of living, and then they quietly make the definition of 'merit' impossible to achieve. Some of them, anyway. Like Lena."

I swallowed a bite of my curried chicken salad. "Huh. Now I know why I can't get her to commit to any goals in writing."

She nodded and took a sip of her iced tea. "You know why we call Frank 'Skip'?"

"The sailing thing," I replied.

She chuckled and shook her head. "That's why the executive team calls him Skip. Some of us call him Skip as in, 'let's skip the raises this year.'"

I snorted, scattering a few crumbs over the lip of my plate. "That's….that's…ah, that sucks, doesn't it?"

"Indeed."

She was right. During the next few months following that lunch, I attempted to knock it out of the park with both Lena and Frank. I churned out news releases and content for the company's blog. I found a local book printer who would expedite Frank's (always changing) proofs with an unwavering smile. I suggested that the cover of *Giving It Away* feature a graphic announcing "100% of proceeds go to charity," which delighted Frank. Noticing that there was no plan in place for communicating during an emergency, I drafted a crisis communication plan that languished in one of the vice president's "we'll get to it someday" folder, its momentum snuffed out by Lena's lack of advocacy.

And still, when it was time for annual performance reviews, I was told by Lena that I would remain at my current salary for another year. Maybe by then, she said, I'd be operating at a "higher level."

Now, I drop the "ask me" pages onto my desk and call up the printer's website on my computer. Logging in to their secure server, I upload and send the new version of Frank's book, then pick up my phone and dial Tom's number. I lean back in my chair, playing with the cord of my phone and staring at the image of Vermont on my computer background. *Soon*, I tell myself. *Seven weeks.*

After a few rings, Tom picks up. "Stop the presses? Really? Are we uncovering Watergate?"

I laugh quietly and look over my shoulder at Lena's now-open door. "I know. Listen, I just uploaded the new version of the book. Do you think you can get the proof here on Monday? If you can hang out while he's looking at it, we can grab a coffee."

"I'll be there."

I exhale, only now realizing that I had been holding my breath. Thanking him, I hang up and grab the newsletter pages. They contain Lena's typical edits, so the "ask me" remains a mystery.

Just get it over with. Angela is waiting for the copy.

I get up and walk the few steps to Lena's office. She's at her standing desk, clacking away on her keyboard. Her tall, thin frame is clad in a tailored navy pants suit. A silk coral scarf is fastened ascot-style around her neck.

Hey! It's Fred from Scooby-Doo, Gilda snickers.

When I come in, Lena stops clacking and raises her eyebrows. It's like she's always a little surprised I managed to find my way into work again.

"Hey there, how's it going?"

"Good," I begin. "The book is all set. Frank has the new numbers, and Kyle has posted the link to the radio show on social media. Angela and I also made the changes, and the new version is with Tom. The proof will be here on Monday."

She nods, the sides of her sleek, chestnut-colored stacked bob swinging gently. "OK. Were there many changes?"

I shake my head. "No. Just wordsmithing." I pause, giving Lena a chance to react. She doesn't. "But we started talking about the online reviews. He wants us to reach out to all of the foundation's grantees and have them write an online review, and then promote the book to all of their members, by email and social media. He wants us to start keeping a record of which ones do and which don't."

Lena nods again. "OK. You can draft some language and run it by me, and Kyle can set it out as an email."

I lower my voice. "But should we? Do you think it's OK to be asking our grantees to do this? To insist on it?"

Lena's face is impassive. "I think it's fine. The more books we sell, the more money goes to charity."

I press on. "We're *telling* them to post a review. And I think the unspoken message here is that it has to be a good review. Those are not good optics. It's leveraging our power over the groups we fund."

"I think most groups will be happy to do it," she says, not even pretending to pause and mull over my concerns.

"And what if they don't?" I press. "Frank is telling us to track the grantees for," I make air quotes with my fingers. "100% participation."

She purses her lips together, the tell that I've come to discover means that she's made up her mind. "It won't be a problem. So. Newsletter?"

That's that, then. Whatever Frank wants.

I hold up the Post-it. "Is there something new I should add to it before I send it over to Angela?"

"Well…" she starts, drawing in some air through her teeth. "I think we need to cut the piece on the outdoor circuit training stations and replace it with something else."

"Really? Why?" I'm surprised. The stations – pull up bars, box jumps, and numerous other equipment – had been placed along a stretch of hotel property that abuts a popular recreation path. I'd recruited some staff members to be my models and written a story about ways for our guests – I mean, our *clients* and *friends* – to stay fit while at a Hudson Hotel.

"Well, I just think that since that particular hotel is the only property to have one, we're positioning this location above the others."

"But I did include other properties, and the places people can go outside to work out," I counter.

"Yes, but those places are *offsite*," she says. "What happens if someone checks in to our site in Maine and expects to see a circuit training course? Frankly, I'm surprised you thought this was a good idea."

"It *is* a good idea," I said. "It's timely for summer. There are some great pictures, and it's clear where the circuit training is. We went through all this in the editorial meeting a few weeks ago, remember?"

"Of course I remember," Lena cuts in, her pale eyes narrowing. It's a look she gives when receiving push back from anyone other than Frank. "I just think the way you've written it will confuse our readers."

"I disagree," I say gently. "I think our readers will get it."

"Well, it's gone. Replace it with another ad for the book and the bike ride," she says, pursing her lips. End of discussion.

I look at her for another beat, and then nod. "Got it."

I return to my desk to make the final edits to the newsletter and swap out my story for a second promo for *Giving It Away*. When it's in Angela's inbox, I lean back and stretch my arms over my head, willing my anger to subside. It doesn't. There's pretty much only one way it will. I click open Jules' email and find Bembé's cell phone.

"C'mon, Book Prophet," I whisper. "Make my day."

Chapter 3

I found Bembé Jean-Baptiste via a new year's resolution. I actually *like* making them. And as long as they don't involve tasks like "return to my high school weight" or "run a 10k at an eight-minute mile pace," more often than not I'll achieve them.

At the start of this year, for example, I resolved to initiate sex with Dan once a week. Don't get me wrong; I like to think that our sex life is, after 17 years of marriage, still better than average. It's just that with two kids, a full time job, and a house to maintain, my libido had somehow taken that left turn at Albuquerque while I tunneled on ahead, oblivious. All the initiation was coming from Dan.

It took him until January 8th to notice the difference.

Last year, my goal was to read 50 books. And not just *any* 50 books, I had a plan in place to diversify my reading. I had to read 10 memoirs, 10 books from other areas of nonfiction, 10 books from the "Best Novels of the 20th Century" list, 10 "wild card" (code for my beloved chick lit) books, and 10 books that were recommended to me by friends or had received good reviews by critics I admired.

In the quest to populate my To Read list, I had taken to

listening to literary podcasts while jogging instead of my 80s playlists. I was shuffling along on the treadmill one Saturday morning to an episode of "Dog Eared," (covering all the books that "you really, seriously, should have already read at least twice by now"), when the hosts introduced their guest. Bembé, they explained, was a rising star on YouTube, and the host of a self-produced online literary show called "The Book Prophet" that had just surpassed the million-followers mark. His focus was uncovering the hidden gems in the world of self-publishing, finding and promoting the talent who – for a variety of reasons – opted against traditional publishers.

As I ran, Bembé's musical Caribbean accent filled my earbuds, thanking the "Dog Eared" hosts for the invitation. Over the next half-hour he won me over, waxing philosophic on his undying love for Stephen King's storytelling ability, his reluctance to fully transition to an e-reader, and the three books he'd bring if exiled on a deserted island (*All the King's Men, The Hitchhiker's Guide to the Galaxy*, and *The Collected Tales and Poems of Edgar Allan Poe*).

When the interview ended, I switched from Spotify to YouTube and became follower million-and-one. He featured the authors – in person or via Skype – in 45-minute interviews that he posted to his channel. The interviews were smart, often wildly funny, and allowed the author's personality to shine. An interview with Bembé now guaranteed the author's book would be downloaded thousands – if not tens of thousands – of times. More than once, I learned, an online interview had resulted in the author securing not just a literary agent, but a new book or screenplay deal.

In addition to being popular, The Book Prophet was difficult to pitch. It wasn't that he didn't want to take recommendations, it was that he *did* want to. He once shared on one of his episodes that, on a slow day, he'll have more than 200 book recommendations in his inbox before his first cup of coffee. But the way I saw it, *The Business of Giving It Away* had two things going for it: Frank's philanthropy and the charity bike ride. Bloated ego aside, Frank's generosity is undeniable. His commitment to pumping much of his hotel empire's profit back into the cities and towns that house his hotels makes the Hudson Foundation one of the top charitable organizations in the state every year.

And the charity ride? My devotion to Bembé's online shows had revealed that – in addition to books, Bembé's other great passion was cycling. VIP treatment during an event like 100 Revolutions was a carrot not many others could dangle.

Bikes and grants. As I dial the number Jules had given me, I pray the combination would be enough.

"Hello?"

He picked up! Gilda squeals. *The Book Prophet picked up!*

"Hi, Mr. Jean-Baptiste," I begin, sounding – I hoped – much calmer than I felt. "It's Georgie Fischer. My friend Julia Martin told you I'd be getting in touch. Is this is a good time?"

"Sure, sure," he says amicably. "And call me Bembé."

"Thank you. I wanted to talk with you about Frank Hudson, the founder and president of Hudson Hotels. Are you familiar with him?"

"I know the chain," says Bembé. "That's all."

"That's not surprising; not many people know Frank's story. That's why I'm reaching out, actually. He's just self-published his memoir, and I think it might appeal to you. Frank grew up with next-to-nothing. His father unloaded trucks for a department store and his mom stayed at home. Today's he's worth more than two billion."

I hear the sound of a mug being placed on a desk. "So it's a rags-to-riches kind of thing?"

"More like rags-to-riches-to-Robin-Hood," I say. "For the last 20 years, millions of dollars in profit goes back into the places where we have hotels as grants."

A pen clicks. Sounds of scribbling. "To whom? Towns? Schools?"

"Towns, schools, fire departments, food pantries, scholarship programs, all of the above," I say. "We're in the final stages of selecting this year's grant winners right now. Every year on Labor Day Weekend, the Hudson Foundation awards the grants at its charity bike ride event." That gets his attention.

"Ah, yes! That's the one with the different distances, yes?"

"That's right. All starting from different hotels and ending up at our headquarters outside of Boston. The event is called 100 Revolutions; it's a play on the number of grants we give out every year, as well as the distance of the longest ride," I pause, giving Bembé time to write. "'Revolutions' is also a nod to the good that these grantees can accomplish, and–"

"The turning of a bicycle wheel, yes. I know the event. There's a lot of local celebrities and politicians who do it; it fills up quickly."

"The shorter rides do, yes. But the party at the headquarters is open to the public. It's a huge event, and great for families," I pause. "A lot of people who participate in the ride are people who have received grants, who have been helped in some way by them, or who have known Frank himself for a long time. You're a cyclist too, right?"

You are. I know you are.

He emits a small chuckle. "I have two passions in my life.

Books and bikes."

"I think participating in the ride this September, and talking to other riders along the way, would be a great way to get a true picture of who Frank Hudson is. And, if you're interested, we could set up an area for you to sit down with Frank on camera at some point during the post-ride event for your channel. That is, if you'd be interested."

There's quiet on the other end of the line, save for Bembé's note-taking. I wait.

"Send me the book," he says. "We'll talk next week."

My cheeks are warm as I hang up. I'm positively *marinating* in pride. I feel like channeling my own version of Paul Revere around the office. *The Book Prophet's coming! The Book Prophet's coming!* But I settle for peering over the partition at Kyle, smiling.

He smiles back. "Was that the book dude you've been talking about?"

"That was, indeed, the book dude I've been talking about. And he's asked for a copy of the book."

Kyle high fives me and stands up. "I take it you're not waiting for the next iteration to arrive from the printer?"

I pretend to mull it over. "Three weeks until 'seemed' becomes 'appeared to be'…what to do…"

Kyle's eyes widen briefly; our established signal that some-one of a certain pay grade is coming and we should look busy. I glance over my shoulder to see Frank heading toward my desk.

"Hi," I say, hoping he didn't catch my dig at his editing style. "I have good news."

Frank hasn't heard of Bembé. Nor does he quite get the appeal of a YouTube review, so I stick to the high points, that a very popular reviewer with a reach of one million and a focus on self-published books is interested in his book.

"I'm sending him a copy right now," I say. "And I'm talking to him again next week."

"Excellent," Frank says. "Now, just think of this as a cat trapped in an elevator."

What the fuck? Whispers Gilda.

"How so?" I ask, glancing at Kyle to see what I'm missing. Was there an oddly worded memo I didn't see?

"Your cat is stuck in an elevator without you," he explains. "You would do anything to get that cat out, right?"

Meh, mutters Gilda. *Now, if it were a* dog...

"Um, sure. Yes."

"OK, then. So getting this Bembé person to review the book is the cat that's stuck in the elevator. Just remember that." Frank nods and continues into Lena's office.

Kyle and I stare at each other. I rub my forehead wearily.

Grabbing the eraser for my whiteboard, I wipe away the *Jaws* quote, then pick up one of the dry erase markers and scrawl "I FEEL LIKE I'M TAKING CRAZY PILLS!!"

"I'm going to mail a copy to Bembé," I tell him as I walk away.

"*Zoolander*," calls Kyle to my back. "That one I know."

∞∞∞

"Why are we doing this, again?"

The conference room table is a sea of Franks. Angela and I are on opposite sides, stacking copies of the book into neat piles of ten. At the table's head, Kyle is carefully slicing open boxes of additional paperbacks.

42

"After the 100 Revolutions meeting, Frank's going to come in and get started on signing the rest of this inventory before the next batch comes in," I explain to Angela. "We're going to send a supply of 'signed by the author' copies to every hotel for the lobby store."

Kyle pauses, looking over the stacks on the table. "Why am I opening up all the boxes? Wouldn't it be better to just open one box at a time?"

I lower my voice. "It would, yes. But you-know-who likes to have a clear sense of the size of the job ahead of him, and his progress along the way."

"Voldemort?" Angela perks up. "There's been a management change?"

I swat her shoulder with the copy I'm holding. "Yes. The Dark Lord is taking over."

"Maybe *he* won't make me buy my own k-cups," mutters Kyle under his breath. Angela and I stare at him. First in disbelief, then with affection.

"Kyle, was that venting I just witnessed?" I ask.

"Look, honey," Angela says to me, wiping away an imaginary tear. "Our little boy's all grown up."

Kyle is still slicing boxes when Lena walks in. "Oooh," she says, with just a little too much enthusiasm. "This is looking great."

Yes. This is exactly *what you want your senior graphic designer and communications manager doing. Piling books on a table. An excellent use of staff resources!*

Kyle breaks down one of the empty boxes and surveys the table. "It's gonna take him forever to sign all these."

"Eh, just take a few boxes home with you," I suggest. "How are your forgery skills?"

43

"My handwriting looks like a river otter's on Pixy Stix," he responds, earning a smile from even Lena.

We sit down as Lena hands out copies of the meeting agenda. For the next hour our focus is the charity ride. I update Lena on any changes to the 25-, 50-, or 100-mile routes due to construction or planned maintenance. Kyle runs through the current registration and fundraising numbers, and the number of staff and volunteers riding in each route as Hudson Hotel ambassadors, charged with providing encouragement to first-time or struggling riders, fixing flat tires, and talking up Frank's life story and book.

"We're set for the 25- and 50-mile routes," Kyle tells us. "We really could use a few more for the 100."

Lena sighs. "Yes, it usually works like that. We'll get there, though. What about in this room? Georgie? You game?" She turns to me and chuckles.

What's so funny?

"I'm already signed up for the 25," I tell her. *As if you didn't know already,* I think. "There are a few reporters riding that route, so I'll be riding with them," I add, trying – successfully, I hope – to keep my voice light, but the chuckle stings. As if on cue, the waistband of my mid-rise underwear slips and plants itself firmly under my perma-pooch. *Et tu, Jockey?*

Finally, Angela shares the latest mock ups of this year's merchandise, and the production schedule for the race bibs, banners, route signs, and event t-shirts.

"Show me the back of the shirt again," Lena says to Angela, who had skipped ahead in her slides of event graphics.

She does. The image is Hudson Hotel's standard back-of-the-shirt double H logo, clean and simple. All the better to stand out clearly in the event photos.

Lena nods. "Let's get creative with the back of the shirt. I think we're losing an opportunity here to promote the book."

Angela pauses to take a sip of her water. *The better to swallow that expletive that's caught in her throat, I'm sure.* "What did you have in mind?"

"I think a call to action, like 'order Frank's Hudson's book *The Business of Giving It Away* online' and then add in the website," she pauses. "Or, '*The Business of Giving It Away* by Frank Hudson, now available at' and then the website."

I clear my throat. *Well, here goes.* "That might be too much copy for the back of a t-shirt. Plus, are we in danger of getting off message for the event?" I venture. "The focus of the day is the company's charity and grant recipients."

Lena inhales while offering a slow nod. Once up, once down. Her signature move for pretending to consider someone else's idea and then explaining why it's utter nonsense.

"I don't think so. Everything we do here is for the charity. The more books we sell, the more goes to charity. And it's not too much lettering for a shirt. Lots of shirts have a lot of wording on them. It makes people wonder what's written there, so they'll make a point of reading it. Annnnd," she drawls, her voice getting that musical quality when she's about to shovel a particularly pungent load of B.S. "Frank thinks that adding the book to the event shirt will almost make it like a 'commemorative edition' you know?" She smiles and stands up.

"I think we're ready for Frank to start signing," Lena announces. "I'll go get him. Let's have some new shirt mockups for Monday, OK?"

The door to the conference room closes, just as Angela's forehead connects with the table in frustration.

"What. The actual. Fuck," she says. "Does she think the shirt's going to be a collector's item or something?"

I lean over, grab Lena's nearly empty glass, and sniff its contents.

"Nope," I say. "Just water."

∞∞∞

Open. Slide. Sign. Wave. Box.

Open. Slide. Sign. Wave. Box.

After some trial and error, Kyle and I have a neat little rhythm going. I open a copy of Frank's book to the title page, slide it to my right, where Frank sits with his pen at the ready. He gives it a quick flourish to produce a dramatic – and irritatingly legible – autograph. Kyle picks it up, gives the ink a few waves with a handy Giving it Away postcard, and places it neatly back into the boxes we unpacked a few hours earlier.

Open. Slide. "Just let me know if you need to take a few minutes break," I say to Frank.

Sign. "I'm fine. Thank you."

Wave. Box.

I consider myself to be an extrovert. Not one of those "I have 900 friends on Facebook and cherish them all" kind of extrovert. But I love being with friends and family. I like concerts, fairs, and other events during which I'm in close proximity to hundreds of strangers. I even enjoy striking up conversations with random people while waiting in a line or on a train.

At the same time, there have been a few times in my life when I'm forced into a professional or social relationship with someone that I just can't seem to engage in conversation naturally. Even my go-tos, like books, movies, and travel get me nowhere. Eventually I end up sounding like an over eager fangirl. I become that dog Chester from the old Warner Brothers cartoons. *"What are we doing now, Spike, huh? Huh, Spike?"*

Frank is one of those people. God, it's awkward. During my first month or so at Hudson, I tried to draw him into a conversation about books while waiting for colleagues to join us in a conference room. I started sharing the plot of a novel set in World War II Poland that I was currently enjoying. He looked at me over his glasses for what seemed like an eternity, then grunted "sounds like a girl book," and turned back to the notepad in front of him, as my cheeks started their slow burn.

What do you like to read, Frank? Huh, Frank?

Ugh.

Not today, though. Screw it. *If he has something to say, he'll say it,* added Gilda.

Open. Slide. Sign. Wave. Box.

"Kyle," Frank says, not looking up from the book he's signing. "Would you get me a cup of coffee?"

Kyle boxes the latest book and heads for the door. He doesn't need to ask how Frank takes it. No one does.

I hesitate. Do I take over the waving and boxing? Or just the waving? The idea of scurrying back and forth behind Frank's chair like a squirrel deciding whether it can beat an oncoming car is unappealing to me. I stay where I am. And apparently it's fine with Frank. He just slides the newly signed copy over to await Kyle's return.

"So," Frank says, still not looking up. "Have you ever done something like this before, Georgia?"

47

"Marketing a book? No, actually. This is a new experience for me."

"Ah, well, that explains it," he responds. And then goes silent. *Where is this going?*

Sign. Slide.

OK, Frank, I'll bite. "Explains what?"

"Why you thought it was OK to forge my signature on these books." He gives me a cold stare as he slides a book away with his right hand and reaches for the one that's waiting for him with his left.

What? I give him the book, but don't reach for another one. "I never suggested that, Frank. I don't know where you would have gotten that idea."

"It doesn't matter where I got it. You proposed that other people sit here and sign *my* name to *my* book. I don't know – and I'm not interested to know, incidentally – how these kinds of things were done at your last place of employment, but it's not how we do things here."

It clicks. My joke to Kyle about how good his forgery skills are.

"Oh, oh, OK," I start to chuckle, relieved. "No, I was just making a joke when we were unboxing the books. I wasn't serious."

"This is my story, and my reputation. I don't want anyone thinking that anything related to this wasn't done by me. That is not how we do things here," he repeated.

"No, I know that. I would never seriously suggest it."

Frank ends the conversation with an extra aggressive autograph and looks back to his book just as Kyle returns with his coffee, and a water for me.

"Thanks, Kyle," I say. *See, Frank? Grownups say please and thank you.*

I go back to focusing on opening and sliding, while I quietly fume. It's clear he doesn't believe me. For Christ's sake, it was a *joke.*

It doesn't matter where you got it, huh Frank? I know *where you got it.*

I picture Lena stepping primly inside his office to let him know the books were ready to be autographed. How would she have phrased it, exactly? I wonder.

Now, just so you're aware, it was suggested that staff sign all the books. I'm sure it was well-intentioned, but I knew that you would never go for that, so don't worry.

She would have known that Frank would hate the idea, that he would see it as someone trying to take away something that was uniquely his to do. She would have known that, just as she would have known that it was a joke. Lena's not that dense. She isn't dense at all.

Open. Slide. Sign. Wave. Box.

It crosses my mind to have Kyle vouch for me. *Of course it was a joke,* he would say. But I can't. Frank already doesn't believe me. He'd assume I was just digging a deeper hole, and dragging a colleague along with me.

I slide a new book to Frank just as the minute hand slides to 4:59 pm. At this moment, a few miles away, Max and Shannon are at my parents' house. Soon they'll be sweet-talking my dad into getting them a pizza. After he gives in and orders one, he'll start putting out the fixings for Friday night happy hour: lemon martini for me, Jameson for him.

Open. Slide. Sign. Wave. Box.

There's no way to tell how long Frank will want to continue autographing, and I can't ask.

The realization that has been dancing in the periphery of my consciousness for months now leaps to the forefront.

Oh my god, I think. *I* hate *it here.*

Chapter 4

"She's a sociopath, Georgie."

My mom, Liz, offers the diagnosis with the certainty of a prophet from her wicker rocking chair on the porch. And by "porch," I mean a three-season room larger than my living room at home. When my parents downsized from my childhood home, there were two conditions during the hunt for their next house. My dad, Colin, wanted a pool, which reduced the inventory available to them. My mom wanted the porch to end all porches. She designed it herself and project managed its construction shortly after they moved.

The walls facing the front and back yards are floor-to-ceiling screened windows. On one half of the porch is a table for six, and on the other is a sitting area for four. The remaining walls are peppered with framed memorabilia from their travels: coasters and menus from restaurants in Europe and the Pacific Northwest, a program from a play in New York, a poster from a transatlantic cruise signed by the passengers they met – and drank with, no doubt – along the way.

I love this room. I didn't grow up in this house, but it feels like home to me. Even in my forties – or maybe especially because I'm in my forties – it's deliciously decadent to come here and be pampered. When I shuffled in this evening close to six o'clock. My dad handed me my cocktail, while my mom waved away my offer to help with dinner and sent me to the porch.

Now, a salmon fillet and second cocktail later, I'm sitting in the wicker chair we've come to call mine. My dad's on my right, his arms folded behind his head and his eyes on the TV, where a hipster couple is "going tiny." My mom is to his right. She's ignoring the TV and dividing her attention between my retelling of my day and a political blog on her iPad.

"Did you call her on it?" my mom asks, looking at me over her glasses.

I make a *meh* face. "Sort of. I went to her office when Frank was done signing for the day and told her about our conversation. I explained I was joking about Kyle signing Frank's name."

"And?"

"She went all innocent on me," I made a wide-eyed *who, me?* expression to demonstrate. "She said that she described it to Frank as a joke, and insisted to me that he either misinterpreted it or just didn't find it very funny."

Mom rolls her eyes. "Nice little dig there, Lena."

"Right?" I shake my head and take another sip of my drink. "The worst part is that people *buy* it. You should hear some of the foundation and event volunteers. They think she is kindness itself. If anyone said otherwise there would be some serious pearl-clutching. I'd be written off as just, you know, projecting my own moral failures onto Mother Theresa."

"Like I said. She's a sociopath."

She goes back to her iPad. On the TV, the hipsters are gearing up for their move from Boston to Tampa.

"Thus raising the IQs of *both* cities," my dad points out, toasting with his whiskey.

I laugh and clink my glass against his. Dad adjusts the cap he's wearing over his blond hair, now nearly white, and turns to me. "You know, think of it like this. In six months, two things will have happened. One, Shannon will have finished almost half of her first year of middle school. Which, by the way, is crazy because your mother and I are still 40."

"Honey," my mom interjects. "You couldn't pay me to be in my forties again." She looks up at me and smiles. "No offense, Georgie."

"By then," Dad continues. "You'll have a sense of how it's going for her. And to be honest," he glances through the kitchen doorway to make sure Max isn't within earshot, then lowers his voice. "She's not going to have the same issues that he's had.

"And two, you'll have had two years at Hudson. Then it's no longer a blip on your resume. You can go out and look for something else, and just explain that it wasn't the right fit."

I drain my drink and nod. "Yeah. That's the timeline I was thinking of, too. I just need to get through the next six months."

And then what?

I'm not quite ready to tackle that one, so I turn my attention to the TV. The hipsters are concerned that the 250-square-foot house doesn't have space for their vinyl record collection.

"Jesus Christ, vinyl records? And you're going tiny?" Dad gives the TV the finger and turns back to me. "That reminds me. There's some stuff of yours from God knows how long ago in a box that we still have from the old house. I found it in the attic this morning and put it on the dining room table"

"All right," I get up. "I'll grab it now and put it in the car, and then I'm giving the kids the 10-minute warning. I told Dan we'd be home around eight."

I step into the kitchen and cross into the pale gray dining room, where a slightly battered box from a now-defunct clothing store rests on top of the Irish lace tablecloth. It's taped shut, and I recognize it as one in which I stashed batches of papers the summer I finished college. There's some heft to it, but I couldn't begin to guess what's inside.

Table for one at Memory Lane this weekend? Fun!

Dad picks up the shaker and rattles the ice at me when I step back onto the porch with the box. "Want one more during those last 10 minutes?"

I suck some air in through my teeth. "Mmmm, I don't know. Have you heard what they say about martinis?"

∞∞∞

Two days – three dance classes, a swimming practice, a spin workout, and 19 errands – later, I finally pull the box out of the trunk of my car and carry it into the house. Max sees me through the wide entry separating the dining room from the family room, where he and Dan are battling over who can reel in the biggest digital fish via Xbox. The late afternoon is warm and bright, whispering of summer.

"What's in the box, Mom?" Max asks, his eyes back to the flat screen, where a rainbow trout is spiraling underwater in an attempt to throw off the hook in its jaw.

"Yeah, Mom. What's in the booooooox?" Dan twists his face into a parody of grief and repeats the question a la Brad Pitt from *Se7en*. The act earns him a chuckle from me and a startled glance from Max. The trout continues its fight.

"Glimpses of my past life, I think," I say. I push aside yesterday's batch of mail and let the box drop the final six inches to the table with a satisfying clap. "I'm not entirely sure."

Dan proclaims Max the fishing champion, checks through the window to our backyard, where Shannon is on the trampoline flanked by two of her friends, and joins me at the table. The dark blue cardboard lid is held in place by four pieces of ancient tape that break easily as my index finger slides under the edges. I cautiously lift the lid, pausing to look at Dan opposite me.

"If there's a diary in there, no grabbing."

He raises his right hand in a pledge. "I promise nothing."

I set the lid down and we peer inside. It's a jumble of paper. Postcards I sent home from my junior year in Europe, the last birthday card I received from my grandfather before he died, concert programs. Reams of a previous version of me.

On top of the pile is the title page to what I assume is one of my college papers. From my perspective, it's upside down. Dan picks it up, a recognizable *WTF?* expression forming on his face as he reads.

"'Diary of a Teenage Drag Queen'?" He glances to see Max's reaction to the title, but he's tuned us out, moving on to larger fish in deeper, saltier waters. "What *is* this?"

I smile and reach for the paper. "I remember this! It's from my Elizabethan lit class my senior year of college. It's a paper on some of the female characters from the plays we read, but it's told from the viewpoint of the actor who would have played them." I wait for Dan to catch on. "You know, a boy. Women weren't allowed to act then. Teenage drag queen, get it?" He nods, though I suspect I started to lose him at "Elizabethan lit."

A quick shiver of delight runs through me. I *loved* writing this paper. I was so pleased and proud of my idea and title. I place it on the table, determined to read it later, and sift deeper into this slice of my past. Dan holds up a purple plastic fork and pries a ticket stub from its tongs. He glances at it and raises his eyebrows. "A-Ha? Seriously? And what's the fork about?"

"Yes, A-Ha. I was young and they were cute." I nod at the utensil. "Scavenger hunt. Summer before college. Do you know how hard it was to find a purple plastic fork on a Saturday night, like, 30 years ago?"

"You signed up for a scavenger hunt?"

"Signed up? We *created* it. Three teams. It was a three-way tie, but maybe that's because we all knew the list a day in advance."

"You think?" Dan chuckles.

"God, that was a fun night. We were fun." I turn back to the box.

A piece of original artwork peeks out from under an Edinburgh postcard. It's one of Jules', I can tell. Drawn in colored pencil, three women sit on stools next to a partition. Above them, "Le Jeu de Rencontres" is written in lights. I squeal. I can't help it.

"Oh my *God. The Dating Game!*" I turn it around to reveal to Dan.

"You mean like, Bachelor Number One?"

"Yes! My high school French class."

"Well, *duh*," Dan says. "Didn't we all play *The Dating Game* in French class?"

"Sorry. You're in the dark on this, I know. I haven't thought about this in years! See, we had to do a project on these plays we had read. Do you know Sartre–"

"Nope, keep going," Dan makes a wrap it up gesture with his hand.

"Well, we could work in small groups, right? So Jules and I and a few others used the characters and put on an episode of *The Dating Game*," I pause, unsure of how much detail Dan needs or wants. "Well, it was funny at the time."

It was more than funny, it was smart. We used the characters Ines and Estelle from Sartre's *Huis Clos* and Daisy from Ionesco's *Rhinoceros*. When the student playing the game show host introduced Ines – famously lesbian – as Bachelorette Number Two, the class snickered at "she enjoys vacationing in Provincetown."

"OK, Chuck Woolery," Dan nudges me and gestures to the table. "I'm calling Shannon in for dinner. You mind clearing off the table so we can eat?"

"Fine. And it's Chuck *Barris*, if you please."

I replace the lid and carry the box to the foot of the stairs leading to the second floor, and add it to the assortment of clean laundry, shoes, earbuds and books waiting to be tucked into their proper place. Eventually.

You're clever, says Gilda. *Did I know you were this clever? It's cool in a, no offense, nerdy way.*

My hand lingers on the box, as if absorbing the energy of its contents, as I wait for Gilda's inevitable follow up.

What happened?

∞∞∞

"Methinks 'tis part of the profession. Even Thomas appears to understand; he has not referred to me as a 'powder-beef quean' since scene VI…but let that pass."

– Great ending remark! Nice work – the concreteness, the humor, the interpolated quotations all contribute to a very effective paper!

I flip back to the title page, place my old paper into the drawer of my night stand, and roll onto my side towards Dan. He's wearing his favorite sleeping t-shirt, a decades-old Monty Python in a faded burnt orange. There's a new hole just under the seam around the neck. "What did you want to be when you were younger?"

Dan blows some air out through his cheeks as he considers. "Oh, you know, the usual. Cop. Rock star. National Park Ranger." He turns and looks at me, his eyes a deeper blue in the lamplight. "What about you?"

"All good choices. But no. I don't mean when you were a kid. I mean when you were a young adult. In college. Like, when you realized you really had to figure it out and do something, what did you want? Was it always something accounting related?"

He closes his book and rests it on his chest. "Well, yeah. I mean, I knew I was good at it, and I *liked* being good at it." Dan pauses, thinking. "That's not to say it's easy. I work hard. But I do like it." He tosses his book to the floor next to his side of the bed and turns more fully to me. "What's up, Georgie? I'm definitely getting a….*City Slickers* vibe from you right now."

"I know." I sigh and adjust the pale green and white comforter around me. "It's just being where I am right now work-wise, and then seeing glimpses of these cool and smart and funny things that I *used* to do and *used* to create…I don't know if 'create' sounds too lofty, but that's the word that fits." I take a deep breath and say what I've been thinking all evening: "I'm underwhelming."

"You're what? Come on, Georgie. I know Hudson sucks, but listen to me. The hotel is your job. It isn't who you are. Jesus, *I'm* the dude. I'm the one who's supposed to base my self-worth on my profession. You're more than what you do."

I sit up, wide awake. "But that's just it. It's more than my sucky job. I'm not succeeding at anything." I start ticking my fingers. "I'm a wife, a mother, a team member, a housekeeper, a cook, and a friggin' activities director, and I'm not doing *any* of them well."

"Georgie, you know that's not true."

"Do I?" I gesture around the room. "This place is a mess. It's always a mess. *I'm* a mess." I reach under the comforter and grab a fistful of my abdomen, shaking it. "I'm fat. I live in elastic waists. I haven't had my hair cut in, like, forever and it looks like shit. I'm behind on setting up summer camps. I cook the same boring food every week. I..." I stop, defeated and embarrassed. I sound like a child.

Fraud! Fake adult!

Dan is quiet, waiting. I start again. "I feel stuck. I get up. I work. I go home. I bring Max to therapy. I go back home. I make a mediocre meal. If I'm heroically productive I might get one load of laundry done. And then it's–" I glance at the digital clock on Dan's nightstand. "Ten forty-seven and I have to go to bed so I can do it all over again the next day. I feel like I'm treading water all the time. All day, every day."

He nods. "That's because we are. Us and about seven billion other people."

I look at him.

"This is life, Georgie," Dan says gently. "It's going to have parts that are boring, crappy, and unfair. This isn't new, and I think you know that. We're just as busy now as we were two years ago, five years ago. But you were happy then, and you're not now. What's different, if it isn't just your job?"

I consider the question. "I'm not sure how to describe it. It's the job, yes, but it's more than that. I see how I used to be, and I'm not that person anymore. I'm staring down the barrel of 50 and I'm not adding anything new or creative or even above average."

"You mean someone who creates scavenger hunts and game show skits in school?" He holds up a hand before I can protest. "I'm not knocking it. I'm not. I get what you're saying. But you're forgetting that you could do those things because you were basically still a kid. You didn't have a mortgage, a son with autism, and the need to do your own cooking and cleaning."

I look around the room again. "Who's cleaning?"

Dan smiles, clearly relieved by my attempt, however weak, at humor. I smile back, but briefly. "I just want to feel passionate about something again," I say. "Does that make me sound ungrateful?"

He yawns and shakes his head. "It makes you sound human. Unforgivable." He reaches over and strokes my cheek. I lean into his palm, absorbing the warmth of his skin and the tenderness of the gesture.

"Thank you for hearing me," I say. "Let's get some sleep."

He turns toward the lamp, then looks back at me. "Are you good, Georgie?"

I nod.

"Will you tell me if and when you're not?"

I nod again. "I will."

Dan switches off the light and we lie back. He squeezes my hand under the covers for a few seconds, his silent good night ritual.

"What *are* you passionate about?" he asks.

"Other than our lottery fantasy games and bad reality television? I have no idea."

I close my eyes, feeling the walls of the room and the weight of his question settle into my chest.

Let's add that to the To Do list, says Gilda. *Parlay in-depth knowledge of TLC and Bravo into purpose-driven life.*

Chapter 5

"Ask me," reads the (regulation!) Post-It note stuck to the copy of Frank's book on my chair.

I pick up the book and wave it at Kyle. "Any insight into this?"

He squints at the note. "Nope, sorry. But I got the sense it would be ready to print today."

I raise my eyebrows. "Optimistic of you."

It's morning on a sunny Friday. After my Sunday night meltdown five days ago, I had arrived at Hudson headquarters on Monday morning to learn that Lena and Frank had delayed the printing of new books. Again. Frank wanted to "punch up" the cover somehow to increase sales. During the last four days he's gone quiet, thinking. It's been lovely.

I drop my purse into its designated drawer and glance at my phone. No messages! I turn back to Kyle. "So. I'm going to follow up with The Book Prophet this morning and see where he is with Frank's book," I put my palms together in prayer, my elbows resting on the cubicle wall. "In my perfect world, he accepts my invitation to 100 Revolutions, and agrees to interview Frank live at the after party."

Kyle grins. "Optimistic of you."

"*Touché*. Anyway, can I pawn off the sales report to you while I call him? Pretty please?"

"New orders, names of new orders, new reviews, names of new reviewers. Have I missed anything?"

I tip an invisible hat. "Got it in one. Thanks, Kyle."

He grins. "Go rescue that cat from the elevator."

I sit down, trying to ignore the flutter in my stomach as I dial Bembé. Why am I nervous? What's it to me if he turns us down? If he does, it's the book, not me.

You're nervous because you care, *dummy. It's your job to care.*

Hush, I tell Gilda. *It's ringing.*

"Hello?"

"Hi Bembé, it's Georgie Fischer. Is this a good time?"

"Ah, Georgie. Yes, of course. Thanks for getting back in touch."

The sound of shuffling papers fills the line. I stay silent, sensing he wants to jump right into it.

"So, I finished Mr. Hudson's book," he begins, reluctance creeping into his voice. "It...it straddles genres a bit, don't you think?"

"How so?" I look up at the poster of the book cover on the wall, relieved it's me getting this feedback and not Frank.

"Well, it's trying to be both a guide to entrepreneurship *and* a memoir, and as a result, I'm afraid it doesn't do either one especially well. Normally, this isn't something that I'd select for the show."

Maybe it's Bembé's use of "it doesn't do either one especially well," which echoes my own insecurities a little too closely. A surge of determination courses through me at his words.

He said normally, whispers Gilda. *He wants to do the ride. He wants to be talked into it. Talk him into it, damnit!*

63

"You know, it's interesting you say that." I look back to the beaming face of Frank on the poster for help. *Why? Why is it interesting?* I grasp onto the thinnest of straws – a coffee stirrer, really – and decide to wing it. "Frank's had the sense lately that something's missing from *The Business of Giving it Away*. He's been working on revisions this week. I think he'd be really interested in this feedback."

HA! Gilda snorts. I ignore her.

"I think the issue of 'straddling genres' is one that he hasn't considered," I grab a notepad and flip to a fresh page. "If *Giving it Away* had to land cleanly in one genre, my gut tells me memoir. Do you agree?"

"I do."

"Great. So, how about this?" I start sketching a mockup of a page in Frank's book to help me think. "What if he pulled the pieces of the book that stray into the 'how to' territory and he placed them at the end as an addendum? The other option would be to close out each chapter with a short 'takeaway' summary. 'What I wished I knew' or something like that."

I stop, giving Bembé a few seconds to consider the idea.

It's not half bad. Actually, it's good.

"I think either of those changes would make it a better book," Bembé says, and I punch my fist into the air. "The heart of the story really is – as you put it when we spoke last week – the Robin Hood aspect, the people and small nonprofits he's helping. I especially like that the grants all go to the cities where his hotels are."

I'm a half-step closer to success. I can feel it.

"You're so right," I say, and cringe. *Don't blow this by being a suck up, you idiot.* "We talked last week about the idea of you joining us for 100 Revolutions, and having the chance to talk to our grantees during the ride. This event is almost like a microcosm of Frank himself: riders put in a lot of hard work for a really good cause." I pause for a beat. *Too much?* Gilda shrugs. *Nah, own it. Work it.*

"If you do decide to join us, what about having a sit down interview with Frank during the party at the finish line? You can weave in your own experiences on the ride – the day, the route, and all the people you talk to."

Bembé chuckles. "I give you an 'A' for effort, Georgie. OK, I'm in for the ride. The full 100 miles."

"Oh, that's *great*," I say, not caring that I'm gushing. "And the interview? Should I plan for that?"

"Sure, let's do it. We'll stream it in real time on my channel."

I promise to register him for the ride. We exchange goodbyes, and hang up. I leap out of my chair and start to dance in place, my arms waving above my head. I look ridiculous, and it feels amazing.

"He's in, he's in," I sing off-key to Kyle. "The Book Prophet is in. I'm a genius. Uh-huh, oh yeah."

Kyle raises and lowers his hands in the universal symbol of *I'm not worthy*. "Pardon the interruption, Einstein. An addendum to the book?" He nods at Frank's face on the poster. "And how are you going to convince Frank of that?"

I smile. "I'll make them think it's his idea."

Kyle widens his eyes. "You *are* a genius. Uh-huh. Oh yeah."

I bow. "Now, if you'll excuse me, I have a victory bomb to drop."

He hands over the book sales report. "Atta girl."

∞∞∞

Frank's at his desk, the sleeves of his white dress shirt rolled up, when I arrive at the doorway. Lena is leaning forward in one of the Windsor guest chairs, examining something Frank is showing her. She's in a long white dress belted with a wide strip of navy leather. Over the dress is a short navy jacket. I knock before Gilda has the chance to start humming the theme to *The Love Boat*.

"Come in Georgia," says Frank, beckoning with his right hand. In his left he's holding down the inside front cover of his book, facing it towards Lena. "Tell me what you think."

He gestures to the second guest chair and turns the book from Lena to me. Inside the front cover, he's sketched out an ad instructing readers to order additional copies on the Hudson Hotels website.

Ugh. They've just bought the book and the first thing they see is a hard sell to buy more?

"Well," I say, pulling the book closer to me. "I like the concept, but I think it would have more impact at the end of the book, on the back cover."

"Really?" Lena jumps in. "I think Frank's vision is for it to be the first thing they see, not the last." There's a light emphasis on "Frank." *Subtle.*

"But wouldn't it be more effective for readers to be prompted to recommend it to others, or buy it for them, after they've read it?" I counter. I turn to Frank before she can respond. "The other thing is, when it's in front, the ad distracts from the title page. That's where you want the eye to go. Without the ad, the first glimpse inside is clean. Professional. Especially if it's a signed copy."

Frank covers his drawing with his hand and studies it, considering.

"You've convinced me," says Frank. He closes the book and slides it to Lena. "You'll take care of it." A statement, not a question.

"Of course," Lena smiles widely at Frank before turning back to me, her eyes instantly going cold. *Perfect time for the victory bomb.*

"I have good news," I pause, drawing the moment out a little. "Bembé Jean-Baptiste is going to participate in 100 Revolutions, followed by a live interview with you, Frank, at the post-ride party. The interview will be streamed in real time to more than a million followers."

He nods. "Good." Lena says nothing.

I wait, but there's nothing more. *That's it? "Good?" But you got the cat out of the elevator! You saved it!*

Of course that's it. In Frank's mind, the idea that The Book Prophet would pass on the opportunity to interview *the* Frank Hudson is ludicrous.

"There's more. We were discussing how your book serves as both a memoir and a guide for new entrepreneurs," I say, making the straddling of genres sound like a *good* thing. "There are a few ways you could make your business advice really stand out. You could compile it at the end of the book, or close out each chapter with the advice that you wished you had been given at that stage in your journey. Which do you think would be more effective?"

"Well, I can see why you'd think that parsing out the advice in stages might work as a storytelling technique, but the guidance that's offered in the book really needs to be in one place so it can be easily accessed," Frank says, turning to Lena for confirmation.

You hooked him, Gilda says. *You should start playing that fishing video game with Max.* "Make the arrangements for the interview," Frank says. "Set it up in a place outside where people can gather around and watch, but we won't be distracted by the party itself. I'm going to work on my how-to addendum for the next printing."

As I rise to leave, Lena clears her throat. "And you'll ride with Bembé, Georgie?"

Umm, excuse me?

I chuckle, but she isn't smiling.

"Bembé's doing the full 100," I explain. "Miles."

"Well, we'll need someone from Communications with him if he's going to be talking to our grantees. Otherwise, we really can't have him in the event."

"I'm supposed to be on the 25-mile route, with the other media," I remind her. "And Bembé will be a much faster rider. I would literally be hours behind him." *You know this. I know you do. You want* me *to be the reason Bembé can't ride.*

"We'll be fine for the 25 miles," Lena waves my concern away. "Those reporters all know the drill. This thing with Bembé is something new. And I think if he's going to be talking throughout the ride, he'll be going a lot slower than usual." Lips pursed. *Oh, Jesus.*

"OK, well," I attempt a smile. "I have some spin classes to sign up for, I guess."

"Here," Frank reaches across the desk and slides the book back from Lena. "Why don't you just take these down to Angela now. With the ad in the back. I'll get you the addendum next week."

I stand. "Sure. I...what's this?" I point to some writing on the cover. Above the title, in Frank's handwriting, are the words "National Bestseller."

Frank smiles. "That was my idea. I want all the posters around the properties updated as well. And I want you to include it in the press releases from now on, and share the new cover to all the grantees so they can post it on their websites. Keep track of that along with the reviews going forward."

I sit back down. "OK...so, on which book list have we reached bestselling status?"

Frank looks at me. "Which list?"

"Yes," my mouth feels like cotton. I don't like where this is going. "I don't know offhand what the thresholds are from list to list, but we have to meet a certain level of sales to be able to use the term 'bestseller' and attribute it to a list," I turn to Lena for support, but she stays silent. "You know, *New York Times* bestseller, *Wall Street Journal* bestseller?"

Frank shakes his head curtly. "No, no. A bestseller can mean anything we want it to mean."

I look from Frank to Lena and back again. "No, it really can't. At some point, especially as you do more media interviews, someone's going to ask how many copies you've sold." I glance down at the sales report, still in my hand, and place it on his desk. "We're under 1,000. People will know that's not a bestseller." There, I said it. I said out loud the only sentence no one should ever say out loud at Hudson Hotels.

Frank is very still. I can feel his anger towards me. "It's *my* best selling book, isn't it?"

It's your only *book, you asshat,* screams Gilda. *Is this a dream? Are we still at home, in bed?*

"We could say 'Frank Hudson's well-received memoir' in the press rel–"

"No. You will say Bestseller."

The enormity of the order is too much. This entire charade

of Frank's to first bully – and now lie – his way to celebrated author is too petty, too crude for words. I look at Lena once more, but she is unreadable. I'm on my own.

So what are you going to do, kiddo? What would Ines from Huis Clos *do?*

"Frank, I'll research every book list I can find. If there's one that qualifies *Giving It Away* as a bestseller, then we're fine. But if I don't, we can't do it. We can't, and I won't."

I leave, holding the book in the crook of my arm to hide my shaking hands.

For once, even Gilda doesn't know what to say.

∞∞∞

Angela is loitering at my desk when I get back. She holds up her hand for a high-five when I'm a few steps away.

"I heard about The Book Prophet, you rock star," she says, beaming as we smack hands. "Was Frank happy?"

I shrug. "Happy is stretching it. He's satisfied, I guess. Where's Kyle?"

"He just left, swapping out the old newsletters in the common areas of the hotel with the new ones."

"Ah. OK." I present the book to Angela, resting it on my arm like a waiter with a bottle of wine. "Here you are, my lady. The scribbling on the first page now goes inside the back cover. Ignore what's on the front cover for now."

She examines the writing, a spiral of one of her long ombre curls falling over her forehead, then looks up at me. "Bestseller?"

I nod, checking to see if Lena is coming up behind me. "I'm going to see if there's a way it can pass the sniff test, but I warned Frank that if there isn't, we really can't do it."

"Good luck with that," she says, rolling her eyes.

"And oh my God, I now have to bike 100 miles with The Book Prophet!" I exclaim. In the "bestseller" madness, I had forgotten. "Lena's making me. Is that even legal?"

"Yikes," she says. "Good luck with *that*."

"Maybe I can Rosie Ruiz that shit," I say, and then pinch the bridge of my nose. "Is it too early to drink?"

Angela laughs and pats my shoulder. "I'll leave you to it. Lunch today?" I nod.

Sitting down, I grab my water and take a long pull, trying to wash out the cottony feel left from my meeting with Frank.

It's nine-thirty, and already this has topped last Friday for sheer lunacy.

I log on to the *100 Revolutions* event webpage and register both myself and Bembé for the 100-mile event, using the staff and volunteer promo code created to waive the entry fee and fundraising requirement. The route map is a long – a *very* long – blue squiggle, nearly four times longer than the Boston Marathon.

Three months. You have three months to get ready for this ride. And you will *be ready. You know why, right?*

"Yeah," I mutter quietly. "Because fuck Lena, that's why."

I click "submit" and turn my attention to the research I promised Frank and Lena. As expected, it's an exercise in wishful Googling. An hour later, I still can't make the numbers work. *Giving it Away* isn't a bestseller. On the plus side, the research I've done may be enough to convince Frank to cease and desist. Maybe.

"Can I see you in my office, Georgie?"

I flinch at Lena's voice behind me. *She needs a bell*, says Gilda.

"Sure," I stand up, notebook in hand, and freeze. She's with Mark.

Mark from Human Resources.

"Hi, Mark," I say, my voice light.

He smiles and nods. It's that lips-closed smile. The kind that the other nominees keep glued to their faces after someone else's name is read. It's not a good sign.

I tally the possibilities. A promotion and a bonus? Highly unlikely. A risk management inquiry into questionable book marketing practices? Warranted, but no. A warning over my push back to Frank?

Ding! Ding! Ding!

We enter Lena's office ahead of her, and she closes the door. She walks around her standing desk and faces me, resting her forearms on the smooth wooden surface. Mark stands to my left. There are no guest chairs; sitting would only give visitors a glimpse of Lena's hairline. It suddenly feels like a courtroom, with Lena as judge and Mark my attorney.

That's pretty much what this is, don't you think? Only Mark's the opposing counsel.

"So," Lena begins. "I'll just get right to it. We're making some changes in Communications, and have decided to eliminate your position, effective immediately."

My stomach flips. That wasn't one of the possibilities I'd considered.

"Changes? What kind of changes?"

Mark answers for her. "There's an identified need for additional capacity in other areas, but no room for growth in the budget."

It occurs to me that, in front of a standing desk, it would be easy to grab his necktie and introduce his forehead to the wood. *Oak, meet Corporate Tool. Tool, meet Oak.*

"Identified need?" I turn back to Lena. "An hour ago you asked me to commit to a 100-mile bike ride in September."

A quarter-sized pink spot appears on each cheekbone. "Yes, well. The decision wasn't final then."

"Look, Lena, if this is about the book cover–"

"Georgie," she snaps, her eyes flinty. "This is business. Don't read more into it than that. I'm sure I don't have to remind you that we've had numerous discussions about your performance in the last eighteen months. If I remember correctly," she looks over at Mark. "You didn't merit an increase in your last review."

Not today, bitch. "Lena, has anyone who's worked for you ever merited one?" I ask. Her eyes flare in response.

Mark clears his throat and takes a step closer to Lena's desk. She places a file folder on top and slides it towards him, and he opens it. "This is officially a layoff due to restructuring, so we won't contest your application for unemployment benefits."

I look back at him. "Noble."

He pauses a beat, and I imagine a thought bubble rising over his head. *I see what you did there, but I'm too professional to acknowledge it.* He continues. "As for your severance, our policy is two weeks in lieu of notice, and one week for every completed year of service. With eighteen months of service, that technically qualifies you for a total of three weeks pay, but Lena has requested we give you four. And a free workshop at a local employment service." He begins handing forms to me for my signature.

This is real. I'm being *fired*. Let go. Given the boot. I'm pushing up the Post-It Notes. I've shuffled off this employment coil. I am an ex-employee.

"Kyle is doing some event-related work offsite right now," Lena concludes. "I made sure you would have some privacy in this area while you pack up your personal items. May I have him call you in the following weeks if anything comes up on one of your projects?"

"Kyle can call me, sure," I say. "But as I'm such an underperforming team member I can't imagine he'll need to."

"Fine. Use the staff only side door, please."

I turn to leave, then stop. "Oh, and it's five to ten thousand."

"Excuse me?"

"In order to *legitimately* call Frank's book a bestseller, it needs to sell at least five thousand copies. Ten thousand, on some lists."

Her eyes flick to her screen, then back at me. I sense optimism. And I have zero fucks left to give.

"Per week, that is," I add. "Just in case anyone here is interested in truth and accuracy." And turn my back on her.

Back at my cube – my former cube – I place my assortment of photos, postcards, and desk accessories into a cardboard box. On Kyle's desk, I leave my pad of extra-large Post-It Notes, *use them wisely* written on the top note.

I round the corner to the hallway leading to the side exit and, to my supreme disappoint, spot Frank ambling towards me.

Terrific.

"Pardon me, Frank," I say curtly. He stops before I can pass.

"It didn't have to be this way, Georgia," says Frank. "But you clearly don't want my book to succeed."

"Are you serious, Frank?" I ask, exasperated. "I'm the one who just got you an interview with The Book Prophet, for heaven's sake. I want your book to be a success; I just want it

74

to be an *honest* success. Don't you?"

"I *am* an honest success. You are not," says Frank, unfolding his arms to jab a finger at me. He lowers his voice. "And if I may say so, you never will be."

Ouch.

"Goodbye, Georgia."

He turns on his heel and casually walks away. I push the door open with my shoulder and leave.

Once in my car, I sit in silence for a few moments, allowing whatever emotions I've tamped down in the last half hour to show themselves. There are none. Yet. Just a hyper awareness of my surroundings. The drone of traffic. The pigeon poking industriously at a crumpled bakery bag.

I pull my phone out of my purse and bring up Dan's number. My finger hovers over the call button, then jerks away. I am not ready to tell Dan I've just lost my job.

"Holy shit," I say to the pigeon. "I just lost my job."

The pigeon is unimpressed.

"Go poop on that blue Mini Cooper," I add, pointing at Lena's car in the next row. The bird continues its excavation of the paper bag.

"I'm...unemployed," I whisper, trying out this new phrase. "I'm unemployed."

What do we do now?

I do the only thing I *can* do. I call Jules.

"Leave early," I say when she picks up. "We're day drinking."

Chapter 6

"**I**'m not making you another one until you've called Dan." Jules and I are on the balcony of her condo. When I arrived an hour earlier, Jules held up a bottle of Tito's in one hand and Tanqueray in the other. "There's wine, too," she added.

I pointed to the gin. "Save the wine for book club next week."

Now we sit in lounge chairs watching the activity on the river and towpath below. Kayakers. Fishermen. A young woman pushing triplets in a stroller.

"Don't you people work? It's barely *two*." I mutter, draining the remains of my second gin and tonic. "Not you," I say to the pink-clad back of the mother, moving out of view. "You've got enough problems."

"Hey, Georg," Jules says. "Can I ask you something?"

I turn away from the towpath activity and towards my friend. "Sure."

"Why was the 'bestseller' stuff the final straw for you?"

I stare at my cherry red ballet flats, thinking.

"Because it's a flat-out lie," I tell her. "I wouldn't be doing my job if I didn't push back. When you're in communications, credibility is currency. If I went along with it and got called

76

on it, not only would Hudson look bad, but *I'd* look bad. In my profession, I'd be the woman who let her CEO author slap a sticker with a big fat lie on the cover of his book."

Jules mulls this over, then nods. "Fair enough," she says. "But seriously, Georgie. Call Dan."

I close my eyes and tilt my chin up, the June sun turning the inside of my eyelids the color of red velvet cake. "How? How do I tell him?

"The same way you told me," she says, reasonably. "That was your practice run."

"What if he's preparing for a meeting or conference call or something?" I point out. "I can't just call him and be all 'Hi honey! Ummm, just calling to remind you that I have book club next weekend so maybe you should make plans in advance with another dad to take all the kids bowling and, oh, I lost my job. Have a great meeting. Bye!'"

I know what I'm really dreading about our conversation are the Follow-Up Questions. Dan is the king of follow-up. Years ago, I stopped agreeing to make phone calls for him unless it was a topic I understood inside and out (and incredibly, he never seems to want me to make phone calls in regard to *Sex and the City)*, because it would usually go like this:

Dan: "Hey, can you call the garage for me and ask about the Honda repair?"

Me: "OK."

Later.

Me: "I called the garage. They said it'll be ready at 5:30 and it's $274."

Dan: "What did they have to do?"

Me: "Umm, fix it?"

Dan: "No, I mean did they have to take apart the (something

something car part) to find the problem or could they identify it by the sound it made on the test drive?"

Me: "….it'll be ready at 5:30."

I can imagine the follow-up questions now: What do mean, laid off? When? Did they say why? What exactly did she say? And then what did you say? What did she say then? And then the big one: What are we going to do now? That's the one that scares me.

"What if he calls you at the office?" Jules asks.

Gilda jumps in. *What if right this very second he's online buying something really expensive. What if you wait and then he buys something huge and nonrefundable, then suddenly he's like the wife in* The Full Monty, *clutching a garden gnome as the television is repossessed and asking, "Why didn't you* tell *me?"*

I sigh and retrieve my phone from the back pocket of my white capris. "OK."

Jules gets up and takes my empty glass. "I'll leave you to it." She heads back inside, sliding the door closed behind her.

I stand and move to the balcony railing, resting my elbows on its warm metal surface. Once again, my finger hovers over the call icon, and this time I press it.

"Hey," Dan answers in what I've come to think of as his Friday Voice. A touch more upbeat, the promise of extra sleep and down time imminent.

"Hey. Do you have a few minutes to talk?" I ask, nervously playing with the hem of my navy blouse.

Here's a silver lining, Gilda offers. *You never have to wear navy and white together again.*

"Is everything OK?"

"No, it isn't. I…." *just rip off the Band-Aid.* "Ah, shit, Dan. I got fired today. Laid off, technically, but Lena fired me."

78

There's silence for a few seconds. "You're kidding."

"Yes, Dan. I'm kidding," I say, exasperated. "Aren't I funny? Wasn't that hilarious?"

"Tell me what happened."

I do. I begin with my conversation with Bembé, and the high I felt on my way to Frank's office. I fill him in on Frank's "bestseller" order, my research, and finally, the meeting with Lena and Mark. By the time I finish, a lump is forming in my throat.

"I'm sorry, Dan," I say, my voice hitching.

"Fuck," mutters Dan, quietly. I don't think he intended me to hear it, and this causes me to full-on cry.

"Look, Georgie, I'm gonna talk to someone here at the firm. This isn't right."

"No shit, but it doesn't mean it isn't legal," I say. "Lena hinted as much when she brought up my review. It's their insurance against a lawsuit. I can't go down that road, Dan. I just can't." I turn away from the river and lean my backside against the railing.

"I get it. I'm just going to talk to them. You don't have to do anything," he says softly. "I need to go, but we'll figure this out, OK?"

"OK. I'll see you later. I love you."

"I love you, too," he says. "We're going to be OK."

I hang up and toss my phone onto a lounge chair. Grabbing the napkin that was serving as a coaster for my gin and tonic, I dab underneath my eyes. The paper is damp with condensation, soothingly cool against my skin. I take a deep, watery breath and crumple it up just as Jules opens the door and steps back outside. She walks purposefully towards me and envelopes me in a long, warm, powerful, lilac-scented hug.

"I'm scared," I confess.

"I know," she says. It's going to be OK."

"That's what Dan said," I reply, resting my chin on her shoulder. A few strands of her red hair dance as I exhale.

"Smart guy."

"Thank you for leaving early today," I whisper.

"Of course," she replies, then releases me. Her eyes have a mischievous glint I recognize and adore. She walks over to the hibachi and opens its cover.

"Here," Jules tosses me a t-shirt I hadn't realized she was holding. I catch the soft charcoal cotton in my hand and unfold it. It's a Ramones shirt left behind by an old boyfriend. I look back at her, my eyebrows raised.

"Navy isn't your color, G.," she says, grinning and reaching for the utility lighter. "Let's burn that bitch."

∞∞∞

Three hours later I'm in front of my stove, stirring ground beef around a skillet and eyeing the clock on the microwave. According to the neon green numbers, Dan will be home in about 20 minutes.

And on a normal Friday, you'd be getting take-out, Gilda says, a little sadly.

"Hush," I tell her, reaching for a can of red kidney beans. "I'm thinking."

I glance over my shoulder, as is my habit during these chats with Gilda, to make sure Max and Shannon haven't busted me. They haven't. Shannon's checking to see if bouncing on the trampoline will translate into steps on my FitBit; Max is defending an online fortress. Loudly.

I walk the dozen paces from the kitchen to the family room and lean against the doorway. "Max? Is screaming essential to winning?" I ask, pointing my spatula at the TV. A series of figures – blue shirts versus red shirts, it appears – are darting around what looks like a dystopian mashup of a coal mine and laboratory.

"Sorry, Ma!" he screams. Volume control and awareness are not his strong suits. "We're planning our attack," he adds, adjusting his headphones.

"Who is 'we'?"

"My friends," he says, a healthy dose of *duh* in his voice. "Joey and Declan."

"Dial it down, OK?" I tell him, as I turn to head back to the stove. "I'm trying to make dinner."

What I'm really doing is visualizing my conversation with Dan, a preemptive effort to steer it in a more positive direction than our history of discussions around money.

I open the beans and shake them into a colander, trying on opening lines.

"I'm not going to be irresponsible," I whisper, rinsing the beans. "This isn't going to be like before."

Why not?

"Because I don't even *have* a credit card anymore, that's why," I answer.

And why not? Remind me.

"I couldn't handle it, OK?" I mutter, angrily dumping the beans in with the seasoned beef. "It was always maxed out. Always. I hid it from Dan, and when I finally came clean we had to pull a chunk out of my 401k to get that fucking monkey off my back." I stir the beef and beans, adding two cups of diced tomatoes. "That was years ago. This is not going to be that."

I cover the skillet and turn the heat down, then sit at the breakfast bar. My neglected glass of iced tea is laced with condensation, and I draw dollar signs in the water. They run.

Just like your money!

"Not really fair," I mutter. "Most of it goes into our joint account."

That's true. Most of our money went to a joint account that covered our mortgage and all the household expenses: utilities, cable TV, phones, groceries and daycare. Especially daycare. Whatever each of us had leftover we left in our own individual checking accounts, with the caveat that it had to cover gas and spending money for the two of us. Cool, right? Effective. Grown-up, even.

I would totally agree…if I could have stuck to it. But for years, I'd get paid on my Friday and think: Wheeeee, I have money again! I can go to Starbucks this morning and get my coffee and breakfast there! Wheeee, we can go out to dinner tonight and I won't cook or do dishes! The kids want a small treat at the zoo's gift shop on Saturday? Why not? Oh, and don't forget to stop and pick up a bottle of wine for book club tonight. Wheeee, book club! And then Monday would roll around and I'd be tapped out. Again. Thus, the credit card.

I clawed my way back to some semblance of financial stability and good credit. And now this.

The lock turns in the front door and Dan steps in. I contemplate getting up to greet him in the living room. It seems like an awful lot of work.

Happy Friday! I got fired!

He appears in the doorway. "Hey."

82

"Hey," I reply.

He sits opposite me at the breakfast bar and starts to trace patterns in the granite top with his fingertips. "What are you making?"

I shrug. "We had the fixings for tacos. I figured tonight would be a good night to start cooking at home more."

He looks at me and nods. "Good call."

We sit in silence for a few moments. I don't want to start the conversation we need to have, and I suspect Dan doesn't either. I take a deep breath and begin.

"So, this is what I haven't been able to stop thinking about all day," I say. "I don't want to repeat that mess from five years ago. I don't want to go back there. And I promise you I won't."

Dan exhales and rubs the back of his head. A lick of his dark hair stays up.

"Neither do I, Georgie," he says. "I don't want us to be who we were then. I like how we are now."

I smile. "Me too."

"We'll need a plan."

"Well," I say. "I think I know a way we can save about four thousand dollars."

He sits up. "Yeah? Tell me."

"We cancel the summer camps."

Dan's shoulders slump. "Georgie, no–"

"Why not? Think about it." I lean over and lay my hand on his forearm. "We haven't paid for all of them, and it isn't too late to cancel and get our money back. They don't even *want* to go to them. It's a no-brainer."

He sits back up and looks at me. "I know I'm going to sound like an asshole, but I'll say it anyway. Don't you need to spend time looking for a new job?"

"So? They're not babies anymore begging me to play with them. They can entertain themselves when I need them to," I gesture to the family room, where Max is yelling at Joey or Declan to duck. "It'll actually be nice to see more of them."

"And what if you land something in, like, two weeks?"

I raise my eyebrows. "That's a bit optimistic, but I appreciate your confidence in me. In that case, they go to camp at the school; you said the other day they have space."

Dan drums his fingers on the bar top and then lifts his hands in a reluctant *you win* gesture. "OK, but I don't want Max on screens all day."

I get up and walk around to Dan's stool. I lean into him and we hug. "It's a start, right?"

He releases me and smiles. "It's a start. Let's eat, and then just relax tonight. We'll figure the rest out tomorrow."

I kiss him and muss the hairs still standing up in back. "You need a haircut."

He grins. "Can't afford it."

"Wow," I say. "You *are* an asshole."

∞∞∞

Hey! Says Gilda. This is like the Sisterhood of the Forgiving Yoga Pants!

I'm standing in the playground behind Shannon's elementary school, where the kids are forming classroom lines for the Pledge of Allegiance. This is all new to me. I was a Before School Mom, in my nylons and heels, rushing Shannon – and Max before her – inside the front door a half hour early.

I still see a lot of parents in office attire, but I have a few new peeps as of this week. There's a clan of us out there at the school yard, standing around with our comfy pants, our travel mugs of coffee, and baseball caps. Maybe we're headed to the gym right after the kids head into school, maybe not. Maybe we'll go home and have another cup of coffee while binge-watching *30 Rock* on Netflix. We don't discuss it. It's our own special version of Don't Ask, Don't Tell.

Shannon waves to me and smiles. *See you after school,* I mouth to her. Her smile widens and she nods. I wait until she's inside and begin the walk home, enjoying my light mood. I pull a set of earbuds out of the small zippered pocket of my black yoga capris, intending to indulge in a little folk punk. Before I can plug in, my phone starts playing "I Am Woman." Mom. I smile at the screen and pick up.

"Ahoy, thank you for *not* calling me at Hudson Hotels. How can I help you?"

My mom laughs. "How's your fourth day of freedom?"

"Lovely, so far," I tell her. "The house is actually *clean*. Can you believe it?"

"Give the kids a few minutes after they get home. Speaking of, it's going to be hot tomorrow. Why don't you guys come over here after school and swim. Dad'll grill."

I trot across the street and wave a thank you to the crossing guard. "I would *love* that. That'll give me the morning to do some job searches and get a little exercise in."

"Job searches already?" she says. "Can't you at least take the summer off?"

"Are you offering to pay my mortgage? Awesome!" I joke. "I'm just taking a little bit of time each day to see what's out there, that's all."

We say our goodbyes and hang up. I forego the folk punk and just walk, taking in the fullness of the trees and the heat of the morning.

The truth is, I feel out of practice. The Hudson gig came to me almost as a fluke. The last time I was unemployed – just before getting my job at the museum – was ages ago. Things were different.

Yeah, agrees Gilda. *There was no Facebook. You didn't even have a cell phone. Hell, you still worked out to* mixed tapes!

I unlock my front door and step inside, unhurriedly. Nowhere to go, nowhere to be. The morning is mine.

A half hour later – with the breakfast dishes done and a load of laundry churning away in the basement – I'm seated at the breakfast bar, a mug of fresh coffee to my right and my laptop open in front of me.

First on the list is my daily networking email. I send a brief and – I hope – unobtrusive message to the head of a small nonprofit I've come to the know and admire from my time at Hudson Hotels. I tell her that I'm in the process of making a career move, and would she be free for a cup of coffee sometime? I hit "send" and then turn my attention to the job boards.

I'm a middle-aged Dorothy for the next hour, following the yellow brick road of job posting email alerts (just click your mouse three times!). Director of Marketing, Director of Communications, Director of Marketing Communications, Director of Public Relations, Director of Media Relations, Director of Marketing Content Strategy. I obediently upload my resume to a few postings, and then spend an additional 10 minutes correcting all the places where the helpful (not) "auto-populate" function screwed things up.

"No, I *went* to UMass; I didn't *work* at UMass," I grumble at the screen. "But hey, are they hiring?"

And then the cover letter. The all-important cover letter. I have the basic template pretty much down. I typically open with "I read with great interest your posting for a [insert title here]," and close with an optimistic "I welcome the opportunity to bring my creativity and leadership to the [insert company] team."

But what about personality? A little line in the cover letter that brings out a sense of who I am? I agonize over this longer than I should before I give up and call Jules.

"Is there room for being cheeky in a cover letter when it's, say, a sporting goods company? Like, 'I spent 13 years working to protect the outdoors (you're welcome). Now I want to help people enjoy it.'"

"There's room. I like a little splash of cheek."

"OK, thanks. How earnest is too earnest when it's a nonprofit?"

"I need some examples."

"'I am passionate about leaving a better world for my children'?"

Silence at first from Jules. "I bet you're a lot of fun at parties."

I sigh. "OK, strike that one. 'I'm hard-working, creative, and don't take myself too seriously'?"

"Meh. The earnest ones will think you're mocking them. And you would be after meeting them."

"Tough crowd. 'I'm creative, hard-working, and thrive on telling a great story'? That last part makes it sound like I hang out in bars a lot. Is that bad or good?"

"It's good. Go with it," Jules says. "And I have to run, sorry. Some of us around here actually work, you know."

"Suckers."

We hang up and I turn back to the current posting. My

favorite part about applying online is the random words scripted in some funky font ("GaSsy CatS" or "ou-yay arted-fay") that the site forces me to fill out to make sure I'm a real person. As if it's my electronic Merlin from 1981 trying to become a marketing director.

As I click "submit" and send it off into the rabbit hole, I remember Jules telling me a few years back that under her HR department's computer-driven screening system, she wouldn't be considered qualified for her current job.

"And these are the systems I'm relying on to help me be employed again," I say, draining my now-cold coffee. I find I'm not excited about any of the jobs I've applied for. Not a single one.

Maybe you should make a change. A real *one*, suggests Gilda.

"To what?" I whisper into the empty cup. "And is that even a good idea at my age?"

I reach for the navy and white folder containing the details of my severance package, and find the notice for the free session at a career management firm. It lists resume and cover letter writing, networking skills building, LinkedIn profile creation, and other services, but my eye is drawn to 'career coaching.' Before I can come up with an excuse not to, I grab my phone and make the call.

Ten minutes later I'm registered for a career building class taking place tomorrow. And I'm in luck, the counselor tells me. There's a women-in-networking social right after the class ends. Why not? I sign up for the social as well. As I hang up, an email notification pops up from the nonprofit executive I reached out to earlier this morning. She was sorry to hear I'd moved on from Hudson, and she'd be delighted to have coffee with me, her reply reads. Does Monday work? I confirm our plans, feeling a glimmer of hope and – could it be? – excitement. I'm on my way.

Ahoy!

Chapter 7

hat the hell?? Gilda shrieks.

I pull open the door and find myself facing a heavyset man dressed in a suit jacket, a button down shirt, tasteful tie, white athletic socks, black sneakers and what can only be described as denim man-capris. I pause and check the door. I'm in the right place. But, again, what the hell? I carefully avoid eye contact and make my way over to the reception desk. Welcome to Career Building Class and Social Hour Day.

Dear God, what if he's the instructor?

This is not starting off well.

As I'm signing in, someone calls "Joe! You made it to Picture Day!"

Picture Day?

My mind automatically goes back to elementary school, and before I can stop myself, I've put Joe and his ensemble in Miss Hatch's second grade class picture. He's sitting in the middle of the seated front row holding the black letterboard with "Washington School, Second Grade." What is *going on* with Picture Day?

In a room off the reception area, a photographer has set up

a miniature JC Penney-esque Portrait Studio, with lighting, a neutral backdrop screen and a bar stool. At the reception desk, a staff member tells a guest that they've hired the photographer for the day to take headshots for use on LinkedIn, business cards and anywhere else a snazzy picture will help get you noticed.

Ah, a *headshot*. Oh, thank goodness.

But really, Joe, whispers Gilda. *You're already halfway there with the coat and tie. Would it have killed you to wear khakis? Or at least pants that reach past your ankles? I know Tommy Lee Jones made the jeans-jacket-tie thing work in* The Fugitive, *but remember Joe*:

I saw Tommy Lee Jones in The Fugitive.

I loved Tommy Lee Jones in The Fugitive.

Tommy Lee Jones was my Hollywood crush.

You, sir, are no Tommy Lee Jones.

A few minutes later, I and the other class participants are given an office tour by Bertie, our chipper class facilitator. Bertie is in her mid 50s with tight, short gray curls and the brightest, hot pink-est dress and bolero jacket combo I've ever seen. That with the hair and perpetual smile gives her a Dolores Umbridge vibe that I find oddly comforting in its familiarity. Bertie tells us we can come anytime during office hours to conduct our job searches; there's a dress code (ahem, *Joe*) of business casual, and the coffee's free. We're shown the cubicles where we can camp out to go online and review job boards, and the printers where we can print out our resumes and cover letters. Then we file into another room for the class.

Over the next two hours, I learn things.

"It's best to apply for a job via email on Tuesdays or Wednesdays," chirps Bertie. "Because on Fridays, HR staff are too excited for the weekend and on Monday's they're too cranky because it's over."

What happens on Thursdays? Gilda wonders. *Are they all looking for new jobs themselves?*

"And as soon as you apply online, you should go to the company's Twitter, Facebook, YouTube, Instagram and LinkedIn profiles and follow them," Bertie holds up an index finger sagely. "This is *very* important."

OK, says Gilda. *Stalking people is bad. Stalking companies is good. Got it.*

"Then, when you've applied online and followed them, print out your resume and bring it to their office personally."

"Uh, you mean like, with no appointment?" says a young man in an overly starched dress shirt.

"Yes!" Bertie beams at him. "Ask if you can have a few minutes with the hiring manager.

Sure! Show up unannounced. People love *that.* Gilda chimes. *I bet that goes over really well at defense contractors.*

I'm not understanding this class. Wasn't this "Career Building"? Wasn't this guidance on my strengths, my interests, and what I want to be doing for the rest of my life? Instead, I'm getting nuggets of wisdom like I should be shamed for still using Hotmail.

"And tell everyone you are looking for a job!" She sings, as the class wraps up. "People *want* to be helpful. Last year, I had a legal secretary land a job just a month after her firm closed down. Do you know how?" She looks at us expectedly, as if someone here would actually know the details of her mystery client's career journey. "Her neighbor had a daughter who knew a judge who knew a lawyer at another firm!"

Wow. Was Kevin Bacon in there somewhere, too?

The Women In Networking social starts promptly afterwards. I had been anticipating a room of a few dozen women milling around, some looking for advice and some looking to offer it. I would mingle, joke about glass ceilings with some female executives and maybe a mentor would emerge.

In reality, the only gainfully employed person in the room is Bertie. The rest of us are a mosaic of job seekers: recent high school or college graduates, many appearing to be in their late 20s to mid 30s, and a few, like me, ticking the "45 and up" box. We sit around a large conference table and she asks us one by one to say our name, our field, and three places we'd like to work. After each introduction, Bertie turns her attention to the rest of us. "Does anyone know anyone at any of these companies? Can you help put her in touch?"

I'm suddenly uncomfortable, and start to shift in my seat. My turn is fast approaching, yet my mind is blank. I can't come up with *one* place I'd love to work, let alone three. What is wrong with me?

The woman two chairs away from me begins to describe her career goals. Wordlessly, I pick up my things and stand. Gesturing apologetically at my watch to Bertie, I scurry out of the room, ashamed.

∞∞∞

I feel shaken and restless. I stand a few feet from the door, taking in slow, deep gulps of air to steady myself. There's a light touch on my shoulder.

"Are you OK?"

I turn. It's a woman I recognize from the networking event. She close to my age – perhaps five or so years older – wearing a cream silk sleeveless blouse with dark maroon slacks. Her ash blonde hair is an elegant twist, a simple string of pearls around her throat.

My hand reflexively goes to my still-too-long hair, tucking one side behind my ear. I smile softly.

"I'm fine," I say. "Thank you."

She offers a smile in return and gestures to the door. "First time?" I nod. "You?"

"Third."

She backs up a few steps while – somewhat contritely – removing a packet of cigarettes from her purse. I wave away her apology and she lights up, blowing the first inhalation off to her right. Her smile turns wry.

"I'd like to say it gets easier, but I'm a woman of a certain age," she says. She holds up her pack of Virginia Slims. "They like to say 'we've come a long way, baby,' but believe me, sexism and ageism are real."

I nod again. "Not the double feature you want to sign up for."

She nods back and flicks a half inch of ash to the ground. "We become more invisible with every wrinkle." She takes a final drag and grinds the remains of her cigarette under her foot.

"I don't mean to be a downer," she says, reaching for the door. "Better get back to it. Bertie's waiting Good luck to you."

I smile. "You, too."

I'm not ready to go home, so I enter a deli a few doors down from the employment firm. The line is a busy bustle of professionals on their limited lunch break. I remember that bustle. Already it seems like a long time ago. I feel like a poser in my (too tight) skirt, blouse and heels. Any moment now, I expect a pharmaceutical rep in a well-tailored suit to point at me across the crowded restaurant and shriek, like Donald Sutherland at the end of *Invasion of the Body Snatchers*.

I bring my turkey wrap and iced tea to a small table in the corner and sit. For the first minute I take a few more deep, purposeful breaths until my heart rate begins to slow down. I'm at a loss to identify what I'm feeling right now, and why I bolted from Bertie.

That was your one free pass at career building, Gilda reminds me. *If you want to go back, you'll have to pay for it.*

"I *don't* want to go back," I mutter into my tall paper cup.

As I eat my lunch, I am determined to do something; to take at least one small action that will shake me out of this paralysis. Pulling out my phone, I create a GMail account that, I decide, will be for my job hunting, career-inspiring, future-envisioning correspondence. My uncool personal life will continue to function under my uncool Hotmail account.

GMail. Check. That was easy. I feel better already. More hip and employable. Energized, I forge on and call up my LinkedIn profile. The one I've been ignoring for the last 18 months.

Whoa, that profile pic. Gilda gasps. *Was that pre-Max?*

My lips twist to the side, a lá McKayla Maroney-is-not-impressed. The photo is embarrassingly outdated, but I'm hard-pressed to find something suitable.

It's not that I'm camera shy. Far from it. Despite being self conscious about the extra pounds I've been carrying around for the last year and a half, I insist on maintaining a well-documented visual history. It's just that none of my photos are quite right for this particular social media channel.

All my hiking, biking and skiing pictures are out. I'm alone in some of them, and look like quite the cool outdoor girl if I'm honest. But no one wants to hire a show off. And really, a LinkedIn profile of me with my sunglasses and fluorescent yellow warm up jacket with a gorgeous blue sky and mountain range around me? Total. Show. Off.

Needing help, I open up my messaging app and text Nora, my old college room mate and current savvy advertising executive.

Hey, I need a new LinkedIn pic. I'm going to send you one in a sec. WDYT?

I choose one from last Christmas. It's the annual cousins-around-Santa (my Uncle Bob) photo, and I was having a particularly good hair day. I use my photo edit function to crop everyone else out, save for my cousin Susan's arm around my shoulders, and send it to Nora.

She responds within seconds. *It's clearly a group shot. I see an arm.*

So? I counter.

This is what people will think: "I don't have a picture with just me, so I cropped one. I guess I just don't like to be alone. Ever. Can I pop into your office two or three times a day, every day, just to chat?"

Really? I text back. *People are mean. How about this one?*

I send one of me taken by Max while sitting at my breakfast bar. I'm alone in it, which is progress. I'm in a medium gray sweater with a moderate cowl neck. A little casual maybe, but not too bad.

Again, her response is quick.

It says to us: "I may be just hanging out in a kitchen having coffee, but the gentle tilt of my head lets you know I'm approachable and a good listener. Talk to me. How can I advance your organizational goals?"

Us? I respond, wary.

Yes! I'm in a meeting. That last one was from the senior copywriter. Send us more; this is fun!

I send a middle finger emoji in reply and close the app. I should have at least taken advantage of Picture Day before fleeing. Joe: 1, Georgie: 0.

I'm leaving the deli when my phone buzzes. I'm expecting a return emoji from Nora – a devil? Tears of laughter? Poop? – when I notice it's not a text, but an email. Once I'm in my car, I open it. It's an invitation to interview for a job I applied to a few days ago. An education group is looking for a communications director, and they want to see me on Tuesday. It's in Boston, as I recall from the job posting, and the salary is decent. On paper, it's a great opportunity.

I reply immediately, accepting, then call a nearby salon and book a last-minute appointment to finally get my hair cut. I input the interview time and location into my calendar, then toss my phone onto the passenger seat and lean back, willing myself to feel happy about it.

∞∞∞

"And now, diving for the United States of America. From Wakefield, Massachusetts, Shannon 'The Eviserator' Fischer!"

Shannon, who's been bouncing at the edge of the diving board throughout my dad's introduction, grins at this cue and leaps into the air. She executes a near-perfect split jump and returns to a stick-straight pencil, slicing cleanly through the water. We wait until she surfaces – her blonde hair slicked to her skull, her eyes immediately seeking ours for feedback – before erupting into applause.

Good to see the dance tuition is paying off, Gilda says, impressed.

"And it's 10s all around," my dad announces, standing up. "Shannon Fischer, in her first Olympics, has captured gold, and the crowd goes wild!" He turns and enters the small room at the back of their house, which serves as a bar-and-snacks area when we're around the pool.

In the shallow end, Max launches into a deliberately off-key rendition of the national anthem, solemnly handing her a goldfish pool toy "medal." The kids occupied, I scooch my chair further into the shade of our table's umbrella and look over at my mom.

"What a perfect day," I tell her, stretching my arms over my head and smiling. Jimmy Buffett is drifting from the pool shed's speaker system. The late afternoon sun is still hot and the sky – through the canopy of old oak trees that surround my parents' yard – is cloudless. "I could get used to this."

My mom smiles back at me as my dad reappears, holding a full pitcher in one hand and three plastic margarita glasses gripped by the stems in the other. He holds the pitcher up. "Are we ready?"

"Ready!" we reply in unison.

Dad distributes the glasses and fills each one to its unsalted rim. Setting the pitcher on the glass-topped table, he lifts his drink to my mom and me. "Here's to us; to hell with everyone else."

My mom pauses before we can clink. "Here's to freedom from assholes."

"Hear, hear," I say. We clink. Or rather, we *clunk* with our pool-safe plastic.

My dad takes a long pull from his glass and sets it down. "So. How's the first week been?"

"It's...different," I say, considering my response. "The first few days were *great*. I got so much done around the house. Like, for the first time since Max was born I feel on top of things at home. That's huge."

"I sense a 'but' coming," my mom says.

"No. Not a 'but,' just this giant 'I don't know.' Before the circus came to town," I say, gesturing to Max and Shannon, who are now bobbing gently in the deep end on swim rings, deep in conversation about Minecraft, or whichever YouTuber they're obsessed with this month. "Everything seemed to just fit into place, you know? I liked what I did. I thought I was good at it–"

"You *are*," my mom says gently. I smile at her, grateful.

"But things are different now," I say. "Everybody always says that your life changes immediately when you have kids. I actually disagree with that. When Max and Shannon were babies, my life didn't turn upside down. I still worked. I still commuted into Boston. It wasn't until they got older that my life changed."

My mom takes a small sip of her margarita and nods. "Yes. They're more independent now, and you'd think that that would make life easier, but it doesn't. Because now they have school, homework, and all this other social stuff to navigate. When they're babies, their problems are simple. 'I'm hungry.' 'I'm wet.' Their problems are way more complicated now, as you found out with Max."

"Yes," I say, leaning forward. I'm relieved, though not surprised, that my mom completely and wholly gets it. She always gets it. "That's exactly it. They don't need me on autopilot, changing diapers or whipping up mac and cheese. They need me on a whole new level." I pause, remembering something, and look at Mom again. "Last week, you made a joke about how you couldn't be paid to be in your 40s again."

She nods. "It's not that I didn't enjoy my 40s; I did. But I was busy to the point of insanity. I never want to be that busy again." She takes a sip of her margarita. "But I didn't have a Lena or Frank to put up with when I was working."

"Speaking of," my dad says. "How's the search going?"

I consider the question. "You know, this whole week I've been looking through job postings, and I couldn't get excited about a single one of them. Ten years ago, I would've jumped at the chance for some of them. Everything's different now. I feel like I need something totally, completely new. Something that will make sure I can put the kids first, but not destroy my soul, like the-hotel-chain-that-must-not-be-named. And I have no idea what that is, or how to figure it out." I lean back again in my chair, momentarily defeated, but relieved to have found the source of my earlier unease. I decide to hold off on telling them about the interview, at least until I talk to Dan.

"Do you have to go back to work right away? In the next few months?" My mom asks.

I smile, a little wryly. "You know that scene in *Titanic* when they're assessing the damage from the iceberg and Andrews says 'the *Titanic* will sink. It is a mathematical certainty'?"

My mom nods. My dad refills my glass and cheerfully admits "nope!"

I turn my palms up and shrug. "Shannon's dance, Max's services, the house, college, retirement, et cetera, et cetera. I have to go back sooner rather than later. It is a mathematical certainty."

"So what's next?" asks my dad.

"That's what I need to figure out," I say, raising my glass.

"Mom!" Two voices shout in unison. Max and Shannon are now out of the pool, wrapped snugly in brightly colored towels, hair still dripping.

I lean forward and make eye contact over my dad's shoulder. "I sense a declaration coming."

"We're hungry!" announces Shannon.

"Are we staying for dinner?" Max asks, for the third time since our arrival more than an hour ago.

"Asked and answered, Max," I say. "The plan hasn't changed."

The kids jog inside, their oversized towels flapping around their ankles. They are, I am certain, raiding the snack drawer in anticipation of post-pool/pre-dinner downtime in front of the TV.

"That's my cue," Dad says, getting up and heading towards the grill.

My mom stands as well. "I'll start on the salad."

"You need my help?" I say, sitting forward. She waves me away.

"No. You sit and relax."

I sink back into my chair and pick up my glass. "That was the right answer."

Chapter 8

"That's amazing!"

Dan is beaming, and it's killing me. I manage a smile. "It could be good, yeah."

We're sitting on the family room sofa, where I'm filling him in on Denim Capris Joe, Perky Bertie, and the interview invitation. I leave out my fleeing from the networking session in a minor panic and my encounter with Ms. Wrinkled Into Invisibility.

"So tell me more about the organization," Dan says.

"Well, the job description made it sound like they were an education nonprofit," I say. "But when I did some quick research, I realized that they're actually a corporation that provides textbooks and online content to public and private schools. I want to do some more research over the weekend. You know, the good kind of stalking."

He smiles and points the remote at the TV, where he's queued up our current favorite British home renovation show. "Well, I'm happy for you."

I adjust the soft pink pillow in my lap and settle in for the episode. But as a Welsh couple attempts to convert a crumbling, three-sided cow shed into a home, my focus wanders.

Why haven't you told him that you need a change, you big chicken? Gilda asks.

I don't have an answer. Gilda does, though. As usual.

You know he wouldn't like it. He'd worry about money. So you avoid the conversation. Great strategy! Cluck cluck cluck!

Of course he would. He knows the mathematical certainty of the *Titanic* sinking as well as I do. I can't burden Dan with this "I've got to find myself" midlife crisis after using him as my personal complaint department during my 18 months at Hudson.

As soon as the Welsh couple unveils their stunning, wood and stone cow-shed-turned-home to the show's host, I stand up and stretch.

"I'm gonna take a look through my closet," I say. "I've got my interview on the brain now and I want to feel prepared. I yield all TV viewing decisions to my distinguished colleague."

"Sweet," Dan says, scrolling through Netflix like a digital parkour champion. "*Star Trek* it is."

"Annnnnd, I'm out," I say. "Live long and prosper."

Two minutes later, I'm standing in front of my closet, phone in hand and Jules on speaker.

"Do you remember that listicle-thing that went around email, like, two decades ago?" I ask. "About the things every woman should have when she's 30?"

"I remember something about having a decent piece of furniture not previously owned by anyone in my family," she said.

"That's the one," I say. "According to that list, I'm supposed to have, and I quote, 'something perfect to wear if the employer or man of my dreams wants to see me in an hour.'"

"Are you on dating apps again?" Jules asks. "We talked about this."

"Funny. Are you here all week?" I say. "I have an interview on Tuesday, and a networking thing on Monday."

"Hey, that's great news! Where?"

I sit down on the bed and fill her in on the details.

"The problem is my closet," I tell her. "I have acres of navy and white, and–"

"Oh God, stop," Jules says. "No. Just no. Where do you want to meet tomorrow?"

"The ink is still wet on my severance package, love," I say, rehanging my navy and white skirt.

"It's an outfit, not a spree," she says. "We'll steer clear of the fancy schmancy stores."

"It's Book Club tomorrow," I remind her.

"That's at *seven*, Georg. It's not like I'm flying you to Paris."

We make our shopping plans and hang up. I return to studying my closet. The news isn't good. I have exactly two decent pairs of jeans, which are out of the question. I have generic v-neck cotton t-shirts in every color (some of them dotted with coffee stains from my inevitable dribbles). And sweaters, of course. You don't live in New England without a collection of sweaters. But there's little here that's interview-y. First impression worthy.

Those extra pounds you're carrying aren't helping, either.

"Helpful," I mutter. "Thanks."

I'm contemplating caving to the navy when my Helen Reddy starts singing from my phone.

"Hi, Mom," I say.

"Hi, honey," she says. "I just realized we never talked about the career session you went to. How was it?"

"It was 10 different kinds of stupid," I reply. "But I *do* have an interview on Tuesday."

"Really?" She pauses. "Why?"

I snort in surprise, and then chuckle with relief. "Oh my God, Mom. That's the question I've been afraid to ask out loud all day." I sit back down on my bed and let out the sigh I didn't realize I was holding in. "Honestly? I don't know why. Because that's what you do when you're out of a job and need to work?"

Another pause. "I just don't want you to find yourself in another Hudson situation in a few months. You have a few months. You should take them."

"It's an interview, not a 10-year contract."

"All right, then," Mom says, suddenly all business. "If you're going ahead with this, you'll have to get dressed up."

"I know," I say. "I will."

"No, I mean *dressed up*."

"Yeah. I know," I repeat. "I'm going shopping with Jules tomorrow." *What is she getting at?*

"You need to wear a blazer." *Ah, we've arrived.*

My mom has always had better fashion sense than me. When shopping, I'll see stray pieces here and there that I like, but putting it all together has just never been my strong suit. But my mom? She has it down. At Christmas, I wouldn't just get, say, a sweater. The box would contain the sweater, the blouse to wear underneath, the perfect pants or skirt to wear with it, the earrings, necklace (or scarf! "A scarf is so versatile!") and bracelet. And sometimes, if I've been extra good that year, there's a blazer.

To my mom, the blazer is the ultimate wardrobe piece. Every woman needs one. Or six. Wear it with boots and jeans and you're casual chic. Wear it with a crisp blouse and a skirt and you're powerful and confident, a woman to be reckoned with.

"I get that, Mom. I do," I say. "There's just one small problem. Lately I look like a Weeble in blazers."

"A what?"

"Google it," I say. "I promise I will look for a non-Weeble blazer."

We exchange *I love yous* and hang up. I fall back onto the mattress, sling an arm over my eyes and lie still.

A Weeble? That's a little harsh, even for you.

"No, it's not," I whisper. "Blazers, big boobs, and bellies don't mix."

You can make it work, Gilda reasons. *I can hear Chevy Chase now. He's saying* Be the blazer, Georgie. *Besides, you suck at feeling sorry for yourself. Get a grip, go shopping, and be the fucking blazer!*

Yes! You're right, Gilda-Chevy! I know I'm on a new budget, but sometimes you have to spend money to make money, right? A new, well-fitting professional outfit is an investment in myself. Ignoring the wreckage that I've made of my closet, I get ready for bed, determined to march into the mall tomorrow with purpose and a positive attitude.

∞∞∞

Late the next morning, I'm standing in a dressing room cubicle, putting the latest batch of clothes on the hook I've designated the No-Fucking-Way pile and absolutely marinating in self-loathing. I feel like Shamu's older, less attractive cousin.

"Well?" Jules asks from the opposite cubicle. "Are you coming out in anything?"

"Uh, *no*," I say.

A metallic clink of a privacy latch slides open, and she's right outside my door. "What's going on in there?"

"In a nutshell?" I say. "If the pants are the right length, they won't button. If I can button them, my feet are standing on six inches of extra hem. The jackets are worse. I feel like I'll split the back seam the second I reach out to shake someone's hand. And they all have pockets that hit me right on either side of my pooch, courtesy of 18 crappy months at Hudson Hotels."

What is wrong with me? Why is this so hard?

"It can't possibly be that bad. And you have heard of tailors, right?" Jules says.

"Yes. I have, in fact, heard the elders speak of such 'thread wizards,'" I reply. "I require their services nearly every time I buy pants. I need a snazzy outfit *now*."

"Right. Then we're outta here," Jules says. "C'mon. Put down the pants and slowly back away. We're going someplace else – that department store a few doors down."

"Do we have to? That place is a zoo on the weekends."

"Yes. Let's try it, anyway. If it's nutty we'll just head straight to my place and start book club early. Just give me a second to change."

"Change out of what?" I ask. "If you're in a sheath dress I'm going to smother you with these enormous pants." I slide my lock back and open the door.

Jules does a slow full circle, her arms out. Her slender frame is hidden in a thick, floor length gown covered in large magenta flowers. The colors clash noisily with her red hair. It's the most hideous thing I've ever seen and I love her for it.

I grin. "You're ensconced in velvet. Just like George

Costanza always dreamed of."

"Velour," she grimaces, tugging at the neckline. "Like Mrs. Roper. Let's go."

We walk a few doors down to the department store. When we reach the women's section, my heart sinks. The place is a disaster. Shirts, jackets, shirts and pants of all sizes are mixed together on racks and the floor.

"What the hell happened here?" I say. "The annual Running of the Hopefully Employed?"

Maybe you should just get another pair of yoga pants and go home and make a cosmo, Gilda suggests helpfully.

Jules and I split up and tackle the racks separately. In the exercise section – of all places – I spot a medium gray skirt with a wide ruffle near the hem. Ruffle?

"Hey, Jules," I say, holding up the skirt. "Too short? Too much ruffle?"

She gives me a thumbs up. "Not too short, and the ruffle will give it a little extra movement when you walk. It'll look good."

I raise my eyebrows. "How do you know that?"

"*Project Runway*. Make it work, baby."

A few rows later, I pull out a forest green short waisted cardigan sweater without buttons.

"That green is great on you," Jules says. "I like that for the Monday networking thing."

"That's what I'm thinking," I say. "But is it too casual?"

Jules looks me over, considering. "No. It's a food rescue non-profit place, right? Aren't most of the staff in jeans carting around crates of broccoli and stuff?"

I laugh. "I think they do, actually. But they do really cool work and I like Kayla, the director. I got to know her when they won a Hudson grant and–" I freeze.

Across the aisle, browsing nonchalantly through a rack of trousers, is Lena. She isn't looking at me, but she's doing so in the telltale way that screams "I've seen you, but I don't want you to know I've seen you."

I turn away from her. Jules is looking at me quizzically. *Lena*, I mouth to her and jerk my head. Her eyes widen.

"Go try those on," she says. "I'll look around a little more."

I speed walk to the dressing room. The six stalls are all empty. I hang the skirt and sweater in the farthest one from the door.

She heard me talking about meeting with a grant winner. I'm certain she did. Should I be worried?

You pissed off the hotel founder and insulted Lena's managerial style in front of HR, Gilda says. *I'd say it's a firm 'yes' on worrying.*

Shit.

I yank the skirt from the hanger, willing it to fit. I'm one disappointment away from burning the mall to the ground.

Thankfully, it does. Jules was right about the hem swinging a little when I walk. Not in a *let's get an egg cream after the sock hop* way, but in a *why yes, I'm a professional woman who doesn't mind letting the world know that I have passable calves* way. My mood lightens a little.

Jules walks in as I'm in front of the mirror at the end of the dressing room hallway. "Lena left. I saw her walk out." She smiles and nods at the outfit. "Done. Green, gray, good to go. And now, try *this*." She hands me a faux-wrap dress in a cool black and tan pattern.

"She heard me talking about the interview with the food rescue people," I tell her before hustling back into my stall with the dress.

"So?" Jules asks. "What does she care?"

"Because she hates me?" I offer.

"I think you're overestimating your place in the grand scheme that is Lena's life."

"Maybe you're right," I concede, shrugging the dress over my head and studying it. The wrap camouflages my midsection, the neckline isn't too low or too high and the pattern makes me feel chic.

"I *love* the dress," I announce. "It's perfect for the Tuesday interview. I declare this expedition over."

I pay for my new treasures, and Jules and I part ways in the parking lot. As soon as I'm back in my car, I pull out my phone and text my mom. Just found great outfits for the meetings next week!

The tension slowly drains from my shoulders on the drive home. OK, I breathe. It's going to be OK. I now have something perfect to wear to my upcoming meetings *and* if (when!) the employer of my dreams wants to see me in an hour. I just have to remember to cut the tags off first.

Ding! goes my phone. Is it the employer of my dreams already?! It's probably Mom, congratulating me on a job well done. At a red light, I slide my phone out of my purse. It's an email from Kayla, the executive director of the food rescue organization.

Hi Georgie,

I'm sorry to have to do this, but I won't be able to meet with you as planned on Monday. I'm concerned that it would be considered a conflict of interest with the team at Hudson. Perhaps I'm being overly cautious, but the grant is too important to risk it.

I hope you understand. Again, I'm sorry. I always enjoyed working with you and wish you the best.

Two short beeps from the car behind me alert me to the green light. I wave a thank you/sorry in my rearview mirror and move forward, tossing my phone onto the passenger seat. My gut is a pit of anger, slowly boiling over to rage.

Bitch works fast, notes Gilda. *It's been, what, a half hour since you saw her?*

"It's possible that Kayla came to this conclusion on her own," I say, unconvincingly, to the windshield.

On a Saturday? Gilda counters. *Shortly after Lena catches wind of it? Don't be an idiot. You played along with Lena and Frank's B.S. for a year and a half, and here you are* still *playing along. Grow up, sweetheart.*

"But *why*?" I exhale, slapping the steering wheel with both hands. "Why would they bother?" I already know the answer.

Because Frank has decided you'll never be a success, Gilda reasons. *And heaven forbid you actually prove him wrong.*

∞∞∞

A few hours later, Nora wraps me in a hug as soon as I step into Jules' foyer for book club. I close my eyes and breathe in her Shalimar scent before we disentangle. She smiles ruefully. "Jules filled us in. Screw that fragile entitled guy."

"Eww," I reply. "No, thank you."

I follow Nora into the living room. Nora's wife Tess, and Tess' twin sister Natalie sit on Jules' smoky gray suede U-shaped sectional, glasses of red wine in hand. Short and fair-skinned, Natalie and Tess are identical save for the lengths of

111

their dark hair. While Natalie's waves brush her shoulders, Tess' thick braid reaches to the middle of her back.

On the glass-topped coffee table are nuts, olives, an assortment of cheeses, salami, and crackers, and three copies of our chosen book, *We Have Always Lived in the Castle*. The unmistakable hollow *pop* of a wine cork reveals Jules' location in the kitchen.

I raise both my hands. "Hey everyone, I got fired. How is *your* week going?"

Tess raises her arm and points down at herself. "I got pooped on by my adorable three-year old-daughter who really didn't enjoy her new potty."

Natalie mimics her twin's gesture and adds "And I got pooped on by an adorable three-year-old lab/beagle who really didn't enjoy her physical."

Jules' walks the two steps down from the kitchen into the sunken living room, holding two empty wine glasses by their stems in one hand and a full bottle of cabernet in the other. She's in a fitted black t-shirt with the *Seinfeld* logo blazed across the front, skinny jeans, and leopard print flats.

I accept my glass and sit on the corner of the sofa I've come to think of as mine, my left leg curled up under my body. I grab one of the burgundy chenille throw pillows and place it in my lap. It's my settling in routine, a bit like a superstitious ball player's ritual at bat.

"Cheers, ladies," says Jules, raising her glass. "Here's to Georgie; may the angels of employment bless her resumé. And," she adds, lifting her cabernet higher. "Here's to Frank; may the offspring of a million bed bugs infest his hotels."

Nora turns to me, her umber brown skin flawless against her chic orange jumpsuit. "OK. I, for one, think Merricat and

Constance can wait. Georgie, love, how are you?"

I make a show of checking my watch. "Right now? Happy to see you all. Eight minutes ago I was mildly optimistic. At four-thirty I was freaking out. Ask me again in five minutes."

"How did the kids take it?" Tess asks.

I chuckle at the memory. "They were overjoyed, running around the first floor shouting 'No more after school!' No more camps!'" I swirl my wine and look down. "I was actually a little scared to tell them. I mean, how do you tell your kids you've lost your job? Especially when they're old enough to know what it means, but still young enough to see you as this–" I make an air quote with my free hand. "All-knowing, all-powerful, unshakable being?"

My friends nod in agreement and empathy, but no one speaks.

"So Dan and I just played it off like it wasn't a big deal. 'Hey kids, I'm not going to be doing my job at the hotel anymore, so if you don't feel like going to After School for the last few weeks of school, you don't have to.'"

"I think that was exactly the right thing to say," Natalie says quietly. "It focuses on how it's a good thing for them."

"It *is* a good thing for them," adds Tess, and I stiffen slightly. Gilda – normally absent when I'm with my friends – awakens, listening.

I take a sip of my wine and reach over for a piece of sharp cheddar. "You know, it's weird. I've had so many people – my mom, my neighbor, some of my coworkers – tell me 'you're so lucky; you get to take the summer off and just relax!'"

"Ah, so *helpful*," Natalie says, rolling her eyes.

Jules is more to the point. "Asshats. Not your mom, though."

Tess glances around the sofa at us. "Is that a bad thing? To take the summer off to relax?"

Oh, you're adorable, Gilda coos. *But Dan doesn't make 200 grand like your spouse, sweetie.*

"No, it's not. But it isn't that," I tell her. "When you've been laid off, the last thing you feel is lucky." I pause and correct myself. "Unexpectedly laid off, that is. It's not unheard of for *some* people" – I catch Jules' eye – "to do Snoopy's happy dance across the lobby as they clutch their severance package to their chest." She winks back. "But right now that's not me."

Nora nods, running a hand over her close cropped hair. "If you want to cheer someone up after a layoff, tell her she's really talented and she'll find a new job she loves. Tell her you're happy to help her network."

"Tell her you'll drink heavily with her when the need arises," adds Jules.

"Check," I salute her.

"But don't tell her she's lucky," agrees Natalie. She turns to me. "What's the Doomsday Clock set to?"

"Four weeks," I tell her. There's a mild groan around the room. "Counting down – second after lightning fast second – to the day when my severance runs out."

Tess sets her glass down. "I'm sorry, ladies, but this is bullshit."

We stare at her. She tosses her long dark brown braid over her shoulder and looks at me. "Would you say the chances are pretty good that you'll be working *next* summer?"

I shiver a little. "God, I would hope so."

"So you're looking at this all wrong. Isn't this a gift summer? A chance to hang with Shannon and Max while they're young enough to enjoy having you around all day?"

I give a half shrug. "I just don't think we can afford that."

"But you don't *know* you can't," argues Tess. "Look, you're already getting full pay for the next month, and they won't fight you on unemployment. This time – this summer – won't be back again."

I grab a handful of pretzel chips and munch one, considering.

"And it isn't like you have to spend a hundred bucks a day, traipsing around Boston and eating at Mistral. This is just… time…*slow* time."

I point my pretzel chip at her. "If you tell me the days are long and the years are short, I *will* mock you."

"We all will," adds Jules.

Tess sighs. "What will Deathbed Georgie say?"

Natalie pops an olive in her mouth. "Way to keep it light, Sis."

"Shut up. You know what I mean. On your deathbed, will you remember that leisurely summer with the kids, or that summer you got laid off and went back to work right away."

"She'll remember not foreclosing on her house," says Jules, a microscopic edge to her voice.

"OK," says Tess, palms raised. "I'll stop."

You know, maybe she's right, suggests Gilda. *I might have to take back that "sweetie" remark.*

"Maybe you're right," I say out loud, more to myself than to Tess.

"You need to do what's best for *you*," Nora says, softly.

"But what if it *is* what's best for me?" I counter. "I mean, it terrifies me, but I hate the idea of letting my fear make all the decisions for me." I turn to Tess. "No. You *are* right. I'm looking at this the wrong way. I've been so…so…mired in everything and everyone *around* me that I have no fucking idea who *I* am or what *I* want." I think of the elegant woman I met at the women in networking event. *We become more invisible with every wrinkle.* "I made a really bad job move for my family, and while it helped them, it nearly destroyed me. I don't regret it, exactly, but I can't do that again. Not unless I have to. This *is* a gift summer, and I'm going to take it."

Tess clinks her glass against mine. "To gift summers."

"No, no," Jules says. She looks at me, gestures to her t-shirt and wags her eyebrows. "You have to say it. It's perfect."

I pause, blinking, then catch on. I stand, grab the brick of cheddar cheese in my hand, raise it over my head, and attempt my best George Costanza voice.

"I declare this the SUMMER OF GEORGIE!"

Jules hoots, and Nora collapses to her side in laughter.

Natalie looks at the cheddar, crestfallen. "You...you just touched all the cheese. That was small batch organic."

Nora sits back up and stares at her sister-in-law. "Seriously? Honey, you were shat on by dogs today."

Chapter 9

"Georgia? Great to meet you. Thanks for coming in on such short notice."

Marvin, the education group's chief marketing officer, greets me in the reception area with a handshake approach so enthusiastic I nearly mistake it for a haymaker. He's tall and slim, dressed in expertly creased chinos and a brick-red V-neck sweater vest over a white dress shirt and half Windsor-knotted navy necktie. His teeth are aggressively white.

"Call me Georgie," I say. "And it's my pleasure. Thank you for the invitation."

Marvin leads me into a modest-sized conference room. One wall is lined with windows overlooking the bandstand in the Common. It's an amazing location, and yet it still doesn't make me want to be back in Boston full time.

The next 15 minutes unfold as if we're reading aloud from *Interviewing For Dummies*. Small talk to break the ice. I talk about myself, my experience, and my interest in returning to mission-driven work. Cue Marvin to outline the needs of the company and the details of the job. When he does, though, something's off.

He keeps saying "sales," Gilda points out. *Why does he keep saying "sales"?*

"So," I say, when Marvin pauses for a sip of water. "I'd love to hear some examples of how this position supports the sales team."

Marvin nods and smiles, but keeps his neon white teeth hidden. "This role is a key member of the team. We're one of the largest providers of K-12 education products – virtual and in book form – in New England." As he talks, I listen for something – anything – that distinguishes "communications" from "sales." Unsuccessfully.

I lean back in my chair and nod back as he wraps up his response. "OK, that's helpful. So, just for my own clarification, when you say this role is 'a member of the team,' do you mean that the communications director is responsible for selling the product?"

He smiles again, this time bringing The Teeth to the event. "Exactly."

Exactly. As in, if there's exactly one career I could never be happy or successful in, it's sales. I simply don't have the stomach for cold calls to strangers that are designed to end in people handing me money. When I meet or hang out with people who *are* good at it – like my lovely Nora – and they start sharing stories about their work, it's like I'm witnessing a horse singing. *My goodness! Look at this strange and wondrous thing!* But me? In sales? No. This is categorically and unquestionably not the job for me.

I should be disappointed. I should be giving myself a *be the blazer*-esque pep talk in order to forge on with the interview. But I'm not. Instead, I feel a relief so palpable that I have to consciously reel in the grin that's threatening to march across my face like Hitler.

"OK, well," I begin. "I'm confident that this really isn't a good fit for my skill set." Marvin blinks. His mouth drops open for a moment, then snaps shut. The smile – sans teeth – returns. "I'm sorry?"

"I view communications as fundamentally different from sales. If you need a salesperson, then I can't – in good conscience – continue to take up your time." I stand and shake Marvin's hand. "I appreciate the opportunity to meet with you. Good luck in your search."

How thoughtful of you! Gilda says. We leave the conference room, and The Teeth and I part ways.

Once outside, I stride towards the train station, enjoying the swing of my new wrap dress as I walk. Making my way across the Common, I pick out a bench and sit, pulling my phone out of my purse. Dan picks up right away.

"Hey, how'd it go?"

"Sales," I say. "It was a sales job."

"Ah, shit," Dan says. "I'm sorry."

"I'm not," I reply. "In fact, I'm happy about it. If I was wearing a hat I'd be tossing it up in the air like Mary Tyler Moore."

Dan is silent. I spot a group of mothers and infants spread out on a circle of brightly colored blankets, a fleet of strollers behind them. I steel myself and forge on.

"So, I was afraid to tell you this on Friday because you were clearly so relieved that I had an interview," I say. "But I'm not ready to settle for a job I'm not excited about. Not yet." I can hear Dan take a breath to interject. "Just listen for a minute. We're already saving a few thousand bucks by pulling the kids out of summer camp, and I have a month's pay for severance. We have some time. We have time for me to really figure out what I want to do next. And I know it freaks you out, but I promise you we have time. We will be OK. But I need you to understand that I can't put myself into another Hudson situation. I just can't."

More silence.

"Dan?"

"No, you can't," he finally says. "Does this have anything to do with what we talked about a few weeks ago? About you feeling 'underwhelming'?"

I consider the question. "In part, yes. But it's not just that. I can't afford to take another bad position and end up hopping from job to job. Not at my age. My next move needs to stick. And it needs to make me happy."

There's another silence. A longer one. "We can't go out as often."

"I know that," I say. "I'll cook more. I might even get better at it. My cooking warnings could be downgraded from 'run and hide' to 'maybe we'll be pleasantly surprised.'"

A gruff laugh from Dan. Then more silence. I know that right now his aversion to risk is triggering a fight or flight response. I stay quiet.

"We have *some* time," he says finally. "Not a lot of time."

I close my eyes. "I know."

"No credit cards, either," he adds. "For me to be on board with this, you need to promise me that."

"I promise."

"I wish you had told me what you were feeling on Friday," Dan says. "You get that I want you to be happy, right? I'm not just looking at a bank balance here."

I look down, feeling my face flush. "I wanted to go through this interview today to be sure. And I am."

We say our goodbyes and hang up. I let out a great, whopping sigh, drawing a startled glance from an old man in a black watch plaid cap. I beam back at him, feeling giddily light.

It really is *going to be the Summer of Georgie,* says Gilda, impressed. *What are you going to do with it?*

I stand. There's half an hour before my train. I make my way slowly uphill towards the State House, glancing with renewed interest at the buildings surrounding the park. Who works there? What do they *do?* Are they happy doing it? When I reach Bowdoin Street I'm slightly out of breath, and grateful that the rest of the walk is downhill. I look at my Fitbit and tap the tiny screen to switch from steps to heart rate.

Yikes, says Gilda. *Maybe spend your summer channeling a little less Julia Child and a little more Gillian Michaels?*

∞∞∞

An hour later, I step off the train at the commuter rail station a half-mile from my house. I'm enveloped in the warm, sugary smell of cinnamon buns from the family-run bakery across the street. Yum. But no. I'm channeling Gillian, not Julia. Resolute, I exit out of the trivia app on my phone and dig my earbuds out of my purse, relying on Blondie to put a little length and speed into my stride.

Ideas for what to do with my newfound summer have been flitting around in my head like pinballs since talking to Dan. Most are of the domestic variety: declutter the house, put our photos from the last seven years in actual albums, plant an herb garden. But now, as I walk home, the one that lingers the longest is the opportunity to really, truly, finally call a truce

121

between me and my body image.

I pause the music and open up my Contacts. I scroll past Jules – she's *working*, after all – and call Tess. She picks up right away.

"Hey," I say. "Is this a good time?"

"Of course," a chair scrapes across a floor. "How's things with you?"

"Why do I think about my weight and my body several times a day, every day?"

"Skipping the small talk; I like it," Tess says.

"Seriously, though," I say. "It has prime real estate in my brain and is my inner monologue's favorite subject. Why?"

"You know why. Because we're women. Because we've been trained by every movie, TV show and magazine. Because loudmouth pricks like that *UK Apprentice* chick say fat people are lazy and weak-willed."

"I'm not lazy, though," I counter. "I climbed Mount Washington. On purpose, even."

"You're not weak-willed, either," Tess points out. "You stood up to Frank."

"That turned out well, didn't it?"

"And you're crushing it being a mom to a lovely boy with autism," Tess adds. "That *is* turning out well."

I smile as I round the corner onto my street. "Thank you, love."

"Want to tell me what prompted the question?"

"Eh, it's stupid," I say. "I've been gifted a summer and want to emerge at the other end with something to show for it."

"That's not stupid, and don't talk about my friend Georgie that way," Tess says. "In fact, we'll do it together. We'll set a goal with an end of summer deadline."

"I'd *love* that," I gush. Reaching my front steps, I scoop up the pile of mail inside the storm door and freeze. Peeking out of the middle of the small stack is an unmistakable navy blue double-H logo. "Thanks for the pep talk, love. I'll talk to you soon. We'll make a plan."

I unlock my door and step inside, tucking the mail under my arm. Oh God, what now? Placing my purse on the foyer table, I gently free the letter from the rest of the pile. It's not a letter, actually, but a postcard. I turn it over and read it.

Ahoy!

Welcome to 100 Revolutions! We're happy to have you on board. A packet with your event shirt, race bib, and ride-day details will be sent to the address on file two weeks before the event. The Hudson Foundation's webpage (see url below) has answers to any questions you may have, as well as information on how you can order copies of Frank Hudson's bestselling new book, The Business of Giving it Away. While you're there, check out some of the book's most recent rave reviews!

See you in September!

"Bestselling," I say, tearing up the card. "And in Comic Sans, too. Asshole."

I head upstairs and swap my dress for my new uniform of yoga capris, v-neck cotton t-shirt, and flip flops. According to my bedside clock, I have an hour before I pick Shannon up from school. I grab the thriller I'm nearly finished with and jog back down the stairs. As I pass the foyer table, I spy the postcard shrapnel and pause to sweep the pieces into my hand.

As I watch them fall into the tall kitchen wastebasket like

confetti, Gilda whispers.

You were *going to ride, though. Weren't you?*

"Yeah, right," I say to the empty kitchen. "A century ride. Me."

You had a reason to ride, though. "Because fuck Lena, that's why," you said.

I can't swing a century ride. My current level of fitness isn't going to see me coasting across the finish line at the Hudson headquarters; it'll get me swept by the ride officials with 20 miles to go.

So you'll have to train. Sounds like you have a goal with an end of summer deadline. "Oh, shut up," I mutter. But there's something to this. There's something about my entry slipping through the cracks just before my firing that's tempting as hell. And then there's the whole "fuck Lena" part.

But to do this right, I have to know exactly what kind of uphill battle I'm facing. I descend the basement stairs to the kids' game room and take out the balance board that goes with their Wii gaming system. I start up the TV, launch the WiiFit Channel and start building my fitness log in profile.

Hey, neat! I can design my own avatar (they call it a "Mii" - clever!), set a goal and weigh in daily.

Ready! says the WiiFit. *Step on!* I step onto the balance board.

Ohhh! it squeaks.

Really? What, *am I hurting you, WiiFit?* Am I, with my extra baggage, actually hurting you? Newsflash: you're an inanimate object. Smart-ass programmers. I make a mental note to draft a friendly suggestion to Nintendo: no editorializing during weigh-ins.

Measuring...measuring...measuring...all done! it chirps.

Upbeat Muzak plays as the program shows me my left/right weight distribution (slightly favoring the right) and balance. Then I watch as my Mii appears on the screen. Awww, look! That's so cute!

Suddenly, the blue "Current" line starts moving up. Rapidly. Through the blue zone, the yellow zone, the pink zone and landing deep into the red zone. Meanwhile, my Mii starts spinning around like a top and then with a *poof!* and some very fat-sounding honks from a tuba, my now-chunky Mii is looking down at herself like "WTF! I was skinny just a few seconds ago!" She even shakes her head in amazement at how I could have let us both go like this.

That's obese! squeaks WiiFit. Oh, you bitch.

My "friendly suggestion" turns into a full on scathing letter in my head. Are they *serious*? What's with the digital humiliation? I can see the programmers now, sitting around a table in a windowless room with crumpled bags of Doritos and empty cans of Red Bull: "Oh! Oh! Guys, I've got it. Listen: We should totally have tuba music if they're fat!"

No wonder you're obsolete, Wii. I bet XBox and Playstation don't mock their owners.

I call Tess again. "I just got fat-shamed by my gaming system," I begin.

"Oh my God, the WiiFit, right?" she exclaims. "I stopped using mine until I lost all the baby weight and then stepped on again just to put that bitch in her place."

I flop down onto Max's gaming chair and sigh. "Were you serious about getting fit together this summer?" I venture. "Because I have an idea."

∞∞∞

125

A few hours later, I'm sitting at the breakfast bar with my open laptop when Dan walks in after work.

"Something smells good," he says. "What is it?"

"Pad thai," I say proudly. "And I've even cleaned up the pans in advance."

Dan leans against the doorframe and peers at me. "Who are you?"

"June Cleaver," I reply. "It's a pleasure."

"No pearls?" Dan takes the stool opposite me and reaches over to give my hand a hello squeeze. "Where are the monkeys?"

"Downstairs. Building a cruise ship in Minecraft. It has an astronomy tower and a petting zoo."

"Of course it does," Dan nods at my laptop. "What are you working on?"

"I'm downloading a training plan," I say. "To train for a century ride in twelve weeks."

"A century ride? As in 100 miles?"

"As in," I say, my eyes on the screen. "Tess said she'd do some training rides with me."

"In 12 weeks," he says, more to himself than to me. "Are you planning to ride 100 Revolutions?"

My eyes slide up to meet his. "I am. I registered before Lena fired me, and a postcard arrived today with event stuff. A postcard that called the book a *bestseller*."

"Ridiculous," Dan mutters. "But you don't have to do it anymore, Georgie, so why would you?"

"I know it sounds nuts, but I kind of think I need to."

"Why?"

I close my laptop and rest my elbows on the breakfast bar. "Well, a few reasons. Fitness, for starters. I could take off the weight I put on during my tenure in hell." I point at him. "I know what you're thinking, and if you start humming Queen or Spinal Tap or any other band with a song about large derrieres, I will smother you in your sleep."

Dan snorts and ducks his head. Guilty. "Please proceed, my lady."

"It's a goal that I have control over. I mean, if I train, I'll do well. If I don't, I won't. And it's something I would be so incredibly proud of doing. Biking 100 miles in one day is a big deal, right?" I look at Dan for confirmation.

He nods. "It's not *underwhelming.*"

I roll my eyes, but still smile. "The other thing is, and I know this might sound weird," I say. "But the training rides could be my contemplation time, you know? My own time to just let my brain run loose. Maybe I'll start to figure out what my next step is."

"You can't 'contemplate' at home?" Dan says, making air quotes.

"What, like while I'm folding laundry?" I say, a warning creeping into my tone. "No, I can't. There are too many distractions here. When I'm here, I'm focused on the kids, on what's for dinner, on the *laundry*. Anything but me."

Dan holds up his hands. "I get it. I'm sorry. I didn't mean to sound all knuckle-dragger there. Honest."

I nod back at him, acknowledging he's not Cro-Magnon Man. Or the state legislature in Texas. "And then, of course, there's the 'F-you' factor to my favorite former boss."

Dan raises his eyebrows. "The F-you factor?"

I nod again. "Yeah. She told me to ride the 100-mile route with The Book Prophet just to be an asshole. I guarantee you she never thought I'd actually do it. Had she not canned me an hour later, it would have been one more thing to flog me for at my review."

"Well, F-her indeed, then," Dan agrees. We sit in silence for a few moments. "Is Tess doing the Revolutions ride with you?"

I shake my head. "No. I believe she said she'd rather spend a day squeezing lemon juice into paper cuts. She'll do some rides with me, but she's not doing the full training plan or the event."

"Are you sure you're OK doing Revolutions by yourself?" Dan says.

I shrug. "I won't be by myself; there'll be a few hundred others riding the century route. And it's not like I'm going to stick around for the after party."

"Good," Dan says, clearly relieved. "You don't need to be around that scene again."

I wave his words away. "I'm not worried about that. I don't work there anymore. There's nothing they could do now to get to me." I pause, and shiver a little. "I think somewhere out there, Lena just said 'hold my beer' to Frank."

Dan laughs. "Or the other way around." He stands up and starts pulling our water glasses down from the shelf. "Well, Georg, I think it's a great goal. I'm happy for you."

"Thanks, babe," I say, then turn around. "We're ready to eat."

Dan walks to the basement door and shouts down the stairs. "Kids! Dinner!"

After an obligatory groan at having to shut down their game, Max and Shannon stomp up the stairs from the game room.

"What are we having?" Max asks.

"Pad thai," I answer, moving off the stool and taking four plates down from the cabinet.

"I don't like that," he says, scowling. "I want a grilled cheese."

This is his patent response to anything I make that isn't, you know, grilled cheese.

I smile calmly at him. "You've never had pad thai, sir. You are busted."

"What's in it?"

"Peanuts, noodles, and chicken. Try it." I start scooping the food onto plates.

"Yeah, Max," Dan says, pouring him a glass of water and catching my eye. "Maybe we'll be pleasantly surprised."

Chapter 10

My life takes on a new and comforting routine. As Max and Shannon slide through their final week of school, I sign up for spin classes. I weep quietly through Shannon's heartbreakingly adorable fourth grade "Moving On" ceremony, and then lug my road bike out of the garage to be serviced.

The first few weeks of summer vacation are bliss. We hike, pick strawberries, visit the zoo, and see movies. Sometimes we band together with other families, sometimes it's our tight little group of three. We take pictures and make short, silly videos to send to Dan at work or show him during dinner so he's up to speed on Fischer Expeditions.

Most weekdays, we camp out for at least part of the day at our favorite country club, Chez Nana & Bop Bop. That's when I get to steal an hour or so to join a spin class or set off on my newly tuned Trek. Channeling Dan's love of spreadsheets, I've started tracking my mileage, average speed, and elevation. I discover that it's actually *really* fun to see my progress laid out so neatly, but I'll never tell him that. Every marriage needs a little mystery.

I've come to love my solo rides. My reptilian brain takes over the bike and, as it pedals and brakes for red lights, I unleash my frontal cortex. It scampers off in a variety of directions, conjuring up satisfying – if unrealistic – scenes of smiting my enemies or achieving stardom. On a steamy morning in early July, I had a long, fictional conversation with a nameless and faceless independent filmmaker. He is smitten with my "Diary of a Teenage Drag Queen" concept – *particularly* the title – and simply must bring me on to co-write the screenplay.

Weekends are for my longer training rides. Today it's 25 miles, the longest I've biked since last year's 100 Revolutions. Tess is with me; we're meeting the rest of our book club for a late Saturday lunch at a bar exactly 25.7 miles from Tess and Nora's place. I've decided I won't tell Tess the .7 part.

"Your calf muscles are scaring me a little," Tess says from behind me, puffing. "They look, like, mad at you."

We've just crested a long hill, the kind that seems to flatten out, but really continues climbing for another tenth of a mile. I hate those hills.

"They're not mad," I say, reaching down to free my water bottle from its cage. "They're just disappointed."

She laughs and maneuvers her neon yellow bike alongside mine. Traffic is quiet, offering us an opportunity to ride side by side. The road is lined on either side by plumes of late-blooming lilac bushes, and their light, sweet scent takes an edge off the humidity.

"We're, what, 20 miles in?" she asks. I nod, taking a long pull from my bottle.

"If this was 100 Revolutions," Tess says. "You'd be a fifth of the way there."

"Huh," I say. "Is that supposed to make me feel good or bad?"

She laughs. "Right now, bad. My butt hurts. The chairs at

this place better have cushions." Tess stands on her pedals and leans her hips back, stretching her legs and back. "You're in Echo Lake all next week, right?" Tess asks me. I nod.

"I'm jealous. Our week on the Cape isn't for another month." She sits up in her seat and shakes a cramp out of one of her wrists. "So how's the Summer of Georgie been? Is it your own unique version of eating an entire block of cheddar cheese?"

"So far, yes," I reply. "I feel so much better than I did a month ago. I can actually find stuff around my house. I haven't botched a meal in, like, days. And my solo rides have become long free-writing exercises, only all in my head."

"Have you cracked the code of personal and professional nirvana yet?"

"No," I say. "But the summer is young." I maneuver my water bottle back into its cage. "Thank you for keeping me company."

"Actually, I'm glad we're doing it this way," she says. "It means I can get nachos. A huge, heaping platter of nachos."

"Oh God, that sounds good," I say. "And you're sure Nora put the bike rack on the car?"

"I did it myself," she says. "With a note tied to it that says 'DO NOT REMOVE.'"

The traffic picks up as we enter a suburban business district, and we ride the last few miles in silence, single file. Gliding into the sports bar's parking lot, we stop and dismount behind Tess and Nora's cute orange Subaru. As we stretch, Nora comes out of the bar to help mount and lock our bikes on the rack.

"I am impressed," Nora says, beaming at Tess.

"My butt hurts," Tess says amicably, returning the smile.

"The nachos are waiting for you," Nora says. "And beer."

"Oh, you goddess," says Tess. "Lead the way."

Inside, Jules and Natalie give us a standing ovation, much to the annoyance of a sun-burned man in an unfortunate red hat at the next table trying to view the Red Sox game.

"Siddown, wouldja?" he growls at Jules. People growl at Jules at their own peril.

Jules gestures around the room. "There are, like, 14 other TVs here," she says to the man. "Every one of them is showing the ballgame, which is actually on a commercial break for a pitching change."

"SIDDOWN!"

Jules glances at the TV, then smiles sweetly at our neighbor. "Ah. I see you were missing out on vital information regarding erectile dysfunction," she sits down. "I'm so sorry. For my standing *and* your penis."

The Sunburn grabs his beer and stalks over to the bar.

"MAGA!" Jules yells, waving.

"Jesus Christ, these places are all the same," she says, shaking her head. "Why are we here again?"

"Because it's 25.7 miles from my house, and no one cares that I'm a sweaty mess," I say. Jules continues her rant. "Nothing but sports on TV, crap wine behind the bar, a bunch of jerseys illegibly signed in Sharpie, and some version of testosterone rock on the speakers. Too damn loud, too."

I laugh. "You might be painting our statewide dining establishments with a bit of a broad brush there, Jules."

"I'm not, but who cares?" says Jules. "Tell us about the ride."

"It wasn't as bad as–hang on," Tess whips around to face me. "Did you say 25 *point seven*? Bitch!" I grin at her.

As Tess fills our friends in on the literal ups and downs of our day, Gilda begins to push in.

133

Is it that *broad of a brush, really? Even if you took down the cheesy jerseys and brought in some decent wine, there would still be the same sports on TV, and the same generic rock playing too loudly to have a conversation. They're all catering to the same people. Dudes.*

My mind is rushing.

What would one designed for women *look like?*

Images flood in. Too many to process. I look around at my friends, and slap the table.

"Oh my God, you guys. I need to open a bar."

∞∞∞

There's a lull in the conversation, presumably so my friends can ponder whether I'm drunk, and if so, how it happened in under a minute.

"Say what now?" says Nora.

"Humor me for a few minutes," I say. "Tell me something that annoys you about this place. Something specific. Right here, right now."

"Right now? OK, at this exact moment I hate that they're playing that over-the-top Lee Greenwood song," says Nora. "Do not even get me *started* on that song. I will put out my eardrums with one of these stale tortilla chips."

Natalie wipes a smudge of salsa from her mouth and nods towards the restrooms. "The doors to the bathrooms are labeled 'Guys' and 'Gals,'" she says. "'Gals' for fucks's sake."

"They are not," I turn around in disbelief. They are. Jesus.

"The inescapable sports decor that permeates every square inch of the place," adds Jules. "I mean, I get it. We're in Titletown. Yay, us. But there are more than four sports in the

134

world. And last time I checked, women – excuse me, *gals* – were athletes, too."

"I biked here," interjects Tess.

I toast Tess with my pint. "Exactly. Where are the photos of Joan Benoit? Where are the shirts signed by Des Linden or Megan Rapinoe? But it's not just the pictures and jerseys," I say. "The Sox are playing right now, sure. But I bet no matter what time of day or what day of the week we walk in, those TVs will be tuned in to a game, or some talk show reporting on a game."

"So, not to bust your balls here, Georg," says Tess. "But it IS a sports bar."

"True," I concede. "But think about it. If any restaurant or bar has a TV, what's playing?"

"Point taken," says Tess, popping a laden chip into her mouth. "So tell us. What does Georgie's Hideaway look like?"

I pause, considering her question. "It's less about what it looks like, and more about who it's for," I say. "Every single bar or tavern I've ever been to caters only to guys. Or at least it skews heavily in the dude direction." I look back around at the multitude of screens showing Fenway Park. "Take the TVs. Now, I love my Sox, but if they weren't playing, I would much rather be sitting here with an episode of *The Amazing Race* or *Chopped* on the screen."

"*The Great British Baking Show*," offers Nora.

"*Say Yes to the Dress*," says Tess. "Any of the *Real Housewives*!"

"Ew, hon," says Nora. "I thought I cured you of them."

"Never," says Tess.

"*NOVA*," says Jules. We stare at her.

"Show off," I say. "And instead of this–" I point upwards to the invisible waves of too-loud guitar surrounding us.

"Wouldn't it be cool to actually hear the TV if you wanted to?"

"How?" asks Natalie.

I shrug. "I don't know…wireless speakers at the table? Old fashioned drive-in style? There's got to be a way."

"OK," nods Nora. "But why wouldn't you just watch the show at home? In your pajamas?"

"Uh, because someone else cooks, serves, and cleans up? No one walking in to judge your taste in shows?" I shake my head. "But it's not about just watching TV. It's having a place to hang out that feels like yours. Ours. A place where MAGA over there wouldn't want to hang out on a Sunday afternoon." I point to our former table neighbor, now sitting on a bar stool and gesturing incomprehensibly at the bartender. "A woman could come alone if she just wanted an hour to herself." I look around the bar again. "I'd have a set of shelves filled with books that people could take or borrow."

"Oh my God," says Natalie. "I hate when I'm alone in a restaurant with nothing to read."

"You could have charging stations at the tables," says Jules, thoughtfully.

"Red carpet parties for the Oscars and Emmys," I say. My friends nod vigorously.

"Hallmark Channel Christmas movies in December?" asks Tess hopefully.

I laugh. "Maybe on Sundays in December, just for you," I say. I drain my water and chase it with a sip of my beer. "And I'd have kick-ass trivia nights. All *Sex and the City* and *Hunger Games* and *Twilight*." Tess groans orgasmically, startling Nora.

"How are we married, you and I?" she asks. "Are you Team Edward or Jacob?"

"As your twin, I advise you not to answer that," Natalie says to Tess. She turns to me. "What would you call it?"

"Jockless?" Jules offers, causing Nora to snort beer foam onto her appetizer plate.

"Playtex Sports?" Tess says.

"Gross, T.," I say. "Hard pass."

"Wine Down," says Nora, thoughtfully. "like 'Wind Down.'"

I nod. "I like that. And the restroom signs would read 'Bad-ass Women' and 'Everyone Else.'" My friends hoot in solidarity.

"Have you ever worked in a restaurant?" Natalie asks me.

Jules answers before I do. "We lasted two days in a bakery on Cape Cod the summer after freshman year," she says, grinning. "We didn't want to work on Saturdays."

Nora laughs. "Nice work ethic."

I shrug. "I've grown. And no, I haven't worked in a restaurant. But I've been planning events for most of my professional life. I know enough to know what I don't know, you know?"

"More importantly," says Jules. "You know a ton of people who *do* know what you don't know." She looks at me, her expression serious. "You could do this, Georg."

Tess looks from Jules to me and back. "Are you really serious about this?"

I lean back in my chair and spread my arms out, palms up. "I have no idea. The lightbulb just went off, like, six minutes ago. It could be a side effect of exercise-induced dehydration and calorie deficit," I say. "And speaking of, let's order. Woman cannot live on nachos alone. This one can't, anyway."

"Well I, for one, would totally hang out at your bar," says Natalie. "I think it's a kickass business concept and investors

137

will be cage fighting each other to see who gets to fund it."

"Ha!" I say, smiling. "Isn't it pretty to think so?"

Jules grabs the last chip a half second ahead of me. "*The Sun Also Rises*," she says. We silently fist bump across the table.

We order, and for the next hour we sit, chat, eat, and laugh. We say no more about our fantasy bar, but quietly under the surface, the lightbulb still glows.

∞∞∞

Hours later, I lay awake in bed, listening to Dan's slow, deep breathing and the quiet *tick tick tick* of the ceiling fan circling above on low. In recent weeks, if I couldn't fall asleep, I would replay a particularly satisfying daydream conjured during one of my solo rides. Or visualize completing my 100 Revolutions ride, now two months away. In my mind's eye I coast across the finish line in a mere six hours. I envision Lena on the VIP bandstand, announcing the names of the riders as they glide to a stop.

"And let's all welcome rider number 467, it's…it's…*Georgie Fischer?*"

My former co-workers scream and clap as a gobsmacked Lena looks on in disbelief. Frank's there as well, having had to give up at mile 12 after experiencing a tiny leg cramp. Sometimes in my visualizations I ride over his foot.

But tonight, my ride is nowhere in the forefront of my mind. Instead I'm at my bar, which is hosting an Oscars watch party. The customers are wearing gowns. Some have dug up old prom dresses and are embracing their tacky ruffled glory; others are loving the excuse to put on the sumptuous gown purchased for a one-time event years ago, which has been languishing in the closet ever since. There are even a few tuxedos in the crowd. Brave spouses, gay men, and dudes very comfortable in their own skin.

And me? I'm in head to toe sparkle and a blond bob wig, keeping the spirit of Joan Rivers alive as I walk from table to table, handing out copies of the Oscars bracket and asking "who are you wearing?" in a thick New York accent.

In bed, I'm smiling. I can't help it. The images are clear and sharp in my mind.

It's a good idea.

I roll over on my side, ready for sleep to come, when my brow furrows in worry.

But has someone already done it?

I try to shoo the thought away, but it becomes insistent. An after-hours Jehovah's Witness. Easing back the comforter, I slide out of bed, fully awake, and tiptoe next door to the office.

I boot up my laptop and pull out a notepad and pen. Opening up the search engine. I pause, my fingers poised in home row position.

What are you going to search for? Asks Gilda. *Women's bars? Bars for women? You're going to end up with a whole bunch of links for brands of organic gluten-free protein snacks.*

"Oh hush," I whisper. I type in "bars near me" and let Google do its thing. Almost immediately, the familiar green map fills my screen, littered with tiny red pinpoints. For a full hour, I investigate the dots. I start with a cursory glance, dismissing every establishment with "sports," "pizza" or "seafood" in its name – which is an alarming number for a small state – and then mentally cross off any with a simple Celtic surname for a title: O'Leary's, McGuire's, Harrington's, and about three dozen more. I love a good Irish pub, but they are not the demographic I'm after tonight. I also exclude the ones in the city proper. My sisters live in the suburbs, for better or for worse.

Tired now, I look at the list of bars I've jotted down on my notepad. There are 30 or so watering holes within 50 miles of my house that I've never heard of and have ambiguous names, each a potential bucket of water to short out my still-glowing light bulb. I take a deep breath and dive in, calling up each one's webpage and – just to be sure – Yelp review page.

Would Bertie consider this good stalking or bad stalking?

One turns out to be a family owned restaurant that specializes in Yankee pot roast. Another has a dynamite martini menu, but gets crossed off when I read about its axe-throwing league. Every time I strike my pen through a bar on my list, I feel simultaneously more hopeful of my prospects and more certain that the very next one will whip them away like a magician's table cloth under a vase of lilies.

Finally, the last establishment on my list – an innocuous-sounding "Dee's" which turns out to be an off-Main-Street pub with tired decor and no specialty cocktails – is crossed off with a thick blue line. No one living within shouting distance has created my dream bar. It's mine for the taking, if I want it.

Do you?

I stare up at the framed black and white photo from a Tour de France mountain stage. Hundreds of skinny men slogging their way to the top of the Alps, more than ready for the screaming descent that lies ahead.

"Yeah," I say to the empty office. "I do. I just have no idea *how.*"

Small potatoes, says Gilda. *That's another Google search for another day. Go to bed now.*

I obey, powering down the computer and shuffling back to the room I share with Dan. I turn over onto my right side – a habit I picked up when heavily pregnant with Max – and gratefully accept sleep.

Chapter 11

We turn off Route 105 in East Charleston, Vermont. The road rises for a few hundred feet, and gradually tapers off. When it changes from pavement to dirt, Max and Shannon snap out of their car-induced reveries and pay attention. I think I know what they'll look for first.

I'm right. When Church Hill Road ends at a lonely T-intersection in front of a farmhouse, the kids shift in their seat, necks craning.

"There he is!" Max says.

"She," says Shannon. "It's definitely a she."

On the farmhouse lawn, sitting regally in a white plastic chair, is a brown goat. At her feet – or really, her hooves – are two German shepherds, stretched out languidly on the grass.

The concept of a chair-sitting goat delighted my kids with its sheer quirkiness when we first spotted her a few years back. Since then, she's become our "Welcome back!" symbol, the second-to-last signpost marking the journey towards our week-long vacation at my happy place.

We turn right onto East Echo Lake Road and begin making our way counterclockwise around the lake itself. Dan's driving, so the final – and Shannon's personal favorite – marker indicating that we've arrived will be on my side of the car. I turn in my seat and meet my daughter's shining blue eyes. She grins at me.

We arc left around the little red house that has all the markings of a school from *Little House on the Prairie*. A few hundred yards later, Shannon sits up at her window.

"Slow down, Dad!"

Dan obliges, and Shannon reads aloud the small sign nailed to a driveway gate, still visible in the evening glow of a northern dusk.

"'I dream of a world where chickens can cross the road without having their motives questioned,'" she says, and she and Max dissolve into giggles.

A few minutes later, we turn left onto a dead end road that dips sharply towards the lake. Within seconds, the pretty yellow cottage comes into view, and we glide into the birch-lined driveway. Dan turns the engine off, and the four of us sit in silence, relishing the moment of arrival before moving on to the process of unloading. I'm in love with this little house on this little lake. Dan found it by accident when another rental on a different lake fell through, and we've been coming back ever since.

Wordlessly, we all unbuckle our seatbelts and step out of the car. Stretching our legs in the gravel driveway first, we each grab an armful of gear and descend the three stone steps from the parking area to the front walk. The door, as always, is unlocked.

Unpacking – nesting, really – for the week takes less than an hour. My and Dan's things are put away in the larger of the two first floor bedrooms. Saving the second bedroom for my parents' upcoming visit, the kids lug their belongings up the ladder to the loft space that they'll share for the week. By the time we finish, it's full dark. Max and Shannon flop onto the long and blissfully comfortable sofa and start up the cottage's small TV. Dan and I pour glasses of wine and carry them onto the screened back porch that faces the lake.

We settle into the cushioned wicker sofa and quietly clink glasses. I let out a sigh of sheer unfiltered contentment. Inside, the sounds of a violent dust storm indicate that the kids have channel surfed their way to *The Martian*. Good. They'll be immobile – and quiet – for the next two hours at least.

"Remember when I asked you if you ever size up houses to see which ones you could hole up in and defend during a zombie apocalypse?" I say.

Dan chuckles. "Vaguely, yes. I believe I dismissed you as a SyFy weirdo."

"You did, actually," I acknowledge. "Well, this is where I'd go. Right here."

"Is it easy to defend?" he asks.

"Very," I say. "We'd sleep in the loft and just pull the ladder up every night. And we'd keep kayaks on the docks so if any zombies came shuffling by we could wait them out on the water."

"Zombie's can't swim?"

I stare at him incredulously. "Duh."

"Well, you're still a SyFy weirdo," Dan says. "But I'll follow you here."

We lapse back into silence. On the lake, an unseen loon calls to its partner longingly.

"You've been really happy these last few weeks," Dan says. It isn't a question.

144

"Yes."

"I'm glad," he says. A few more seconds pass. "Let's not talk about it during vacation, but when we get home, can we start brainstorming about what's next for us?"

"You mean, what's next for me?" I ask. He looks down and nods.

I take a sip of my wine and keep my eyes on the lake, dimly lit by the rural starscape. "Of course we can. Actually, I have an idea. It's…still half baked, but I've done a little research on it. I'm kinda excited about it."

"Tell me."

I laugh nervously. "Now?"

"Why not?"

"I haven't put together the elevator speech for it yet."

"Try me anyway."

I shift on the sofa so I can face him. "OK. But listen, this is just a random, pie in the sky thought that came to me after a bike ride. No waving it off like my brilliant zombie apocalypse housing plan, OK?"

"I would never wave off your disturbingly well thought out zombie apocalypse housing plan."

I take another (and larger) sip of wine for fortitude. "I think it would be amazing – and profitable – to open a bar. For women."

"Just for women?" Dan asks.

"Yes. No. I mean, guys can *come*, obviously. But it would be designed around what women like to do with their friends."

Dan feigns indignance. "I don't think I like your tone," he says. "What's wrong with making a bar for guys, too?"

"Oh! They have those places, too," I say. "Maybe you haven't seen them. They're called *every bar that ever existed*."

Dan drains his glass. "Hang on." Getting up, he leaves the porch and walks through the living room to the kitchen and back again. This time with the bottle. He refills both my glass and his and settles down again, fully facing me.

"Tell me everything. From the beginning."

∞∞∞

Why is this hill here? This doesn't feel like a hill when we're driving.

Having read somewhere that "arms climb hills," I lower my head and pump my arms to propel myself up the – if I'm honest – really small hill. Just as I'm about to give myself a minute of walking, I feel the road level out. Thank God.

I keep plodding along in my slow jog and take deeper breaths. *This is the last hill you have to run up, right? The final one is during the cool down.*

Yes, I respond silently (because I don't – or perhaps *can't* is more accurate – talk to myself out loud when I'm running). *That's why it's going to be Des Linden on the wall of my bar and not me.*

It's our second full day at the lake, and the late afternoon has grown overcast. A half hour ago, the idea of holding happy hour on the porch while watching the rain on the water motivated me to lace up my sneakers and burn off my cosmo in advance. Two and a half miles later at the opposite shore, I feel conned. I glance across the lake and spot the yellow dot of our house. I'm wearing a bright blue tank top. Can they see me?

If you wave, will Dan come get you?

Thankfully, I know from previous runs over previous vacations that the road tips gently downward for the next half-mile. Letting gravity lend a hand with my momentum, my thoughts shift from *why the fuck are we still running* back to my conversation with Dan the night we arrived.

"You've heard the part where more than half of all restaurants fail the first year, right?" he had asked, after I explained my vision for the bar.

"Ah, I thought you might say that," I said, pointing at him. "That's not actually true. It's way less than that."

"And who told you this? Lisa Vanderpump's blog?"

I smile. "Shockingly, no. I read it in *Forbes*. I'll show it to you, along with all the stats I've found on what the average bar owner makes per year. And anyway, I'm not talking about just a 'restaurant,' it's an experience. When the kids were younger, we never went to Chuck E. Cheese for the pizza; we went because we could sit down for five seconds while they ran wild, burned off some energy and played Skee-Ball."

I grabbed Dan's arm. "Remember how crowded it always seemed to be when we went there?" He grimaced and nodded. "Exactly! Because there weren't a lot of places where you could take young kids to eat and let them run around. Well, I've been searching online for places in Massachusetts that cater to women the way I'm describing. They don't exist. Mine – ours – would be the first."

"Ours?" He looked at me then, eyebrows raised.

"I'll need an accountant," I countered. "I thought you could moonlight for me."

He laughed, and a knot I hadn't realized was there loosened in my chest. "Let me guess, pro bono?"

"Aww, see? Look at us on the same page."

A few seconds of silence went by. I took a deep breath and continued. "It's an *idea*, Dan. That's all it is right now. I need to put together a business plan, talk to some of my old contacts in the event space to sketch out some costs, and see what kind of financing opportunities there are. I wouldn't have brought it up tonight if I didn't think there was something *there* there, you know? Maybe I won't be able to get it off the ground, but it's something I really want to dig a little deeper into."

I settled back into my side of the wicker sofa. "So, that's everything so far. Any other questions you want to ask me right now?"

He puffs up his cheeks and exhales slowly. "Um, yes. About a million. But let me sit with it for a while, and let's have a fantastic week, OK?"

I smiled. "Agreed."

We clinked glasses again. "Is there anything else that *you* want to tell *me*?" he asked.

"Actually, yes," I said. "How the hell do you know who Lisa Vanderpump is?"

Now, my circumference of the lake nearly complete, I walk slowly on the road sipping water from the small bottle I keep strapped to my waist on runs. Or in my case, slow jogs. I'm lighter for having opened up to Dan on the first night. I feel strong and happy.

Not bad for someone who conned herself into running five miles.

Rounding a corner in the steep road down to the house, I spot my parents' black Camry. I force myself to spend a few minutes stretching out my quads and hamstrings, delaying the gratification of a glass of iced water. And then perhaps something a little stronger.

The first fat droplets of rain are falling when I bounce lightly up the steps to the front door, the unmistakable rattle of ice against metal ringing in the kitchen.

My dad grins at me. "Saw you through the window," he says, handing me a cold martini glass and planting a kiss on my cheek. "We're on the porch."

"Well, I was going to do water first, then booze," I reason. "But I can flip it around."

"That's my girl."

I fill a second glass with water and carry both onto the porch, where I greet my mom. She's sitting neatly in one of the collapsible chairs-in-a-bag they brought, a half-finished bottle of iced green tea in the mesh cup holder. Since arriving, she's laid out a happy hour spread of guacamole, tortilla chips, sharp cheddar cheese, rice crackers, and salty smoked almonds. Max and Shannon are sitting at the small formica table on the far end of the porch, devouring a bowl of cheddar popcorn and flipping cards over in an earnest game of War. Both of my children are still in their swimsuits and wrapped loosely in oversized beach towels. Shannon's long blonde hair is still damp and mildly tangled from her recent swim. Lake life.

I take the seat on the part of the wicker sofa I've come to call mine and raise my glass. "Cheers to your safe arrival," I say, and take a long pull. "Oh, God, this tastes good. Thanks, Dad."

"So how's the entrepreneur?" my mom asks, smiling. I look over at Dan, innocently nursing his wheat beer.

He shrugs. "I wanted to get their uncensored opinion," he says. "And I think you'll be glad I did." He gestures towards my mom with his bottle. I look back at her.

"What?"

She smiles wider. "Three words, Georgie. 'Woman-owned business.'"

∞∞∞

I'm sweaty, still clad in my damp aqua blue tank top and black workout shorts. A minute or two ago, I had been contemplating bowing out for a quick shower, but at my mom's words, I kick off my sneakers, tuck my left leg underneath me, and nestle a throw pillow in my lap. I'm in, sweaty or not. If I offend, it's my mom's fault.

"As Frasier Crane would say, 'I'm listening,'" I tell her.

She grins, briefly, then snaps back into wisdom mode. "If you decide that this is something that you want to move forward on, and you're the owner-slash-proprietor, that makes your bar a woman-owned business," my mom says.

I nod thoughtfully. "It would, wouldn't it?" The relevance of her words hits me. "And that would help me when trying for a business loan?"

She gives me a small smile, the one usually reserved for my dad when he's not catching on fast enough for her liking.

Dang, Georgie, Gilda says. *Keep up, girl.*

"So despite outnumbering – and outliving, thank goodness – the men in our fair country, no offense, honey," she glances over at my dad, who is – I suspect – pretending not to be listening. "Women haven't quite caught up to men in terms of business ownership."

Dan leans over to my dad. "I sense a sermon. Should we leave?"

"Nah," my dad says. "We voted Democrat. We're good."

My mom turns her sharp, intelligent gaze to my husband and father. "Isn't it interesting that I've only just started discussing women in business and you're already feeling uncomfortable. Have I accidentally stepped on your privilege?"

150

Yeah, you picked the right ringtone for her with that Helen Reddy number.

"I think there's going to be some lightning," my dad says to Dan. "Should we walk out onto the aluminum dock and hold up a TV antenna?"

"You first," says Dan. "I'll be right there, honest."

My parents sit in silence for a few seconds. My mom's face stays impassive. I know my parents are teasing each other, as I've watched it my entire life. Still, this is way better than Max and Shannon's card game. Who will flinch first?

"May I make you two smart, beautiful and independent women a drink?" asks my dad.

My mom smiles, a genuine one. "Jameson and water. More water, less Jameson." He bows dramatically, and points at my glass. I shake my head, and he heads inside. She turns back to me.

"As I was trying to say," she continues, casting a *don't interrupt me, Testosterone* glance at Dan. "There are some real benefits to being certified as a woman-owned business."

I scoop up a generous dollop of guacamole with a tortilla chip and hold it over a napkin. "Like what? Aside from being my own boss, that is," I say, then pop it into my mouth.

"There are special lending programs for women in business," she begins. "A lot of them offer better interest rates. And there are grant organizations out there that will award funding to women entrepreneurs. I'm not saying it's going to be easy, but it might not be as daunting as you think to get the start up money together."

Beyond the porch screens, the rain is light but steady. Mist has obscured the opposite shore. The bright red of our rented paddle boards is the only spot of color amidst the gray sky and water. My mind is reeling.

"Holy shit," I say to my mom. "So this could really happen."

She smiles and nods. "And based on what Dan's told me, it would be amazing."

Once again, she totally gets it. I look back at her, the smartest woman I've ever known. The smartest woman I'll *ever* know. Her approval means everything, even as an adult. "Really?" I ask.

She nods again. "Really. It's genius, Georgie. The theme, the Oscar parties, the trivia nights. I love it. I love everything about it."

Remember your To Do item when you found your old box of memories? Gilda asks. *'Parlay in-depth knowledge of TLC and Bravo into purpose-driven life'? Well, this could really tick that box, kid.*

I swing my head around and look at Dan. "I'm going to try to open a bar, Dan." He's smiling. To anyone else, it looks real. Only I, after nearly 18 years of marriage, can see the worry underneath.

You're going to have to make it OK with Dan. He's going to be the tallest hurdle, but he's also the most important. There isn't a shortcut to this.

My dad steps back onto the porch, carrying my mom's drink and his own in his hands, and a fresh iced water for me in the crook of his arm.

"My favorite thing about this house is its big glasses," he announces, handing my mom her whiskey and water. "Make sure your bar has 'em, too, Georgie."

I stand up. I glance down at my mom, and she rises from her chair. Dan, tuned in to the mood of the group, joins us. At the far end of the porch, Max and Shannon are focused only on the cards and the remaining popcorn in their shared bowl.

"I think we're toasting," I say. "Toasting to my new business venture."

"To Georgie," declares my dad. "To the success of – do you know what you're going to call it?"

I grin. "Book Club."

My dad and Dan look puzzled, but my mom laughs out loud. "Oh my God, that's *perfect*," she says. "I can see it now, hundreds of women saying 'Honey! I'm going to Book Club tonight!"

I beam at her, grateful that she got it immediately.

"Hey, I read," says Dan. "I get to go too, right?"

"So do I," adds my dad. "And I hardly even move my lips."

"OK," I say magnanimously. "My bar will cater to women, but allow men."

"To Book Club," says Dan.

"Book Club!" We clink glasses and take generous sips. A few seconds later, we're seated again. Something big has happened, right here in my most cherished place in the world. I feel amazing. Amazing and utterly at a loss as to what to do next.

"I haven't felt this…this…*energized* in a long time," I say. "But I'm not gonna lie; I have no idea what I'm doing here. I mean, I know I've worked in special events and all, but opening a *bar*? What the heck do I actually know about opening a bar?"

"The caterers you've worked with might be a good place to start," my mom says. "But you do need to talk to someone who actually runs a bar or restaurant."

I consider this. "Well, there are the restaurant managers at Hudson…"

"No," clips my mom. "No way." She's right.

I look up at the ceiling. "I think I need a fairy godmother; I feel like I'm sitting here in rags and not going to the ball."

"I know people," offers my dad.

I sit up. "Yeah?"

"Do you remember Jasper Lewis? Neil and Rita's son? He owns a couple of restaurants. I'm sure he'll meet with you."

"Or god*father*," Dan says. "A fairy godfather will do."

Dad raises his ice-filled tumbler. "Bippity boppity boo."

Chapter 12

The rest of the week passes quietly, blissfully. We swim. We hike. We read on the porch. We paddleboard across the lake to the bridge and leap, shrieking with joy, into the clear waters below. Mom and Dad depart for home a few days ahead of us, allowing us to spend the second half of our vacation as a foursome. Before they leave, Dan and I take on a 40-mile round trip bike ride to the Canadian border, pedaling along the forests and ponds of Route 114. It is wild, hilly, and gorgeous. To my delight, I can actually keep up with Dan. My legs are powerful and steady on the long inclines. One hundred miles doesn't seem so laughable anymore.

On the morning of our departure, I strip the sheets off the beds in the loft and stuff them into a pillowcase, singing snatches of Blondie songs. A few feet away, Max is glumly pushing t-shirts and socks into his duffle bag. Mixing the clean with the dirty, no doubt.

"Why are you *happy?*" Max asks, irritated. "We're *leaving.*"

I lean over the railing of the loft and gently toss the sheets onto the floor below. "I dunno, Max," I answer. "I guess I just can't wait to spend four hours in the car with your stinky feet perched on the headrest of my seat." He grins and wiggles his toes at me.

"P.U.," I say. "Get out of here. Bring your bag to the car. And those sheets, too, pretty please."

As I walk through the rooms, looking for forgotten flip flops or swimsuits, I consider his question more fully. A year ago – when I was six months into my stint at Hudson Hotels – I was morose when we were preparing to leave Vermont. It wasn't the regular end-of-vacation-blues; it was full-on, lead-weight-in-the-belly despair. I certainly wasn't belting out the lyrics to "Dreaming."

Come to think of it, comments Gilda. *Do you even* have *the regular end-of-vacation blues right now?*

I plump up the cushions on the porch sofa and take a final, long look at the lake. I give it a two-fingered salute. "Until next year, old friend," I say.

I'm excited to get home, I realize. There's a lot I need to do and figure out for Book Club, and I can't wait to get started.

An hour into the ride, we cross from Vermont into New Hampshire. Dan and I are quiet, taking in the northern New England landscape. In the backseat, Max and Shannon are absorbed in their tablets. Earbuds in, oblivious.

I reach over to Dan and place my left hand on his thigh. He smiles and covers it with his right. Freed from shifting gears for the next few hours, it's our go-to highway pose.

Dan and I avoided any further discussions on the bar after the rainy happy hour on the porch. I let him sit with it, knowing he'd bring it up at some point during the ride home. I was betting on just after Franconia Notch.

He glances at me, then back to the road. "So. Book Club," he says.

156

About 17 miles early. I was close.

"Yes," I say.

"I like it," he says. "It's clever."

"Thank you," I say, grateful. "I like it, too."

Dan lapses back into silence. I wait, sensing he's considering his next words. There are three hours left in the ride. We have time.

"Your mom's right about the women-owned businesses," he says. "That hadn't occurred to me when you first told me your idea." He seems disappointed.

Because Mom thought of it first, or because it makes the idea more possible?

"I didn't think of it, either," I say. "But it sounds promising."

"That first night of vacation, when we talked about it, all I could think of was you asking to cash out our retirement fund to go open a bar."

"Dan, come on," I say, sitting up and turning towards him in my seat. "You *know* I'd never ask that. You had to realize I'd be looking for a business loan."

"I know," he says, and sighs. "I guess my mind always runs to the worst case scenario with a big change like this."

"Well, tell it to pull a U-turn and meet us over here in Best Case Scenario-land," I say. "The view isn't so bad. I might be able to get a decent loan, or even a *grant*."

"A grant would make me feel a million times better," Dan confesses, not looking at me.

I glance out my window, tensing.

"If you can fund a chunk of the start up costs through a grant, I'm on board," Dan says.

"A grant would be fantastic, I agree," I say quietly. "But it isn't a sure thing. And I really want to do this."

"I know," he says. "And I'm telling you what will help me sleep better at night. This is huge, Georgie. And right in the middle of when we need to be saving, for retirement *and* college." He gestures to the back seat.

I fixate on the endless forest outside, as resentment builds inside. But whether it's resentment over Dan's condition of a grant, or over the fact that it's actually a fair one, I'm not sure. It's probably a little of both.

You wanted to get him on board, Gilda reasons. *He literally just used the words "on board."*

I exhale, my breath clouding the glass. "OK," I say. "Book Club needs a grant."

Dan squeezes my hand again, and I draw it gently back into my lap. A sense of uneasy truce hangs over the car. It's not the excitement of toasting with my parents on the porch from a week ago, but I'm chalking it up as a win.

Hours later, we swing the car into our driveway. As I open the car door and step out, my phone buzzes. It's a text from my dad.

Georgie, thanks for the great time. Hope the ride home today was uneventful. When you're ready, call Jasper at the number below. He has two restaurants in Boston and is opening up a third. He's expecting to hear from you. Love ya, Dad.

"Who's that from?" Dan asks.

I smile at him. "My fairy godfather."

∞∞∞∞

The perk of having fun parents is they have a lot of friends, and they hang on to them for a long time. Their network reaches far and wide.

Neil went to Boston College with my dad. He and his wife, Rita, are part of a circle that my parents affectionately call "the BC crowd" which, nearly 50 years after graduating, still meets for dinner four times a year. I have vague memories of playing Atari with their son Jasper, then a gangly high school freshman, during a holiday party when I was in sixth grade, but we hadn't seen each other since.

Still, when I called a few hours after receiving my dad's message, Jasper cheerfully agreed to take me on a tour of his soon-to-be-opened third restaurant the following day.

Now, I drive to Boston's Seaport District following the guidance of Crystal, the name I had given the patient and soothing voice of my phone's GPS app. The moniker had been Max's inspiration. "Because she's crystal clear!"

I pull up to a sleek building of steel and glass facing the harbor, where two men are standing, hands on hips, staring at something near the roofline. The taller one, with a widow's peak and salt and pepper hair, is a 50-year-old version of my former Atari partner. As I step out of my car, Jasper greets me warmly, dismissing his companion with a genial clap on the back.

"Jasper," I say, as he pulls me into a hug. "You must be so busy. Thank you so much for seeing me."

"Not at all," Jasper says. "I'm happy to help."

"You'll be happier when I tell you that I plan to stay in the suburbs with one little bar and the last demographic that would want to step inside are Power Lunchers."

Jasper purses his lips for a moment, then nods. "You're right. I am happier now."

159

He leads me inside for a tour. The floors are a checkerboard of black and white tile. Two walls are floor to ceiling glass, the other two are painted a deep and luscious red. The main bar is a glossy black lacquer.

"It's stunning," I tell him. "Congratulations."

The restaurant isn't furnished yet, so we sit on a pair of battered gray stools at the bar to talk. For close to an hour, Jasper shares the process of opening his first restaurant. He walks me through calculating the monthly versus yearly square footage rental rates: "For a 3,000 square foot retail space, a yearly rental rate of $25 per square foot works out to the same as a monthly rental rate of $2.083 per square foot."

"You know that, like, just like that?" I ask. "My head just exploded."

He grins. "Watch. You'll have it memorized after your third location viewing."

He breaks down start up costs versus ongoing business maintenance costs, and shows me how to figure out what I'll be spending on inventory, insurance, and staff. I shudder a little, and send a silent prayer of thanks that Dan isn't here to faint or vomit on the beautiful new floor.

He shares small tricks of the bar trade ("if you serve real food over snacks, people stay up to an hour longer and spend more money!"), offers advice on drafting a business plan and applying for loans, and explains the quirks of the Massachusetts liquor license laws. All the while, I scribble notes into my blue spiralbound diary.

"This is new construction," Jasper says, waving his hand around the empty space of his third restaurant. "This is *not* the route that I'd advise you to go for your first place. The way I see it, you have three options." He ticks off one finger.

"First, you could buy a building. That's a good option if you're going to be there for a while, and you'd be building equity, appreciation, and getting some tax benefits."

"What's a while?" I ask, as I continue to scribble.

"Generally, seven years is when it pays off to buy space over renting it," says Jasper making a seesaw gesture. "And I'm assuming you know what everyone always says about the success rate of new restaurants in the first year?"

"That they all fail and we should run screaming from the endeavor?" I say. "So what you're saying is, renting is for insecure pussies." Jasper laughs. "Besides," I tell him. "My good friend *Forbes* says the more than 50 per cent thing isn't true."

"Well, the variables of that particular statistic are pretty much endless, so run with the one you like the most," Jasper says, smiling. "The other thing you could do is *lease* a space, which, as you've just pointed out, is the, uh, scaredy-cat option. But it could save you some on maintenance and insurance."

"M'kay," I say. "And the third?"

"You could buy a bar that's already up and running."

I look at him, my brow furrowing. "Yeah? Is that done a lot?"

"Sure it is," he says. "You know, you walk in one of your regular places and there's an 'Under New Management' sign on the door?"

Duh. I silently curse my non-mastery of the obvious. "Of course," I look at him sheepishly. "Stupid of me not to think of that."

Jasper shakes his hand in a *don't worry about it* gesture. "Not stupid at all. Anyway, it's worth looking into, because in a lot of cases the price of the business will include some of the big-ticket items like the liquor license and furniture. That would save you a ton of hassle."

I click the end of my pen a few times, thinking. "And if the customer base overlaps with the audience I'm after, I might be able to get them to keep coming."

Jasper taps his nose with one index finger and points at me with the other. "Bingo," he says. "For a first-time restaurant owner, it's the method I'd encourage you to look into first."

I glance at my watch, mindful that Jasper has another meeting in a few minutes. I tuck my diary and pen into my bag and step down from my stool. "This has been so helpful, Jasper. I can't thank you enough," I tell him. "Is there anything else I should be doing right now that we haven't talked about?"

"Yes, actually," Jasper says, walking me to the door. "Have you ever taken a bartending course?"

I shake my head.

"Sign up for one. Right when you get home," he says. "It'll help when you're planning your menu of signature cocktails. But more than that, I can guarantee you there will be nights when you're short staffed and need to jump behind the bar. Best to be ready."

"Well, I already have the witty repartee down," I offer.

"See?" Jasper says. "You're halfway there."

∞∞∞

My phone rings on the drive back to my parents' house. I glance at the screen in its hands-free holder. Angela. I put it on speaker.

"Ahoy, there!" I say, delighted.

Angela chuckles quietly. "I bet that felt good."

162

"A little," I confess. "How've you been?"

"Eh, you know, the usual," Angela says. "Hudson is Hudson. Frank is Frank. Listen, it's been, like, a month since we last talked, and I'm sorry about that."

"Stop, Angela," I say. "Don't even think about it. I know what it's like this time of year at Hudson."

"Yeah. And it's official. *100 Revolutions* has entered the madness phase."

"I can imagine," I say. "I saw the postcard from a while back. The 'bestseller' one."

Angela is quiet for a few moments. "Yeah, well. Not all of us can afford to stand on principle."

I cringe. *You asshole, Georgie.* "Oh my God, that's...I didn't mean it like that, Ange. I was just venting a little. I'm sorry."

"Forget it," Angela says, sighing. "It's a ridiculous ego stroke, and everyone knows it."

"So was the Comic Sans your small contribution to the resistance?"

She snorts. "No. Frank picked it. I didn't dissuade him."

"Rebel," I say. "Uh, I also noted that the postcard said something about rave reviews. Please tell me he didn't go through with his plan to demand reviews from grantees."

"OK, I won't tell you that," Angela says. "I'll be lying, but I won't tell you that."

"Frank Hudson, everybody," I say. "Hotelier, author, and now pimp. Have any of the grantees pushed back?"

"Several so far," she says. Her voice lowers. "They were strongly encouraged to reconsider, and reminded of the timeline for their upcoming grant renewal."

"Ugh. That's unconscionable."

"That's our guy," Angela says. "Listen, I called because I

really do want to hear what you've been up to, but I have a work question first."

"You can't use the k-cups in the lobby, Angela," I say with mock exasperation. "You have to bring your own. We've been over this."

She laughs. "It's about The Book Prophet guy."

"Ah, how is Bembé?" I ask. "Which of my former colleagues will be riding the 100 with him as chaperone?"

"No one, actually," Angela says. "Lena insisted it wasn't necessary."

I shake my head. "So much for 'he can't ride without someone from Communications,'" I say. "So what's up with the Prophet?"

"Lena's starting to prep Frank for the live interview with Bembé after the ride," Angela says. "She wants Frank to get a feel for how he can expect the interview to go."

"Makes sense," I say.

"She asked Kyle to watch a bunch of them and then narrow it down to a short list of episodes, including, as she put it, 'time stamps of the most relevant pieces of the discussion.'"

"For fuck's sake," I say. "*Time stamps?* That's days of work."

Angela exhales. "I know. And she wants it tomorrow."

I roll my eyes. "Of course she does. Bembé's been running his show every week for years; there's going to be hundreds of hours of it. Poor Kyle. Like he doesn't have enough to do."

"Well, that's why I called you," she said. "Kyle is stressed out. Neither of us have ever watched this guy's show. I was wondering if you can suggest some that are, uh…"

"Frank-friendly?" I offer.

"Yes," she says, relieved. "I told Kyle that I'd ask you; he would have called you himself, but was a little paranoid that

Lena would overhear and, you know, be Lena. Can you save him?"

"Partly. I can tell you which episodes I think Frank might like, but he's on his own for the time stamping part, is that OK?"

"More than OK," she says.

I recite a list of some of my favorites, which Angela promises to pass on to Kyle for viewing and "time stamping."

"Thank you," she says. "This is going to prevent Kyle from breaking out into the hives that I *know* are lying just beneath the surface."

"For you, my dear, anything," I say. "How else may I be of service?"

"That's all I need. Now I want to hear about you," Angela says. "Tell me everything."

I do. I share my *Seinfeld* moment at Jules' house. I tell her about the half-interview at the education place, and my conversation with Dan about the summer. I tell her about receiving the postcard, and making the decision to ride.

"Do you think that will be a problem?" I ask, suddenly nervous.

"Nah," Angela says. "No one'll care. And even if Lena *did* care, she's at the finish line all day. What's she gonna do, make you ride back to the start?"

"Still, though...don't point it out to her, OK?"

"Of course not."

We talk about my training rides, Echo Lake, and her recent vacation to Belize. Finally, I tell her about Book Club. I describe my vision for the place, my conversations with my family, and Jasper's advice.

"I love this idea," Angela gushes. "Save me a seat for Oscar night, would you?"

"I'll save you a table," I say. "But seriously, Ange. I'm so excited about this. It's completely crazy, but I'm going for it."

"I'm really happy for you," she says. "And I'm proud of you for doing this. A little jealous, too, I'm not going to lie. But still proud. I miss you here, but I'm glad you're *not* here, you know?"

"I know. I miss you too."

"Keep me posted, and thanks again for the Book Prophet stuff," Angela says. Her voice lowers again. "Also, Kyle and I don't plan on telling Lena we talked to you about the episodes, so–"

I laugh. "I'll be sure to avoid the subject on our nightly girl-talks, then. C'mon Angela."

"I know. Just covering my ass. So hey, I have to run to another event meeting, but I'll look for you in September at the finish line, Georgie. Good luck."

I'm about to say *don't tell anyone about Book Club*, when I hear the chirp indicating that the call has ended.

I drive for another minute, thinking of my last conversation with Frank.

You are not a success. And if I may say so, you never will be.

I find that I don't want Frank to know anything about what I'm doing. A fissure of worry is opening up in my gut. An unnecessary one, I'm sure. She would never tell Lena or Frank. She wouldn't.

Would she?

I try – and fail – to dismiss the thought. At a red light, I call Angela back. It goes straight to voicemail. I clear my throat.

"Hey Angela, it's Georgie again. Umm, before we hung up before I wanted to ask you to keep the whole Book Club thing quiet, OK? Frank and I didn't end on a good note and, well, I just feel weird about him knowing what I'm working on. Thanks."

I hang up and drive the last few minutes to my parents' house. The worry rides with me.

Chapter 13

"Is there a difference between a mixed drink and a cocktail?"

My dad's hand shoots up. "A mixed drink has two or more ingredients, whereas a cocktail is a combination of liquors, sweetener, bitters and water," he answers. "A cocktail is always a mixed drink, but a mixed drink isn't always a cocktail."

I give my dad a sidelong glance. "Whereas?"

He shrugs. "I'm educated. Sue me."

"Thank you, Mr. Miller," says Ben, our mixology instructor. He looks around the room at the rest of us and gestures to my dad. "This guy's way ahead of the rest of you."

We go back to pouring. "I had to twist your arm to do this with me, and you're showing me up," I say. "You should work at Book Club. You're like the Hermione of bartending classes."

My dad looks up from his muddler. "Who?"

I laugh and shake my head. "I can't think of a similar character from your formative years. Mr. Peabody, maybe? Here, taste this."

It's day four of our week-long bartender certification class. Each morning, I drop the kids off at Camp Nana and hitch a ride to the course venue with my dad. Today, we're experimenting. *Think of different flavors and how they can work together*, suggested Ben. My goal is to concoct at least one Book Club signature drink before the end of the course. Right now I'm testing out a combination of gin, rosemary infused simple syrup, and a splash of pink grapefruit juice.

Dad samples my creation. Our kelly green aprons are spattered from overeager pours and leaky martini shakers, and our socks are drenched inside our sensible-for-standing-all-day shoes. It's been so much fun.

He swishes the liquid around and swallows. "For me, I'd say a little less syrup and just a bit more juice. But you're the boss."

"I like the sound of that. The boss," I say. I take a small sip and consider his feedback. "I agree. I shall call this 'The Miranda.' Outwardly sour but with an undercurrent of sweetness."

"I have no idea what that means," says my dad, putting the finishing touches on a pineapple mojito. "But I will assume it's genius."

"May I?" Ben appears at my station. Our instructor is British, my height, with a mostly bald head and rimless glasses. He takes a microscopic pull from a straw, pauses, and then nods. "Yes. Definitely a 'Miranda,'" he says. He looks at my dad. "It *is* genius." Ben winks at me, and moves on to a pair of recent college grads to my right.

"He's going on Book Club's mailing list," I say.

"Speaking of," Dad says. "What else is happening on that front?"

"A lot, actually," I say. "I've written most of my business plan, and had Jules review it for me. And I've started visiting bars and restaurants in the market for new owners. Dan and

I are having dinner at one of them tomorrow to check out the Friday night crowd. And then Tess and I are going to stop at another one for lunch on Saturday during our training ride."

"Is that the route you're going? Buying someone out?"

"If I find the right place, then yes," I say, rinsing out my shaker and checking out my ingredients for inspiration. "I like that when I'm applying for the business loan – and the grants – I can have some real revenue numbers to add to it."

"Did mom's women-owned business tip pan out?" Dad asks.

"Definitely," I say. I grab the bottle of pineapple juice from my dad's station and pour in a few tablespoons. "I have some really good options for loans, and I found an organization in Boston that awards grants, and is looking specifically for women-owned startups. All I need is the right place, then I hit 'submit.'"

"Sounds like it's coming together," he says, admiringly. "I'm proud of you."

I smile. "Thanks. I'm proud of me, too."

Writing the business plan had knitted the pieces of this fantasy into a structure that felt real and attainable. Seeing my market analysis, business concept, and marketing strategy on paper filled me with pleasure...and determination. It solidified just how much I wanted this.

And heaven help the one who gets in our way, adds Gilda.

Dad and I work in silence for a few minutes. I measure out some vodka and add it to the pineapple juice in my shaker.

"The kids seem really happy," Dad says. He dries his hands with a clean bar towel and pulls his phone out of his pocket. "Mom sent me a photo from the whale watch."

I look at it and laugh. My mom has captured the last glimpse of a breaching humpback just before it disappears beneath the surface. In the foreground is Max's profile, his face a mask of surprise and awe. "They're having a great summer. It's exactly what I wanted for them. For all of us."

"Have you thought about what kind of hours you'd be working if – sorry, *when* – Book Club is up and running?" Dad asks.

Only multiple times a day, every day.

"Some, yes," I say. "I want to fix it so that the kids aren't in After School every day, so I may make Monday and Tuesday my new weekend."

"And on real weekends?" He asks.

I shrug, feigning nonchalance. "I'll have to put in some time on those days, sure. But I have no desire to stay open really late like other places. The customer base I'm after is like me; they all have sitters and spouses to get home to. It'll be a different schedule from what I'm used to, but as 'the boss,' as you pointed out, I'll have more flexibility. I can do a lot of the administrative stuff from home."

The truth was, as the business plan coalesced, Dan began to voice concerns about my potential new schedule.

"You'll be home for dinner occasionally, right?" he'd asked me recently. "Will we see each other beyond breakfast and bedtime?"

I tried, successfully, to not roll my eyes. "Of course we will."

"OK, because the more we dive into this business plan, the more it feels like you're going to be working longer and later hours than when you were at the museum. Are we going backwards here?"

I turned to him, defensive. "Would you be saying this if I were a cop? Or a doctor or nurse? Or if I taught night classes? Lots of people work irregular hours."

Dan was quiet. I sensed his own anger building. "I know, Georgie. All I'm saying is, didn't you leave the museum to give yourself – us – a little more flexibility?"

"And this will do that," I said, more gently. "I won't have typical office hours, it's true. But there will be days during the week when I'll be home when the kids get out of school; that's worth something. And I'll be happy. *That's* worth something. A lot more than I realized before."

In the end, we cobbled together a blueprint for a new schedule that satisfied both of us. It added a part time night manager's salary to my budget, but we went to sleep that night happy.

Now, I peek inside my shaker. It needs something else, but I'm not sure what. I glance back over at the bottles near my dad's station.

"Are you using that coconut water?" I ask.

Dad shudders and passes me the carton. "Did you really just ask me that?"

"I'll hire you," I caution. "But you can't mock my customers."

He turns to me, serious. "Well, where's the fun in that?"

∞∞∞

The following evening, a bartending certificate in my hand and dry shoes on my feet, we drive 20 minutes to an Italian restaurant, Fiorentino's, one of the restaurants for sale that – I hope – has the potential to be Book Club. Shannon and I are belting out the lyrics to Blondie's "The Tide is High," and Dan is pretending not to enjoy it.

"I feel like a spy," I say to Dan gleefully, as we exit the highway.

He smiles at me and lowers the radio volume, quieting Blondie. "So what are my orders?"

"Just watch and listen," I tell him. "Does it seem busy? How would you describe the customers? Does it seem organized and well-run? Does the staff look like they enjoy working there? That kind of thing."

We pull into the parking lot, which is half full at seven o'clock on a Friday. The building is painted an avocado green and trimmed in a deep shade of plum. It looks big to me, but whether it's too big for Book Club, I don't yet know.

The four of us spill out of the car and walk to the front door. The entrance is sheltered under a small portico supported by a set of columns. Pots of bright pink geraniums flank the door.

"What do you think, kids?" I say. "We've never been here before."

"I want grilled cheese," says Max. Dan looks at me wordlessly. *What did you expect?*

We enter. Inside the front door there are stairs leading both up and down. The dining room is upstairs. We climb the short flight and present ourselves to the hostess, who seats us in a booth right away. Shannon opens her menu. Max ignores his and turns to the graphic novel he's brought with him.

"The book goes away during dinner. OK, Max?" I remind him. I get a noncommittal "Mmmm" and chalk it up as a yes. I lean back and look around.

The room is good sized. The walls are lined in booths clad in plum vinyl, with individual tables set up in the center space. Most of the booths are occupied, as well as a few of the tables. There isn't a bar, but I spot a set of wooden double doors marked "Lounge" on the wall farthest from our booth.

Dan taps the edge of my menu with his own. "First

impressions?"

Before I can answer, we're approached by a server in his early twenties. A college student home for the summer, perhaps. His name tag reads "Dustin."

"Welcome to Fiorentino's," he says. "Can I get you started with drinks?"

The kids opt for ginger ale, and Dan a half carafe of the house white. I scan the cocktail list, choosing a martini that resembles the pineapple concoction I made the previous day. When Dustin leaves, I catch Dan's eye and nod towards the lounge. "I'll be right back," I say, and slide out of the booth.

The lounge at Fiorentino's is dark, small, and noisy. Most of the room is consumed by a horseshoe-shaped polished wood bar. Three quarters of the stools are occupied, the diners being served by two bartenders. The rest of the space consists of about six high top tables – all of them full, a good sign – and an old fashioned self-serve popcorn machine. Four flat screen televisions are all tuned to a soccer game. An 80s hair band whose name escapes me is playing on the sound system.

Ugh, snorts Gilda. *I bet this is where the guy in the MAGA hat goes after dark.*

I retreat back to the main dining room and our booth. Dan and Shannon are in a heated battle of tic-tac-toe, scribbling Xs and Os on the paper placemats. From what I can glean from Max's book, Godzilla is retreating into the sea, wounded.

"So?" Dan asks, as Shannon draws a line through three Xs in victory.

"The lounge is small," I say. "I'd definitely want to knock down the wall that separates it from the rest of the room."

Dustin arrives with a tray bearing our drinks. I smile at him. "So, what's downstairs?"

He sets my full martini glass down without spilling. *Nice technique,* admires Gilda. "Banquet room for private functions," he says. "Weddings, showers, bar mitzvahs, that kind of thing. Any questions on the menu?"

We order – shrimp scampi for Dan, baked haddock for me, spaghetti with meatballs for Shannon, and in a surprising turn of events, chicken parmesan for Max – and Dustin glides to another table. I look at Dan and shake my head. "This isn't it. I mean, it's fine, but it's too big, for one. And it just doesn't have the layout I'm looking for. It isn't Book Club." I'm disappointed.

"Well, you haven't seen that many," Dan says, reading my expression. "Don't get discouraged."

I nod and take a sip of my drink. It's too sweet. Amateurs. "Well, I've looked at – and rejected – about two dozen others without having to see them. But you're right. I'm not going to worry about it. Yet. And anyway," I raise my glass. "I'm here with my three favorite people in the world. Happy Friday, family."

The four of us clink glasses. "What are we doing tomorrow?" Max asks.

"A bunch of stuff," I say. "I'm going on a bike ride with Tess. You guys are going swimming at Walden Pond."

"How far are you riding this time, Mom?" Shannon asks.

"60 miles. Can you believe it?" I say. "The big ride is just a month away."

"Oh, hey. That reminds me," says Dan. "Send me the route when you have a chance. We'll meet you at one of the rest stops to cheer you on." Max and Shannon nod vigorously.

"Really?" I'm touched. "I'd love that."

"Nana and Bop Bop are coming, too," Shannon says.

"Well, that's fantastic," I say, then turn to Dan. "But I forbid you to offer me a ride. I might be too tempted to take you up on it."

He laughs. "That's exactly what your mother will do."

I shake my head. "I'm serious. Do *not* let her. I'm doing this. I didn't come this far to only come this far, you know?"

"I know," he levels his eyes at me. "You won't need me to stop you from quitting. I'm pretty convinced that you can complete this journey all on your own."

I return his gaze, then shake my head. "Not all alone. Never all alone."

We clink glasses again. Just the two of us.

∞∞∞

The next afternoon, I'm straddling my bike at the side of a long, shady road. There's a stretch of state forest on one side and a series of lovely houses I'll never be able to afford on the other. I've just summited a long and difficult hill, and am waiting for Tess to catch up. We're about two miles from Dee's, the next bar/restaurant for sale on my list of possibilities. The water in my bottle has grown lukewarm, and I'm craving an iced tea so badly I could weep.

I spy Tess chugging around the final bend of the hill. I lean over to get a better look and place my left foot on my bike pedal.

"Hey!" Tess shrieks. "No 'fuck you' breaks!"

I wait until Tess pulls up just behind me on the shoulder of the road. "A *what* break?"

Tess unclips her shoe from the pedal and looks at me. "A 'fuck you' break," she responds, breathing heavily from

176

exertion. "If you wait until the moment I catch up with you and then take off, that's a 'fuck you' break." She folds her arms onto her handlebars, and rests her head on them. "Fucking hills."

"Right?" I say. "And I wasn't about to leave, I promise. Take your time; we're only two miles away from food and all the iced tea we can drink."

Tess straightens up again. "And then how many more miles?"

"Umm," I say. "Only 18."

Tess looks at me and shakes her head. "I hate you a little right now, you know," Tess says.

"I know," I reply, sipping my water. "Will you like me more if I tell you that the next mile and a half is downhill?"

"Much more," she says.

We glide the rest of the way towards the busy center of a town five miles from my house. Our destination is a pub set back one block from the main street. I'd first discovered Dee's in my insomnia-driven research earlier in the summer. When it appeared again in my search for businesses for sale, I added it to my list for the smallish size and the proximity to home. Now, I'm not so sure it was worth the time. The building is a dreary gray, squatting between a Parisian-themed salon and a kitchen-and-bath design firm. The small neon logos of below average beer conglomerates glow in the large, front-facing window.

"You're sure about this?" Tess asks as I'm locking our bikes to the post of a street light across the road.

"Nope," I say. "But I'm hungry, thirsty, and here."

We walk in and approach the hostess station. Beyond, Dee's opens into a modest-sized rectangular space. At the center of the room is the bar, also rectangular, with stool seating around its entire perimeter. Behind the bar is a long mirror with "Dee's" in gold-painted script. One end of the room hosts a semi-separate seating area for about 20, the other a small dance floor and shallow stage. The lower third of the walls are clad in wainscoting, and the upper two thirds are painted a faded gold, perhaps originally intended to match the script on the bar's mirror. It's a little dark and a lot run down, but the space appeals to me.

Why? Gilda challenges me.

I consider the question while Tess and I wait to be seated. I like that it's one big room, but each end has its own purpose. People who are here to dance will gravitate to one area; those here to talk or watch so-bad-it's-good TV will go to another. It's got good bones.

No hostess appears. "Let's go sit at the bar," I suggest to Tess. We walk over, the cleats of our biking shoes ticking on the wooden floor, and climb onto two stools. Within seconds, the bartender approaches, her eyebrows raised in the universal gesture for "what can I get you?"

We ordered our iced teas, and I grab a sticky, laminated one-page menu that's within arm's reach.

"How far did you ladies ride?" the bartender asks, setting pint glasses before us. "The shoes gave it away."

Tess and I smile, and she smiles in return. "Just over 40 miles," I say. She's in, I'm guessing, her mid-to-late 60s, with a braid of silver hair reaching down to her waist. Its sheer length would be pooh-poohed by stylists who use phrases like "women of a certain age." I get the feeling that our server would have a choice phrase of her own in response.

"Nice," she says. "Did you bring your water bottles in? I can fill them up with fresh water if you want when you're done.

Are you eating?"

I order a chicken quesadilla, and Tess opts for chili. Our server withdraws to the far side of the bar and starts chatting familiarly to several men in golf shirts.

"What do you think?" Tess asks.

I look around again. There are no booths. Instead, the floor is filled with movable tables for four and two. Flatscreens are mounted above the mirror at the bar and on the outer walls, probably a dozen in all.

There's a lot of potential here, whispers Gilda. My inner voice may be the queen of snark, but she's still on my side.

"There's a lot of potential here," I say out loud. "I actually like this place."

The bartender returns with a basket of tortilla chips and salsa. As she's setting it down, I turn my head slightly to read the script of a tattoo on the underside of her forearm. "Dreaming is free," it reads.

I gasp. "You're a Blondie fan!" I say. "I love her."

"Them," she corrects. "Blondie is a band. Debbie Harry is an individual."

I nod, conceding. "I love *them*," I say. "I'm Georgie, and this is my friend Tess."

"Deandra," our server says. "Call me Dee."

"The owner," I say. It isn't a question. Dee nods.

"How long have you been here?" Tess asks.

Dee leans against the bar's internal counter and squints. "Mmm, been running this place for about 20 years, and in New England for 35. I'm originally from South Carolina. Myrtle Beach."

"Really?" Tess says. "What brought you here?"

Dee gives us a wry smile. "Followed a guy who became my

second husband. That didn't stick, but the place did. I'm actually planning on heading back south." Another smile. "Tired of the winters. I'd rather hang out on the beach with my sister."

We laugh. I like Dee. She excuses herself and retreats to the kitchen for our food, and Tess heads to the restroom.

Alone at the bar, I now sense a buzz around me. The same buzz that came when I first saw what my version of a bar could look like, and the one I felt at Echo Lake when I realized it could actually happen.

I like this place. This could be Book Club.

Tess returns, wincing. "Georg, don't hate me, but when we're done eating I'm calling Nora to pick me up. I can't do another 18 miles."

"My place is closer," I say. "We'll call Dan."

Tess looks at me, understanding. "You think?"

I rub my palms on my Lycra-clad thighs, thinking. "Yeah. I think so. It's worth a conversation, at least."

Dee returns from the kitchen, carrying my quesadilla and Tess' chili. She grabs our now-empty iced tea glasses and starts to refill them. I open my mouth, but nothing comes out.

Do it! Gilda shouts. *What are you waiting for?*

She's about to drift back to the quartet of golfers when my voice kicks in. "Dee," I stammer. "Do you have some time to talk?"

Chapter 14

"How short are you?" Dan asks. "How much is the loan?" He's standing in the doorway of our home office in khaki shorts and his maroon UMass t-shirt, holding two tumblers of iced seltzer with lime in his hands. I'm at the computer, the response to my loan application open on the screen and our financial binder open on the desk.

I look up at him and offer a weak laugh. "Did the binder give it away?"

He doesn't return the laugh. "Just tell me."

The last two weeks have churned with activity. I've been back to Dee's nearly every day. With her help – and her last six months of balance sheets – I was able to submit both the loan application and the women-owned business grant. I included a suite of "before" photos, and Nora tapped an intern in her firm's Art Department to provide pro bono "after" mock ups. They are gorgeous sketches, with bright new decor and cool dining sets. I queried contractors, created renovation and inventory budgets, and spent more than one late night polishing and perfecting the numbers with Dan. Every night before bed, I would call up the designs Nora sent and stare at them. They are Book Club. They are my blood, sweat and tears of the summer.

And it worked! I officially have a business loan. It just isn't enough.

Dan is still in the doorway, waiting for me to respond. "About sixty-five," I say.

He exhales, loudly, and enters the room as if a force field had just been removed. "Oh, OK." He hands me my glass and pulls another chair up beside me.

"You seem relieved," I say, surprised.

"I am, actually," he says. "I thought it might be more. Show me the spreadsheet again. There's still the grant, right? Isn't that for fifty thousand?"

I minimize the congratulatory email and call up my Book Club budget. I type in the loan amount I've qualified for and look at the balance. Sixty-five thousand dollars short of the number Dan and I agreed – at the end of those late nights – we both felt comfortable with to move forward with buying Dee's. In another row on the spreadsheet, the space reserved for a grant award is taken up with an ominous "TBD."

Too Big a Deficit.

"Yes," I say. "I should find out in a day or so if I've made it to the final round. And Jules thinks she has a lead on a second grant. But even *if* I get the first grant, I'm still short. I know you didn't want any of our retirement savings going into the pot."

Now Dan laughs. "Georgie, if you get the grant, it's a done deal."

I look over at him. "It is?"

He nods. "*Yes,* dummy. You think I'm going to throw up a roadblock over fifteen thousand? Can you imagine me trying to explain that to your family? Your mother would kill me.

Slowly. And with pleasure, I might add."

I consider this. "Yeah," I nod. "That tracks. She might even record it to play back every now and again if she needs cheering up." I pause. "I just want you to be sure."

He swivels my chair so I'm facing him. "Listen, you have worked so hard on this," he says. "You've been meticulous, creative, and resourceful. You've taken an idea and made something real and impressive. Look at this loan, you did that." He points at the screen and looks back at me. "Do you think the Georgie of five years ago would have qualified for that?"

I smile. "Definitely not," I say, touched. "Thank you for that." *No fake adult here, toots,* says Gilda. *Not anymore.*

"You've convinced the bank, and you've convinced *me,*" Dan says. "If you get the grant, we've got the rest."

I flip the binder shut and pull Dan's chair closer to mine. "I have to say, all this supportive partner foreplay is sexy as hell." I lean in and kiss him.

"Well, in that case," Dan says. "You should know that I just did the dishes."

"That's hot," I tease. We kiss again. "Where are the kids?" I ask.

"Game room. Two floors away working on their cruise ship in Minecraft," he says. "Apparently it needs an obstacle course for the sheep. They'll be hours."

"*I'm too sexy for my cat, too sexy for my cat,*" trills my phone. Jules. I raise my finger in a *hold that thought* gesture to Dan. He shakes his head vigorously, *don't pick up!*

"She was looking into a second grant for me," I explain. He sits back, resigned.

"Hello, my lovely," I answer.

"Hey," she drawls, and I know it's bad news.

"Ah, dang," I say. "No go, huh?"

"Sorry," she says. "The deadline was a while ago. I feel like an asshole."

"Don't," I say. "A while ago I didn't even have this idea. Not your fault." Dan tugs at the scooped neckline of my cotton lemon yellow shirt. I slap his hand and point to the vintage Tour de France print. "Not in front of my mentors," I whisper.

"What?" Jules asks.

"Nothing," I say. "I have to run. But listen, I really appreciate your checking it out for me. You're the best and I love you. I'll let you know when I hear about the other grant."

We hang up. I place my phone back onto the desk and turn to Dan. "Well, I have fifty thousand eggs in one basket now. Dan, if this grant doesn't come through–"

"Shh, sexy supportive partner here, remember?" He stands, and then grabs my hands to pull me up with him. Suddenly he cocks his head to the side and looks at me, eyes bright. "When you open Book Club, will I get my own barstool, like Norm?" Dan asks.

I grin. "With your name engraved on it and everything."

We kiss again, deeply, and then Dan wordlessly leads me towards the door.

If I get the grant.

As we tiptoe into our bedroom, I try to shrug off the question simmering under the surface.

What if I don't?

∞∞∞

Later, I slip out of the room, closing the door gently on my sleeping husband. I pause at the top of the stairs to pull on Dan's pilfered UMass t-shirt and listen for sounds of life downstairs. After a few seconds of straining, I hear Shannon and Max chatting companionably two floors away, clearly still engaged in their digital world. I tiptoe back into the office, slide into my chair, and turn my attention back to the computer. I close out of Book Club's budget spreadsheet and call up the website of the foundation that – fingers crossed – will award me a grant in the next few weeks. The organization, focused on supporting women entrepreneurs, is called, simply, "B♀ss."

"Empowering a new generation of women entrepreneurs in Boston!" the organization's website boasted when I found it during my research earlier in the summer. The group, I read, awards dozens of small grants – of $5,000 – locally throughout the year to women seeking to launch their own business. *That's all well and good*, I thought at the time, *but 5k isn't going to get me there. I'm gonna need a bigger boat. Where's my* Orca?

I found it a few minutes later. B♀ss' signature award, I learned, is an annual $50,000 grant given to a local aspiring woman-in-business. The windfall is intended exclusively for first-time woman entrepreneurs, like me. When I first found the award program, I fervently scrolled through the page. *Please please please don't let the deadline be last week*. It wasn't. In fact, the timing was damn near perfect.

"Yes!" I shouted at the time, slapping the top of the oak desk in delight. Palm stinging, I downloaded the application. *This is what I need to get Dan fully on board*, I thought then. *This will get me my Book Club!*

Now, looking at the screen, my attention is drawn to a new link on the foundation's homepage reading "An important update for potential grantees!" I click on it, suddenly nervous.

To our B♀ss grant applicants:

This is the week! Five up and coming "B♀sses of Boston" will be chosen to make a two-minute video about their business for our volunteer selection committee. We encourage all potential grantees to review their application materials to ensure we have the most up-to-date contact information.

I confirm my details, and lean back in my chair to think. A two-minute video. The most important pitch of my life to date. What do I say?

I clear my throat. "Hi, I'm Georgie Fischer, and I'm opening Book Club…" I trail off, suddenly self-conscious. I've been talking to myself out loud my whole life. Hell, I even named the voice in my head I converse with every day. *Now* I'm shy?

I try again. "Have you ever noticed that every bar you've visited is designed for men?"

Oh. You're Andy Rooney now?

I utter a low growl of frustration and start over.

"Walk into a bar, any bar, and look around. You'll find that…" I stop, not feeling it. They should know my story, how the idea came to me.

"It all started when some crank in a MAGA hat yelled at my friend Jules…" I start to giggle. I can't help it.

You need to take this seriously, Gilda snaps, bringing me back. *You want to be a "B♀ss," don't you?* I draw in a deep breath and shake out my arms lightly. Exhaling slowly, I close my eyes and envision the selection committee. They appear as a group of six women in crisp jewel-toned suits, walking in slow motion to a long table. They sit, and turn to me in unison. *Hit me with your best shot*, their faces say. What are they hoping to hear? What do they need to feel?

"Women in the U.S. outnumber men," I say, suddenly all business. My brain begins to pull whole paragraphs from my research. "We make up nearly half of this country's workforce. Single women are more likely to be homeowners than men. We vote more than men do, too. Women in households make the decisions about what a family eats and wears, where they go on vacation, and what products they bring into the home.

"And yet, despite being a driving force of our country's economy, women are largely ignored when it comes to casual entertainment outside the home." I stand and begin pacing the office, my gaze fixed on the gray patterned rug. "I want you to pause and remember the last time you visited a bar. Or the last three bars, for that matter. Think about what it looked like, what was playing on TV, and who its customers were. Who did those establishments cater to, really? I'm willing to bet the answer isn't women. Or rather, women who were simply going out to enjoy the company of other women.

"I want to offer a different vision. I want to offer a place where women can go and revel in what they enjoy with their sisters, friends, and cousins. A place where the purpose is *not* to meet men, or entertain their children, but to be themselves. Without worrying about being judged for how old they are, what they look like, or which guilty-pleasure shows they secretly love. I want to offer a sanctuary where women can go – in groups or alone – to say *piss off* to the real world for a while and sit in peace. Or in laughter. Or in contentment.

"I want to offer...Book Club."

"I like it. Not sure about the 'piss off,' though."

I whirl around. Dan is standing in the doorway, clad in his

boxer briefs and a rumpled gray t-shirt.

"Jesus Christ!" I exhale. "You scared the crap out of me."

"Sorry," he says. His grin says otherwise. He points at that stolen shirt that I'm wearing. "Aha. I was looking for that. What are you doing?"

"If I make it to the final round for the grant, I have to record a two-minute video about Book Club, so I was trying out a few approaches," I say. I shift from one foot to the other. "So. You liked it?"

He nods. "But, as you pointed out so delicately when you first pitched me the idea, I'm not your audience."

"Good point," I say. "What the hell do you know?"

∞∞∞

The weekday summer traffic is light. I pedal up and down a series of rolling hills, my cadence steady. There are 10 miles to go in my last ride before 100 Revolutions. I'm biking 75 miles, the longest ride I've ever done. For the next week and a half my training program will focus on yoga and light weights. My bike, which has become a reliable friend over the summer, will be driven to a repair shop for a wheel-to-wheel tuneup and cleaning.

Today's daydreams have been centered on the upcoming ride, as well as last year's, when I biked the 25-mile route as a member of the Hudson communications team. A year ago, I huffed and puffed my way through, taking a too-long break at the midpoint rest stop and finishing in the back third of riders. I remember being hyper-aware of my stomach flab as I leaned forward to grip my handlebars, as well as the feel of my helmet straps pinching into the fleshy underside of my chin.

You didn't like yourself very much back then, Gilda says. *And I enabled it. Often. I'm sorry.*

"It's OK," I whisper, turning to face an expanse of reservoir to my right. "I like me now. A lot."

I shift my mind's eye from last year's ride to this year's. Having decided to "store" the official navy and white riding jersey in my kitchen trash can, I've chosen to wear a cheerful and bright tangerine one on the day of the event. I visualize myself in it, straddling my bike at the start of the ride with hundreds of others. This time, I imagine being hyper-aware of my strong core and my easy breathing during the ride. I see my legs churning through the miles like crankshafts. It isn't a *fuck you* to Lena and Frank anymore. It's an *amen* to me. To my abilities, my creativity, my strength, my courage, and my happiness. I've learned this summer that my happiness does, in fact, have a lot to do with it.

Now, as the final miles tick down, I'm feeling a strange mix of pride and sadness. Pride for everything I've accomplished in the last three months, and sadness for the time I lost mired in self-loathing and doubt. As I glide around the final corner and onto my street, I make a promise to be kind to myself. Or try to, at least.

Shannon is sitting in one of our beach chairs and occupying a patch of shade in the driveway, an open book on her lap. I coast to a stop, then give her my best jazz hands. She grins.

"How far did you go, Mom?" she asks.

"Seventy. Five. Miles." I dismount and wait for her to be suitably impressed.

"What's for dinner?" She asks me. I'm sure she's simply too overwhelmed by my raw power to express her admiration.

I chuckle and glance at my watch. "It's only two thirty, so I have no idea." I start my post-ride stretching and look at her book. "Is that from your summer reading list?" She nods.

"Are you getting excited about going back to school?"

"Kinda," she says. "I like seeing my friends every day."

I nod in agreement. "Makes sense. Have you had a fun summer?"

She smiles. "Yeah, it's been awesome."

"Yeah?" I ask. "What's been your favorite part?"

"Everything!" Shannon exclaims. Her blonde braids are starting to show wisps of escaped hair, and there's a smudge of something – chocolate or dirt? – on her lower right cheek. She looks rested and happy, and a rush of gratitude courses through me.

Thank you, Summer of Georgie.

"Everything, huh? Well, that narrows it down," I say. "Give me a top three."

She cocks her head to one side to think, a gesture that I've seen Dan do a thousand times. "All the time at Nana and Bop Bop's pool, learning to do a flip on my trampoline, and the time we picked all the blueberries."

Things she wouldn't have been able to do if I were still working at Hudson. This is exactly *why you did this.*

"Nice," I say. "The pool time with you and Max is on my top three list, too. And then our week at Echo Lake. But since I never did a flip on the trampoline, I'm gonna put all my bike rides as my third."

We sit in silence for a few minutes. She reads. I stretch.

"Am I going to Before School this year?" Shannon asks quietly.

I stand up, my stretching complete, and walk over to the

190

beach chair. Squatting down to her level, I hold up my right hand, pinky extended. "No," I say. "No more Before School. There will be some days when you'll go to After School, but not every day. Deal?"

We lock pinkies. "Deal," she says.

I head inside. Dan and Max are on opposite ends of the family sofa, noses in books.

"Hey," I greet them, leaning on the door frame. "Is this library hour?"

Dan looks up. "Yep. That summer list isn't going to read itself. How was your ride?"

"Long, but good," I reply. "How was your day off?"

He smiles. "Fantastic. I should not work on Wednesdays more often."

I step into the room and give him a kiss. "Good in theory, but bad in practice. I'm going to jump in the shower. Carry on, bookworms."

I think about my pinky-promise to Shannon as I rinse off 75 miles of sweat, road grit, and bicycle grease. I know it's one I will keep, bar or no bar. But it'd be better with the bar.

As long as you get good news from B♀ss.

I dry off and head to my bedroom, where I pull a cotton Madras skirt from the closet. Last summer, I didn't wear it once. It pinched my waist, but I couldn't bear to let it go. Now, the zipper slides up effortlessly. I'll never be a size six, and that's OK. I feel like me again.

Having finished my ride, stretched, and showered, there are no more excuses to delay checking my email. I've tried this week to limit myself to only doing so twice a day, in the morning and afternoon. The first five times, there was no message from B♀ss. I sit down in front of my laptop and power it up, a fight-or-flight war raging in my gut.

Maybe the sixth time's the charm?

It's the first message I see when my inbox fills the screen. "We'd like to learn more about you! A message from the team at B♀ss"

Oh my God! That's good, right? That has to be good.

Shaking, I open the message.

Dear Georgia,

Congratulations! You've been chosen to advance to the final round of candidates to receive our annual "B♀sses of Boston" $50,000 grant. The preliminary selection committee was very impressed with your proposal. We think your business concept is creative, fills a need that's missing in your chosen industry, and shows strong promise for expansion as a brand.

I clap my hands over my mouth in surprise, and they remain there as I read the rest of the email, noting that the deadline for the two-minute video pitch is just two days away, with the grant announcement on Monday.

"DAN!" I shriek and clatter down the stairs in my bare feet. I round the corner to the dining room and nearly collide with him. "I made it! I made it to the final round for the grant!"

He whoops loudly and we hug. Max pads in from the family room. "What's going on?"

We turn to face him, beaming. "Your mom is wicked smart, Max. She's WICKED SMAHT!" Max retreats back to the sofa, shaking his head.

"I have to send in the video pitch by Friday," I tell Dan, my heart thumping. "I gotta go call Jules."

My friend screams into the phone when I tell her. We spend

a minute or two gushing over the news – "my concept shows strong promise for brand expansion! I show promise, Jules!" – before settling down to discuss the video. I recite my pitch from a few days ago. "I should do the video at Dee's, don't you think?" I ask her.

"Yes, definitely," Jules says. "Let's go tomorrow. All of us. Book Club goes to Book Club. We'll have dinner at Dee's, and torment you until you nail the pitch."

We hang up. I allow myself a few moments of solitary joy.

I did it, I think, glowing with satisfaction. *I did it, and it's going to happen.*

Chapter 15

"Why so fast, do you think?" Natalie asks me.

The five of us are sitting around one of the larger tables at Dee's and brainstorming where in the room I should shoot the video. The bar is lively, but not full. It feels like an upbeat Thursday-is-the-new-Friday cocktail crowd. Dee herself has joined us for a few minutes, curious to meet the rest of my band of Book Club boosters.

"This is how they've done it for the last several years, according to what I've read," I say. "Once they've narrowed it down to five, they toss us all into the deep end to see who can swim. Thus the two-day deadline. The winner is chosen from a different selection committee – a smaller one."

"Speaking of, I vote that you get right behind the bar for the video," says Nora, turning around in her seat to get a better view. "They'll see customers in the background, hear the buzz of conversations. It'll make you look like a boss." She puts the last word in air quotes.

"I don't know," I say. "Isn't that tempting fate a little? Acting like I own the place already?"

"Toughen up, cookie," says Dee. "There's no room for superstition."

"You could give a virtual tour," offers Tess. "You could even start outside and 'invite' them in, and then walk around the place and explain what you want to do."

I consider this. "I like the concept," I say. "Would it be weird for me to be walking around, and everyone else just having their drinks or dinner or whatever?" I chuckle softly. "I really don't want my video to have people in the background looking at me like I'm nuts."

"So make them part of it," says Jules. "Make all of us part of it."

We all look at her. I lean forward. "How?"

Jules smiles. "Put us in it. Put Dee in it. Put anyone in this bar who wants to be in it, in it." She gestures to Natalie, Nora and Tess. "We can vouch for how smart, creative, and dedicated you are. Dee can talk about the importance of handing her business over to another woman. And everyone else here can say that they love the idea of Book Club. Put us *all* in it."

"Yes!" Nora says. Natalie nods vigorously.

"I'm game," adds Dee.

We all look at Tess. She looks sheepish.

"I hate being on camera," she says. "You have Nat already, it'll be just like having me."

"Get over yourself," Natalie teases. "This is for Georgie."

I place my hand over Tess'. "I need someone to shoot the video," I say. "Know anyone?"

Tess nods. "Sold," she says.

"Chicken," says her twin good-naturedly, then turns to Dee. "Think we can round up some of these revelers?"

Dee smiles and stands up. "Leave it to me." She strides over to the bar and has a brief exchange with the bartender. He nods and turns the sound system down. At the sudden drop in

195

volume, the customers involuntarily pause and look around, curious. Dee pounces on the opportunity.

"Everybody listen up for a minute!" Dee bellows, her voice carrying easily around the room. "Most of you know that I'm looking to pack things up and head back to Myrtle Beach."

"Booooo!" a few people respond, not unkindly.

"Yeah, I love you too," Dee says. "But there's a fabulous woman right here who wants to take it over, and I know there's a lot of folks here tonight who are going to love what she's gonna do." She turns and points at a group of 10 or so women taking up a line of tables along one wall. "I'm looking at you, Thursday Night Hockey Moms." They cheer, clearly delighted to be singled out as regulars.

"But she needs our help to win this, uh, contest. Now, anyone who wants to can come right up here around the bar, and when I give the word, I want us all to yell 'we want Book Club!' Got it?"

I sit in stunned silence, watching two dozen or so customers - most of them women - hustle over at Dee's command.

This woman is a badass, says Gilda, awed. *She's a BΩss.*

"Get over here, G!" Jules calls. I hurry over to where Dee has turned a high-back bar stool so it's facing outward.

Tess has pulled a chair to an empty spot about 15 feet from the bar. She gingerly steps onto it holding my phone, and turns it horizontally to capture the full gathering. She gives the group a thumbs up, and Dee counts down from three.

"WE WANT BOOK CLUB!" Everyone cries in unison, glasses raised.

I am flushed with pleasure. The Thursday Night Hockey Moms circle me briefly, wishing me luck before trickling back to their tables.

I turn to Dee. "That was incredible. Thank you."

She hugs me. "We needed to do that part first to get you in the right frame of mind. Now it's *your* turn."

Buoyed by my impromptu cheering squad, I deliver my "I want to offer Book Club" pitch with renewed energy. I'm focused, passionate, and articulate. I nail it on the first try.

"No more takes," I tell Tess. "Now we celebrate."

"No, now *you* celebrate," says Dee, handing me a cosmo. "The rest of us have some filming to do." She turns the bar stool back around. "Sit. Enjoy. You've earned it. Tess and the rest of the original book club, you're with me."

They walk to the far end of the bar, where I can watch them set up and discuss various video angles, but can't make out what they're saying. I give up trying to eavesdrop, trusting implicitly that they have my back. Instead, I lean back in the stool and sigh, soaking in the memory of the people gathered around me, cheering for an idea they didn't even know about. They did it because they clearly love Dee. And Dee, apparently, likes me. So they like me.

I am radiating happiness. I don't even mind that I'm sitting by myself at a bar without a book.

Not for long, Gilda reminds me. *Soon this place will have its own lending library.*

Inspired, I turn around and scan the room, searching for the ideal place to house a collection of paperbacks. I'm sizing up a nook near the hostess station when a movement near the door catches my eye. I look over, and freeze. My stomach hollows and drops to the floor.

Standing just inside, looking around with suspicious interest, is Frank Hudson.

∞∞∞

Why the hell is he *here?*

I whip around and face the bar, turning my back on Frank. Using the mirrored "Dee's" sign behind the bar, I can study him as he studies the crowd. He's in pressed Chino pants and a short sleeved navy golf shirt, the recognizable white double-Hs of the hotel logo on the upper left side. His face and arms are deeply tanned, no doubt from numerous sailing adventures on his boat over the summer. The hostess approaches him, and Frank chats with her, smiling. She nods and gestures to the bar.

Shit.

I pick up my cosmo and slide off the stool, keeping my back to Frank, and casually circle around to the opposite side of the long rectangular bar. Now the mirrored sign is hiding his face, but beneath it, his branded shirt gives his position – three stools down from where I just sat – away.

What's he doing? Gilda asks. *And why are you hiding? You have nothing to hide from.*

It's weird that he's here. With all due love and admiration to Dee, this is not a place that Frank Hudson would frequent.

"Georgie!" Tess yells. "There you are!"

I grit my teeth as she, Natalie and Nora make their way around the bar to where I sit. Beyond the mirror, and under the pretense of adjusting something out of sight – his sock garters, maybe? – Frank ducks, bringing his head below the bottom edge of the mirror. He sees me.

Double shit.

Jules appears on my right and grabs the empty stool beside me. Dee slips behind the bar and makes her way over to our

198

group. Nora hands me my phone.

"I sent all the video clips to my email," Nora says. "Would you let me have a crack at editing it down to two minutes?"

"Seriously? I would love that," I tell her. "But are you sure? With the deadline tomorrow, I'd understand if you can't."

Nora smiles. "I got this. I have it all planned out already. You'll have it first thing in the morning. Listen, Tess and I have to relieve our sitter, and we're giving Nat a ride home. We are so proud of you, G." They both hug me, and leave.

Dee places a drink in front of Jules and looks at me. "Everyone here is in your corner tonight, hon," she says.

Not everyone.

I reach over and squeeze her hand. "Thank you again, Dee. You were amazing."

"So were you," she says. "I gotta get back to work. Don't even think about paying for those drinks." She winks and moves on to another group a few stools away.

I glance over at Frank. He's sitting up straight again, a neat Scotch untouched in front of him. His fingers idly drum the bar-top.

I lean towards Jules. "Ebeneezer Gates is here."

Her eyes widen slightly, but she doesn't look around. Ever the reliable wingman. She picks up her glass and smiles. We're just two friends chatting. "Where?"

"Other side of the bar and a few stools down to the right. Navy shirt. He can't see us now, but he knows I'm here."

"It's weird, isn't it?" Jules says. "It doesn't feel like a coincidence."

"Right?" I feel validated for hiding. "I want to know what's going on, but I'm not just waltzing up to him and saying hi. Not after the way they canned me. And definitely not after my last conversation with him."

I am a success. You are not. And if I may say so, you never will be.

"Want me to try to chat him up?"

I shake my head. "He saw us together. But thanks for the offer."

Jules pauses, thinking. "You could just go over and tell him to go fuck himself."

"It's tempting," I say. "It won't help me find out why he's here, but it's tempting." I peek over again. His stool is empty. His drink is resting on one end of a $20 bill, the other end curling lazily up the side of the glass, retaining its shape from living inside Frank's wallet.

"He's gone," I tell Jules. "That was fast."

"Maybe *you* scared *him* away," she says. "Maybe ex-employees tossing drinks on him is an occupational hazard."

"Maybe," I say, knowing that's not the case. Not with Frank.

"Well, good riddance," Jules says, "Anyway, guess what? I forgot to tell you on the phone the other day, but I met Bembé Jean-Baptiste."

I forget about Frank. "You did? When? Where?"

"A fundraiser for Pediatrics. You know that nurse who's friends with his wife? She's in pediatrics."

"What's he like in person?"

She laughs. "You're totally fan-girling on me. He's a normal guy. Friendly. He mentioned how much he was looking forward to the ride, so I told him the real story behind you getting canned. He was actually pretty annoyed about the whole 'bestseller' thing."

I smile. "Really? Thank you." I drain the last of my cosmo. "You know what? Screw Frank. I'm going to go home and find something productive to do while I wait for Nora to send me the video. Actually, no. I won't be productive." I pick up my phone and wave it at her. "I'm going to sit on my couch and watch videos of my friends saying lovely things about me."

I climb down from my stool and sling my purse over my shoulder. "Want to walk out with me?"

Jules shakes her head. "I need to hit the bathroom, and there's a line. Promise me to fix that when it's yours, OK?"

"Number one item on the list," I say, and walk outside. The late August night is humid, offering no trace of the approaching fall. No stars are visible, though whether they are hidden by clouds or light pollution I can't tell. I look up at the bar's entrance. The yellow neon "Dee's" tugs at me a little. I pull out my phone to snap a picture of it, and notice that Nora has left it in video mode.

"Georgia."

Frank is across the narrow street, standing next to a street light – the very one where Tess and I locked our bikes a few weeks ago – and working his way through a petit cigar. I don't trust him, not one little bit. I have no idea why he's here, but I know it can't be good. Still looking at my phone, I tap the red button and begin filming.

My phone casually at my side, I walk over to him, standing far enough away to avoid the worst of his puffs. "I didn't realize you smoked, Frank."

"Very infrequently," he says. "I limit myself to three or four a year. Sometimes fewer."

"Really," I say, cautiously. "What's the occasion, then?"

He doesn't answer right away. He drags on his cigar, and exhales a perfect ring into the beam of the street light. "Do you know why I'm successful, Georgia?"

201

"I could recite the relevant lines from your foreword," I say. "I've edited them enough. But why don't you tell me, Frank?"

"I see opportunities," he says. "I meet needs that are missing. I had no interest in taking my hotels national because there's a sizable percentage of the population who do not venture far from home. They want the mountains, yes. They want to visit beaches and lakes, but they want to feel like they are home, and know exactly what to expect. I remained regional to offer that local not-so-far-from-home experience exceptionally well."

I say nothing.

"And they keep coming back because now they know that when they stay at a Hudson Hotel, they are ultimately funding a charity that will pump money back in their homes. To fire departments, food pantries, and youth groups. That kind of generosity gets attention."

"Why are you here, Frank?" I ask.

He puffs again. "Did you really think, Georgia," he says, "that a foundation seeking to award grants to future business owners wouldn't place a successful and philanthropic entrepreneur on its selection committee?"

∞∞∞

It occurs to me that I could just leave. I could simply lean back onto one heel, execute a neat little spin, and walk away. I also know that there's no way in hell I'm doing that right now.

"You know, Frank, I knew they would," I say. "My mistake was assuming they wouldn't choose a misogynistic blowhard like you."

Frank chuckles. "Blowhard, I'll give you," he says. "Just this once. But misogynistic? Come on, Georgia. You know that's not true."

"I know *you* think it isn't," I counter. "Have you read any 'girl books' lately?"

He looks at me thoughtfully, clearly not remembering our one conversation about books that didn't include his own. "I don't follow," he says.

"Of course you don't," I reply. A mosquito has landed on my arm, but I refuse to swat it. I'm willing to risk its itchy after-bite – or even malaria – to avoid showing any sort of weakness in front of this man. "I'll ask you again, Frank. Why are you here?"

"Because I see opportunities," he says again. "In all my decades running my business, I'd always viewed my customer as part of a couple or family, or as a traveling professional. I've known, of course, that most family vacations are planned by the mother or wife. But until I read your proposal I hadn't considered how the needs of a female customer traveling on her own or with friends would differ from her needs when she's with her family."

"But who's misogynistic, right?" I say. "Get to the point, Frank."

His eyes flared briefly. "My point is that when I first overheard office gossip about your little idea, I dismissed it as a novelty."

Angela told somebody, Gilda whispers, disgusted. *You* knew *she would tell somebody.*

"Imagine my surprise when I'm handed a dossier from the lady-boss foundation that includes you. A person of *principles*. And even better, they seem to think that your idea – your fad – could actually be something worth funding. Worth replicating. Well, I had to see it for myself."

"Why?" I ask, coolly. "Because you're on the committee or because you once told me I'd never be a success?"

"Neither," Frank says. "It's business. My largest hotel is a mile from here. And if, as these lady-boss experts seem to think, it's worth replicating, a chain of bars would certainly start regionally, wouldn't you agree?"

"And why would that interest you?" I ask. "You already have a restaurant."

He waves his cigar at me. "The restaurant is a cheap breakfast buffet followed by short order room service, and you know it. I see an opportunity, and I'm here to make a deal."

"I'm not interested, Frank."

"Humor me, then, will you?" Frank says. "Forget the grant. Forget your business loan, for that matter."

Inwardly, I cringe. Having access to my grant proposal, he knows *everything*.

"I will invest in your idea. You can launch your bar here, in this space. You will be the manager, and I will own it. If it's successful, as you claim it will be, we'll eventually expand. At that time, we can discuss your taking ownership of a franchise."

"No," I say. "You will have nothing to do with this. And I'm certainly not working for you again. Ever."

Frank smiles, and takes another deep drag from his cigar. *He's enjoying himself*, Gilda notes. *What an asshole*.

"If you turn my offer down," he says. "I can assure you that you will not receive this grant. And if you don't win the grant, you won't secure this space."

"And why is that, Frank?" I ask. "Why are you so certain?"

"Well, for starters, I can sink your proposal," he says. "You don't give out millions upon millions over the years and not have your opinion hold weight. One word from me, and you move to the bottom of the pile."

I shrug, determined not to be rattled by him. "Whatever, Frank. Pull your petty little strings. Have at it. I'll get my funding somewhere else."

"I have no doubt that you will, Georgia," he says. "But will it be in time?"

Despite the tumultuous storm in my gut, I am very still. "In time for what, Frank?"

"In time for me to buy this place, of course," he says. "The proprietor won't wait forever for you to find a new source of funding. And as I said earlier, it appears to others to be a nice little idea you've had. I may just build a girl bar of my own."

"A *girl bar*?" I spit the words onto the sidewalk. "Are you serious? You know nothing about how to make this work. You don't even *want* it to work. You just don't want *me* to make it work."

"Nonsense," Frank says. "I know exactly how to make it work. You spelled it out so carefully in your proposal, and for that I thank you."

Images from my perfect summer are rushing at me, causing a sense of vertigo. My bike rides. My epiphany about Book Club. My meticulous research and discussions with Dan, Jasper, and my parents. The bartending course, and finally, meeting Dee. I planned for everything. Everything except the sheer viciousness of my former boss, and I want to scream.

"But why? Why would you bother? Why do you even care?" I ask. I can hear desperation creeping into my voice, and I hate myself for it. "Is it because I refused to lie and call your book a bestseller? Because I pushed back on pressuring grantees to pimp it for you?"

"Of course it is," he says, simply.

I'm shocked into silence. He smiles again.

"Don't be ridiculous, Georgia," he says, shaking his head. "I'm doing it for the bottom line and the expansion of my brand. But the fact that it's you is the mint on the pillow, as we say in the hotel business. Think about my offer. You have until first thing Monday morning."

"Monday," I say. "The day the BQss grant winner is announced. How convenient. That's not a coincidence, is it, Frank?"

"No, it is not. The selection committee is meeting at ten o'clock that morning, and the winner will be announced at noon. Good night, Georgia."

He saunters away, leaving me with nothing but a smoke ring and my helplessness for company. I look down, seething. I stare at my hands, fully comprehending what just happened. My options, limited as they are, start coming into focus.

Monday. I have three days to decide what to do.

Chapter 16

I didn't fill Dan in on my encounter with Frank outside Dee's when I arrived home the previous night. In part so he wouldn't lose sleep until he needed to, but mostly so I could sit with it for a while myself. I laid awake long into the night, thinking. This morning, bleary-eyed and gripping my favorite *Yellow Submarine* coffee mug a little more tightly, I kissed Dan goodbye as he headed to work, still keeping this new obstacle to myself.

Now, a fresh mug of coffee in hand, I sit down at the breakfast bar with my laptop. Nora's email is waiting for me, having arrived in my inbox at 7:10 am. I open it. *So excited for and proud of you!! xoxo N.* it reads. I click on the video file attached.

The first few seconds hold an image of Dee's yellow neon sign, the sounds of clinking glasses and soft chatter creating a relaxed cocktail party mood. With the bar soundtrack still playing, the sign dissolves into a new image, with the words "Book Club, by Georgie Fischer" appearing in the same script and color as the original sign.

And then there I am, delivering my Book Club pitch in front of the bar. I tune the words out – I was there, after all – and take in the visual of myself with fresh perspective.

I look good. My skin has a healthy glow from a summer of fresh air, sunshine, and exercise. My dark blonde hair has streaks of honey running through it. The sea glass green wrap dress draws out the matching color of my eyes. I am not skinny. I'll never be skinny. And that's fine. I'm strong and happy, and I realized this summer that I like that even more.

"Welcome back, Georgie," I say. "I've missed you."

Then my happy, smiling, confident self fades, and Jules appears.

"Hi Team B♀ss," she says, waving at the camera. "I'm Jules Martin, and I've known Georgie Fischer since middle school. You've seen her proposal, you've read her business plan, and you like her idea. Now you're wondering about the woman herself: can she see this through? Is she worthy of this award? I can tell you, without hesitation, that she is. She has the grit, the heart, the passion, and the leadership to revolutionize girls' night out."

"Oh, honey. I love you so much," I say to the screen. Seconds later, Jules is replaced by Dee. Even on video, her presence commands attention.

"You're looking to help more women become their own bosses," she begins, her long silver braid draped over her shoulder. "I've been the boss here for the last two decades. This place has made me work, sweat, scream, and cry, but it's also given me a joy that I never thought I'd experience. There is no one, *no one*, I'd rather pass it on to than Georgie Fischer."

Dee's face transforms into an enormous smile. "But don't take my word for that, let me tell you what my Thursday night regulars think about a change in management."

The crowd of customers, gathered around the bar on Dee's

say-so, fills the screen. "WE WANT BOOK CLUB!"

As the video ends, I start to weep. I'm overwhelmed by the love and support of my friends, Dee, and the dozens of strangers who gamely stepped up to help. I'm also overwhelmed by a fresh wave of rage, and I'm determined to never – *ever* – allow Frank Hudson to come within shouting distance of this vision again.

I download Nora's video and send it to the team at BΩss, fulfilling my final requirement for consideration hours ahead of the deadline. Then I pick up my phone and call Angela.

"Hey! How are you?" Angela says. "I've been thinking about you since we last talked."

I decide to get right to my point. "You got my follow up voicemail right after that, right?" I ask. "About keeping it on the down low."

She hesitates. "Yeah. Yeah, I got it." I wait for her to reassure me. She doesn't.

"Who did you tell, Ange?" I ask.

She sighs. "Kyle. I told Kyle. It was right after we talked and I didn't get your message about not saying anything until later. Lena was in her office, and I was sort of bragging about what a cool idea it was because I knew she'd be eavesdropping and I enjoy pissing her off. Why? What happened?"

I give her a synopsis of my run-in outside Dee's.

"Jesus, there is no rock bottom, is there?" Angela says. "Georg, I'm so sorry. I feel awful."

"It's not your fault," I say, resigned. "He would've seen the proposal anyway. I just needed to know how he found out for my own peace of mind."

"What are you going to do?" Angela asks.

"That's what I'm going to figure out today," I say. "I'm

209

weighing a few options."

"Listen," Angela says, her voice lowering. "If there's something I can do to help you, please tell me, OK? I'll do it."

I pause. "There might be, Ange," I say. "But you really don't have to get involved. This is my fight. I don't want you to end up a victim of 'an identified need for more capacity,' you know?"

"Well, I have an identified need to not work for a despot."

I laugh. "Good for you. How's the ride planning going?"

"We're in the calm before the storm," she says. "Lena has Kyle giving her weather updates twice a day. Friday it'll be all hands on deck here setting up for the after party." She lowers her voice again. "I assume you're not riding now?"

"Screw that, I'm riding," I say forcefully. "Watch for me. Listen, I gotta run. Hang in there this week, OK?"

Hanging up, I check the clock on my phone. I have an hour before I have to hustle Max and Shannon to my parents' house and get to one of my last pre-ride yoga classes. I turn to my laptop with renewed interest, determined to unearth additional sources of funding to make up for a grant that seems to be drifting out of my reach. A carrot on a string, with Frank holding the stick. As I search, fragments from my recorded conversation with Frank begin bubbling to the surface. Another kind of plan emerges. One saved just for him.

∞∞∞

"You need to call the people at BⱣss, Georgie."

Dan and I sitting on the small deck in our backyard, sipping tall glasses of seltzer. Max and Shannon are getting in a

210

few final minutes on the trampoline in the deepening dusk. Since filling him in when he got home, Dan's fit of apoplexy has gradually subsided into pleas for me to blow the whistle on Frank, peppered with musings on what kind of blunt instrument would make the most interesting imprint on his forehead.

I watch Shannon execute another flip. I adore the moment when she is nearly right side up again, her golden ponytail sticking straight up with momentum. Max is sitting on the side of the trampoline, pressed up against the safety netting and offering details on her vertical lift. They have become friends this summer, and that is everything.

"Kiddos!" I call from the deck. "Time to read!"

They climb down and jog across the yard to the deck. Shannon is carrying her flip flops. Max is, as usual, barefoot.

"You're going to have to start wearing shoes again soon, buddy," I gently remind him.

"Nope!" The deck door slides closed with a definitive snap.

"Well," I say to Dan. "That's case closed on the shoes, I guess."

"Seriously, Georg," Dan presses. "Why not call them?"

I adjust my chair so I'm facing Dan instead of the trampoline. "Believe me, I thought about it," I tell him. "But no matter how I look at it, it's pretty clear that telling them won't get me the grant."

"Why not?"

"Because if they *do* give it to me, knowing that I've come to them with a story about one of their selection committee members blackmailing me for my business concept, then it looks like *I'm* the one blackmailing *them*," I say. "There's no way that would end well. Say I call them and tell them what I know. To begin with, I deliberately left my time at Hudson

211

off my grant application, so I might have to explain why. And if they want to talk to Lena...well, I don't have to tell you how *that's* going to go.

"At best, they'll kick Frank off the committee. They'll ask him to recuse himself given the fact that I once worked for him. Then they'll tell me to apply again next year. They will insist that the award was already going to someone else – and it might be for all I know – and *maybe* they'll toss me a five grand mini-grant to keep me quiet."

Dan is quiet for a moment. "Yeah, I see it. So why not just *tell* Frank that you're going to call B♀ss and expose him?"

I tilt my head back and study the sky. A few stars have crept out while Dan and I have been talking. "Well, a few reasons. It's mostly because Frank would have already thought through the whole 'what if Georgie calls B♀ss?' scenario. I'm sure he already has a whole speech prepared in the event they call him on it. It's probably something along the lines of 'my heavens, I had no idea Ms. Fischer worked for me. It couldn't have been for very long. No, no, it isn't true. Of course I'll recuse myself. The poor girl must have felt so desperate to make up a story like that.' And he knows that even if they don't buy it, they still won't give me the grant. They've worked too hard on their reputation. They will want to avoid a mess like this."

I lift my legs and stretch them out in front of me. It seems strange to know they'll be biking 100 miles in just over a week. "But you know what else? If I *threaten* Frank before the grant is announced, how does that make me better than him? There's a chance – maybe it's a small one, but it's there – that he *won't* torpedo my proposal. That even he wouldn't sink that low. Maybe he thinks he can scare me into accepting his offer, and make some money off my idea in the process. But isn't it possible that he has no intention of abusing his power as a committee member? As long as this possibility exists, I can't threaten him. I can't. I'm better than that. I would rather lose the grant than win it by holding a knife to someone's throat, even his."

"But Georgie, I hate that he's even threatening to do it!" I can sense Dan's anger radiating. "And the absolute gall of him to try to steal it from you. We need a backup plan, now. What are you going to do when – and for me it's *when*, not if – he *does* nix your grant?" Dan asks.

I grin. "Then it's on."

He looks at me, curious. "What are you playing at, Georgie?"

"A game of chicken," I say, picking my phone up from under my chair. "I'm going to see if Frank blinks."

"You realize I was talking about a backup plan for the actual money, right?" Dan says. "But now I have to know; what's your plan?"

I show Dan the video recording of my conversation with Frank, and divulge the idea I've been formulating since earlier today.

"Wow," he says, admiringly. "You are vicious. I am so turned on right now."

I laugh.

"So, if you don't get the award, would you entertain the idea that you genuinely and honorably lost it to someone else?" Dan asks.

I pause, thinking, then grin again. "Nah. No way. First of all, how could they reject Book Club? And second, Frank deserves payback regardless. This gives me license to go after him with a clear conscience."

"Huh," he says. "Vicious *and* ethical. A surprising combination."

Dan gets up from his chair. "It's Friday night, and while 'need' may be too strong a word, I officially want a drink. Can I get you something stronger?" he offers, motioning to my now-empty seltzer glass.

I shake my head. "I'm teetotaling until after the ride, but thank you."

He nods. "Makes sense. But I think you just wanted to use the word 'teetotaling' in a real sentence."

I shrug. "I was an English major. I need to flex those muscles every now and again."

"Vicious, ethical, and show-offy," Dan says, mulling it over. "Now maybe I'm the one who should feel underwhelming."

∞∞∞

I wake up early on Monday morning, nearly an hour before the alarm. The weekend had been two days of solid rain. Far from feeling disgruntled, we leaned into it and hid from the world for a while. We chucked our normal rules about screen time, which awed and delighted the kids, and allowed Dan and I optimum sofa space. During the day, the two of us sprawled in the family room with our books, listening to the rain lash against the windows while Max and Shannon huddled in the game room watching the eight *Harry Potter* films. In the evenings, we splurged on our favorite takeout – pizza one night and Thai the next – and introduced the kids to the "old" movies, *Ferris Bueller's Day Off* and *Sneakers*.

After our discussion on the deck Friday night, Dan and I avoided the grant subject. There was nothing to do but wait until I hear from *BQss*.

Now, I lay in bed, listening to a mourning dove and feeling the warmth of my husband next to me. After a few minutes, I give up on falling back asleep and get up. The clock on Dan's night table reads 6:16 am. Two hours and 44 minutes until it's officially "first thing Monday morning." Frank's deadline.

I wonder if he's up yet, and if he really thinks there's a chance I'll accept his b.s. offer.

I peek into Max's room. He's lying on his side, one earbud plugged in and the other dangling off the edge of the mattress. He's clutching his tablet like a teddy bear. I make a mental note to revert back to our regular rule about screens in bed.

I tiptoe through the office and open the door to Shannon's room. Her daisy-patterned comforter is pulled up nearly over her head. Quietly, I step into the room and gently pull it back. She's on her stomach, her arm curled over a small stuffed duck designed and sold by one of her favorite YouTubers. I feel a surge of love for my family, and place a soft kiss on Shannon's head before retreating and closing the door.

Downstairs, I bypass the programmed setting on the coffee maker and start it brewing. The sun has returned, so I take my mug outside and sip it on the still-damp deck, feeling strangely at peace. Shouldn't I be freaking out right about now?

Nah, Gilda says. *That isn't you anymore.* I lift my mug slightly in a silent toast of thanks.

I stay on the deck until the sound of the shower tells me Dan is awake. Back in the kitchen, I set about scrambling some eggs and put two pieces of sourdough in the toaster. When Dan walks in, I present his breakfast with an exaggerated curtsey.

He sits down at the breakfast bar and smiles. "You didn't have to do that," he says. "Monday is one of my mornings to

215

cook."

I give him a good morning kiss. "It's no big deal; I was up." He nods, understanding why.

We eat in companionable silence for a few moments. Then Dan puts his fork down. He lets it go an inch higher than he should have, causing it to clatter on his plate. I look over, startled.

"What?" I ask.

He draws in a gulp of air, appearing to steel himself. "If you don't get the grant, let's take the fifty thousand out of one of our retirement accounts. We'll have to pay a penalty – *and* taxes – but we can do it."

I can't believe what I've just heard, but I don't dare ask him to repeat himself. I know how difficult it was for him to say what essentially amounts to *hey, let's blow some of our life savings on a dream that isn't remotely guaranteed to work!* My eyes fill. I swallow the lump forming in my throat. "Are you sure you're comfortable with that?"

He laughs quietly. "I'm not comfortable at all. But I *am* sure, if that makes sense."

I slide off my stool and into his arms. Hugging him tightly, I whisper into his shoulder. "Thank you, Dan. Thank you." Keeping my arms around his neck, I pull back so I can look at him. "But no."

He blinks. "What?"

"I can't do that, Dan. I'll find another way to get it. But you have no idea how much I love you for volunteering it."

"I love you, too," he says. "Call me when you hear from BΩss. And then take that asshole down, will you?"

When Dan leaves for his train, I find I'm eager to get out of the house. Partly because of our two days of living the hermit life, but mostly because I can't be near my laptop all morning, imagining it taunting me until the grant winner is announced at noon.

At nine, I flip my clock a ceremonial bird – *pass this on to Frank, would you?* – and rouse Max and Shannon with promises of a pancake breakfast at their favorite diner and a hike around a nearby pond. They grouse a little about the hike, probably immune to nature after the 48-hour movie marathon.

When we return, it's 11:58. I send the kids to the backyard and creep up to the office. I'm shaking, and need to enter my password three times before getting it right.

The email is there. This time, the subject line reads simply "A message from the team at B♀ss."

Dear Georgia,

We're sorry to let you know that your proposal has not been chosen for our annual "B♀sses of Boston" $50,000 grant. This was an extraordinarily difficult decision, as the final selection committee felt that each candidate was worthy of a grant in her own right. In the end, they selected the proposal that they felt had the most potential to flourish as a business.

I stop reading, unable to stomach the rest. Tears spill onto my cheeks and drip onto my shirt. I ugly-cry for a solid ten minutes, feeling Dee's – and Book Club – slipping away. When I am finally calm, I head to the bathroom to splash water on my face, and then call up B♀ss' website. I need to find out who this woman with the most potential to flourish is. Did she beat me fair and square, without Frank's help?

The winner's story is up on B♀ss' homepage. In the photo,

she's in a pantsuit and standing, arms crossed, in front of a meadow filled with wildflowers. She's launching a luxury vegan spa with her grant prize. Hair, skin, and nail treatments with vegan products, vegan refreshments, and vegan decor.

I lean back in my seat, trying to consider her plan objectively. Is it a good idea? Sure.

But does it fill a need that's missing in the spa industry, and show strong promise for expansion as a brand? Gilda whispers. *Does it* really?

I'm not sure. Vegan spas already exist. And this one will cater to a wealthier clientele; Book Club is for any woman who can budget for a nine-dollar quesadilla.

I'll never know for sure that Frank screwed me, but still. I *know.*

"OK, asshole," I say. "Don't say I didn't warn you."

You didn't, actually, Gilda points out. *But that's totally fine. It sounded good. Carry on.*

I shut down my laptop, pick up my phone, and make a call.

"Angela," I begin. "You asked if there was something you could do. Well, now there is."

Chapter 17

T he sky is streaked with pink when I wake at five a.m. the morning of the ride. The hotel – *not* a Hudson Hotel, thank you – is on the ocean, and I listen to the surf for a few minutes before getting up. I stretch my arms and legs out fully, enjoying the rare treat of a queen bed all to myself. In the room's second bed, Jules is still asleep.

Jules drove me and my bike to the mid-Cape last night. "It seems weird to be biking from the Cape back up to the Boston area," she said during the ride down. "Isn't it better to ride from Boston to the Cape?"

I shrugged. "Not really, actually. I mean, sure, it's more *fun* to end up at the beach, but it's harder to manage the event," I explained. "The headquarters has the most outdoor space for the size of the after party, and because it's pretty much the bullseye in the map of Hudson Hotel's properties, it lets the hotels north of us be part of the event. Some of those hotels are the starting points for 50- and 25-mile rides."

I slip into the bathroom to dress, pulling on a black biking skort and my bright tangerine UV protection shirt. As I slather sunscreen on my exposed skin, I gauge my mood and find that I'm excited. Nervous, but mostly excited. I know that I'm physically capable of riding 100 miles today. The questions circling in my head are: can I pull off my little parting gift to Frank? And can I finish the ride in time to see it?

Jules is up when I come back into the room. She's wearing a beachy blue sundress and pulling her long red hair into a high ponytail. "Ready for battle?" She asks me, smiling.

I nod. We high five and head for the door. I carefully maneuver my bike outside and mount it to the rack on Jules's car.

The atmosphere at the starting line is decidedly festive. Even this early – an hour before the ride – people are gathering at the hotel. They're stretching, chatting, laughing, tuning gears and pumping tires. And everyone's smiling. Some nervously, of course; but the mood is light.

I park my bike and immediately join the porta potty line for the first of what I'm sure will be three times before we ride. Once inside, I reach for one of the white paper seat covers and pause. Above the dispenser, someone's written "Free Cowboy Hats." It's fabulously inventive graffiti, and I take it as a sign that it's going to be a good day.

My bladder lightened, I head for the breakfast buffet table, surreptitiously scanning the crowds for Hudson staff through the sea of navy and white event shirts. Jules joins me as I'm grabbing a foil-wrapped sausage egg and cheese biscuit. I pause, and then take a second. Need to up my calories today, after all.

"Do you need to check in or anything?" Jules asks.

"No, thank goodness," I say. "I got my bib number in the mail."

We take our breakfasts to one of the picnic tables set up in the hotel's parking lot. Beside us is a group of six riders, wearing Hudson riding shirts with "16 MPH," "14 MPH," and "12 MPH" printed in large font on their backs. It dawns on me that these are the pace riders.

"That's so cool," I say, more to myself than Jules.

"What?"

I nod to the table. "These guys are pace-setters. They are volunteering to ride 100 miles at a certain pace so that the other riders know how fast to go if they have a time goal."

I find I'm impressed – a little awed, even – by the fact that people have voluntarily given up any attempt to ride a personal best, and instead are riding to help others achieve theirs. I look around, suddenly unsettled. This is a really good event. What am I doing?

It is *a great event*, Gilda whispers. *But Frank is not a good man. This is about him.*

"Are you OK?" Jules asks me.

I swallow the last of my biscuit, which feels suddenly dry in my throat. "Yeah," I say. "A sudden case of cold feet."

"Why?"

I gesture to the riders and volunteers around me. "Because this is so…inspiring. Everyone's happy and nervous and excited. I'm starting to feel like a bitter party crasher."

She nods. "That's because we are. Let's own it."

I glance at her in surprise, then realize she's right.

"Am I being selfish?" I ask my best friend.

Jules places her hand on mine. "No. This is between you and Frank. It has nothing to do with today."

I nod and crumple up the napkins and foil from my breakfast. "Let's go. I need to get my legs moving."

We get up and mill around the lot, watching the crowd. At the bike mechanic's tent, I spot Bembé Jean-Baptiste. Seeing him in person for the first time, I'm stuck by how tall he is. Taller than Kyle, even.

Thank goodness you don't need to keep up with him, Gilda whispers. *Those legs are a mile long.*

I nudge Jules. "There he is."

We make our way over, the cleats of my bike shoes grinding on the concrete parking lot. Having met Bembé at a hospital fundraiser just a few weeks ago, Jules takes charge, calling his name when we're 10 feet away.

They hug. "Jules! So lovely to see you again so soon," Bembé says. "I'm glad you found me." He turns to me. "You must be Georgie. Jules told me you'd be here."

We shake hands. "It's great to meet you," I say, giddy and beaming. "I'm a huge fan of your show."

"I appreciate that," he says, his deep brown eyes crinkling with his smile. I'm reminded of Sidney Poitier in *Guess Who's Coming to Dinner* and I melt even more. "And thank you for getting me into this ride. I've been looking forward to it for months," Bembé's smile deflates. "And I was sorry to learn from Jules that you were no longer working at Hudson."

I shrug lightly. "Thank you. Onward and upward. Are you ready for the ride?"

He nods. "Speaking of–" Bembé pulls a piece of paper out of the back pocket of his riding shirt and unfolds it. "Would you mind helping me find some of these people? These are the ones Lena has suggested I speak with today."

I step closer to look at the list. "Knowing Lena, I think 'suggested' is being generous." His chuckle in response lets me know I'm right.

I skim the paper; I recognize it as the short list of event volunteers and staff from a few grant-winning organizations that I asked Angela to text me a few days ago, along with a few other things. A surge of anger courses through me, quelling my earlier doubt. It's exactly the list I would have put together had I still worked for Frank and cared about making him look good. Unfortunately for Frank, I don't care about that anymore.

"These two will be milling around the stage that's set up for the start," I say, pointing at the list. "The other two will be at the 50-mile rest stop." I give Bembé quick descriptions of them so he'll know whom to look for. "Any one of these folks will be warm, articulate, and tell you exactly what Frank wants you to hear."

He looks at me with interest. "And are there people here that would tell me what Mr. Hudson *doesn't* want me to hear?"

I smile, and pull out a list of my own.

∞∞∞

I optimistically line up with my bike behind the pacer wearing the "14 MPH" shirt. Riders are hemmed in around me, all of them with one foot already locked in to a pedal. On the stage, a Hudson Foundation ambassador is wrapping up her spiel on this year's 100 Revolutions grant winners, and acknowledging the local celebrity riders who have signed up for the full century: a local TV news meteorologist, a Cape Cod native who won a stage in the Tour de France last year, and a runner-up from the most recent season of a reality TV show.

"And finally," she says. "I'm excited to share that this year we have the popular YouTube personality The Book Prophet riding with us, Mr. Bembé Jean-Baptiste! Bembé will be interviewing Frank Hudson live after the ride and discussing his bestselling memoir, *The Business of Giving it Away*."

I look over at Jules, standing behind the safety barricade the event staff have set up at the starting line, and mouth "bestelling." She rolls her eyes in return.

"If you haven't read the book yet, you'll have a chance to buy a copy at the post-ride celebration!"

Of course they will.

"And if you're really lucky, you can get Frank Hudson himself to sign it!"

*Well, if that isn't motivation to ride 100 miles...*Gilda reasons.

"Riders get ready...and go!"

0-10 Miles:

We're off! Jules jumps up and down, waving her arms. There's the typical speed up, slow down and jockeying for space one finds at the start of any race. For the first few miles, we wind our way from the oceanfront through quintessential Cape Cod neighborhoods with weathered shingle houses. People are lined up on sidewalks to cheer us on. Traffic is stopped by police officers as hundreds of riders swarm the narrow streets like bees at peak hive mentality. Television camera crews film us. I wave to them. While we are grouped tightly on the road, I chat amically with the strangers who have instantly become comrades in the day-long undertaking we've taken on together. It's festive, and it's good to be part of it.

11-30 miles:

I lose my handful of chatty fellow riders as the peloton thins out. Which is fine by me. Despite my verbosity during the first 10 miles, I tend to be quiet when I'm being active. You know those people you see having full-on conversations while running seven miles an hour side by side on the treadmill? That's not me. Never has been. The talking part, that is. Well, the running seven miles an hour part isn't me, either, if I'm honest.

I roll in to the first rest stop - a Hudson Hotel just one town away from the Cape Cod Canal - at mile 20-ish feeling energized and upbeat. Rest? Who needs to rest?? I hit the porta potty (free cowboy hats...heh heh), refill my water bottles, munch a banana, and dump a bag of trail mix into my jacket pocket. I feel great!

I glance around, unsure if I should make myself known to the Hudson staff working the event. I decide against it; this ride – this day – is for me. Bembé is nowhere in sight. I spotted him close to a 16 MPH pace setting at the starting line, so he's likely come and gone, but I'm delighted to be part of such a big pack. There are still a lot of riders hanging around the rest stop when I hop back onto my bike, eager to reach the bridge, which is my first mental milestone. I should be finished by 2:30. That's *way* before the volunteers start sweeping the route for stragglers at 4:30.

31-50 miles:

Why are there so many hills? I thought the Cape was flat.

I notice I haven't seen the 14 mph pace setter in a while. Nor the 13 mph guy, come to think of it. Hmmmm. But there are still plenty of people at the second rest stop with me. I stretch, slather on another layer of sunscreen and stuff a few packs of energy gels into my pocket. I'm doing *fine*, I tell myself. And

I'll be at the bridge soon.

THERE IT IS! I see the steel exoskeleton of the Sagamore Bridge peeking over the treetops. I'm thrilled. I've been driving over this bridge several times a year, every year, since I was a child. Never in all that time have I ever crossed it on my bike. Until now.

There's no bike lane on the bridge, so all cyclists have to walk their bikes on the sidewalk spanning the bridge. I savor the chance to get off the saddle and take in this milestone, pausing to snap pictures of the plaque and the Cape Cod Canal and post them to my Facebook page. I'll be in Plymouth in no time. Once I hit Plymouth, I'm practically in the suburbs of Boston. I'll be done by three o'clock. Three o'clock isn't bad.

51 70 miles:

Plymouth is China. No, it's Narnia. You wander in, convinced of its reasonably-sized expanse, and it goes on forever. No wonder the Pilgrims landed here. How could they not? It takes up the whole Eastern Seaboard. Fucking Plymouth.

71-90 miles:

This is officially the longest I've ever biked and now I know why. My hands ache. My back aches. My butt aches. I'm on the border between too hot and not-so-hot that I would bother to stop and remove my wind jacket. Besides, if I pull over and take my jacket off I'll finish 30 seconds later than if I just tough it out. If I stop, I won't make it by 3:30. 3:30 would be a win.

I compromise at the Mile 80 rest stop, peeling off my jacket and tossing it to Dan. He and the kids have staked out a small patch of grass, and they shower me with packs of my favorite energy gels.

"How are you feeling?" Dan asks.

"Like roadkill," I respond, emptying a pouch of strawberry banana gel into my mouth. "But I still don't want a ride."

He smiles and pushes a hank of sweaty hair off my forehead. "I'll see you at the finish line," he says. I reluctantly leave them after a ten-minute rest and grimly return to my bike to churn through the last stretch of the route.

My internal monologue has run out of things to say. I desperately need music to get through the last 20 miles. I pull my phone out of my pocket and, keeping one hand on my handlebars, manage to start up my workout playlist without crashing. That'll kill an hour. I put my phone back in my pocket, but can't hear it. And riding with earbuds is, well, dangerously stupid. There's just one option left. I unzip my bike shirt halfway and slide the phone into my sports bra, making sure it's centered so that the speaker faces outward while also covering any cleavage. I'm nothing if not classy.

That's better. The rhythm helps my cadence on the bike, gets me out of my own head and back to focusing on the road. As other cyclists pass me – and I'm starting to worry about the frequency at which they do – some do a double take at my MacGuyver-esque stereo setup. I keep waiting for one of them to exclaim "lucky cell phone!" but none do. They're nothing if not classy.

Miles 91-100:

Please don't let me be last. Please don't let me be last. Please don't let me be last. Please don't let me be last. Please don't let me be last. Please don't let me be last. Please don't let me be last.

I don't even know what's keeping me going at this point. Is it the mile-by-mile countdown signs that the volunteers set up in the last ten miles ("Just eight and you'll feel great!" "Just four and then no more!")? Umm, no. My brain jumps from one thought or memory to the next. *Gosh, remember when we saw The Monkees perform on Cape Cod in 1985? That was such a fun – ooo, I wonder if there'll be good beer at the finish line?*

The end is tantalizingly close; I am intimately familiar with the roads surrounding the Hudson Headquarters, so that when the ride route turns away from it I find myself becoming irrationally angry about it. And then there it is: the logo! The double H's! The bad memories! Crowd control barriers begin to line the ride route, the universal symbol of the end of the course.

It's 4:00. I finished 30 minutes ahead of the race closure. Navy and white bunting swings gaily from the arch set up at the finish line. The hotel grounds are packed. Most riders have swapped their bike shoes for sandals and are into their third beer. But plenty are still in the post-ride stretching phase, and more are still riding in (behind me!) from the 25- and 50-mile rides, which always start later in the day.

I'm exhausted, sweaty, thirsty, hungry, achy, and happy. So, so happy. I did it. I set a goal – a difficult one – and achieved it. I'm not a fraud. I am not a fake adult.

Now, where's Bembé?

∞∞∞

I park my bike with the others, accept a finisher's medal from a volunteer, and grab a water bottle. I pause for a minute to surreptitiously pull my phone out of my bra and text Dan I've finished. He replies immediately with confetti emojis and a promise to pick me up in an hour. I spend a few minutes stretching and sipping my water before turning my full attention to the scene.

The party is in full swing. Music blares from the sound system. Two large tents form a wide rectangle of shade covering the majority of attendees. There's an enormous buffet, acres of tables and chairs, and a stage set up at one end for Frank's annual event speech. An area in front of the stage has been artfully sectioned off with navy velvet ropes. The seating area within the ropes has tablecloths and elegant centerpieces. There's a private bar and waitstaff.

Ah, the VIP section. That's where Frank will be, so steer clear of that. But where's Lena?

I scan the crowd for her stacked bob, unsuccessfully. Would Frank have told her to keep an eye out for me? Possibly. He'd never fill her in on our conversation outside of Dee's, but would he suggest to her that she be watchful for people "who might want to dampen our celebration"? Definitely. She can't know I'm here. I text Angela.

I'm done! I type. Where r u? Where's L.? Want to avoid.

My phone buzzes with her reply. L at interview area in garden. Meet me at beer table in first tent.

I make my way to the spot, craning to peek through the crowd and into the small oasis of green on the other side of the tents. Located in a corner of the Hudson Headquarters's main parking lot, the garden was designed to serve as a handy beauty shot for hotel marketing pieces. Photographers could frame the hotel entrance in the distance, with the garden's lush flowering bushes and free standing double H logo in the foreground.

Now, I see two square armchairs placed in front of the logo, angled towards each other. In between the chairs is a side table with three copies of Frank's book stacked, spine facing the camera, and one propped up on a mini book stand on top of the pile. Above the books, a large flatscreen TV is cycling through a slideshow of the photos appearing in the book.

A streaming webcam is set up on a tripod a few feet away, connected to a laptop resting on a second side table. Lena is bent over the laptop, presumably studying the image of the interview set as it will appear on camera. She's wearing the same *Love Boat* get up she had on the day she fired me.

Bembé, showered and wearing a fitted red v-neck t-shirt, is standing off to the side, watching Lena fuss with the books on the table.

Looks like you finished just in time, Gilda says. *Good thing you didn't stop to remove that jacket, hey?*

I reach the tent where a local brewery has set up, its staff lining the tabletop with plastic cups nearly overflowing with beer. Angela is there, waiting, a full cup in each hand. She places them back on the bar top's edge when she spots me and we hug.

"Holy crap, Georgie," she exclaims, looking me over. "You look amazing."

"Thanks, love," I say. "The interview is starting soon, isn't it? Fill me in."

We pick up our cups and move towards an empty table. I grab a foil-wrapped cheesesteak sub that I plan to murder as soon as I sit. I wonder what's being served in the VIP section?

"I'm technically not supposed to be drinking while working the event," Angela says, after a deep sip of her beer. "But what the hell. Next Friday's my last day."

My eyes pop. "Please tell me you quit."

She nods, grinning. "Heading to an ad agency in Boston."

"OK, I want to hear everything," I say. "But *later.*"

"Right, right," Angela says. She glances at her watch. "Frank's supposed to start speaking in just a few minutes. The interview with Bembé will take place right after that. It'll be live streaming on his web channel."

"Have you talked to Bembé?" I ask, then take a big bite of my sub.

She nods, and looks over her shoulder, as if expecting to find Frank or Lena right behind her. "We had a nice long chat when he finished the ride. He's talked to everyone on your list today."

I swallow my bite. Bembé knows everything I wanted him to know. The rest is up to him. "OK," I say. "And you? Are we good?"

She nods. "It's all set up. And it was my absolute pleasure."

We tap our cups in a toast. "There's nothing left for us to do," I say.

As if on cue, the music stops.

"Good afternoon, everyone!" Frank's voice booms through the speakers dotted throughout the tents.

Angela and I turn. He's standing, comfortably and causally, at the far end of the tented area on the small stage, an easy smile on his face.

"What an incredible day," he says. "Thanks to the efforts of all of you – the nearly 1,000 riders of this year's *100 Revolutions* – we have raised more than a million dollars with today's ride.

A new record!" The crowd cheers.

"And as always," Frank continues. "Hudson Hotels is matching that amount, times five!"

More cheers.

"That's six million dollars being pumped right back into *your* community," he says. "To *your* libraries, *your* food banks, *your* schools, *your* youth groups." By this time everyone's standing and applauding. I feel the same wave of doubt that enveloped me at the starting line.

"Where are my century riders?" Frank asks, scanning the crowd. "Who rode the full 100 miles?" Throughout the tents, people hoot and wave their arms. Mine stay down.

"Every mile you rode today represents one organization getting a grant," he says. "All of your hard work is paying off in the support of the hard work these groups do. They will continue to do this work because of you."

"It's because of *you*, Frank!" someone shouts. "This is all you!" Frank grins boyishly in response.

I look at Angela, eyebrows raised.

"A plant. Lena's idea," she says.

I shake my head. *Of course it was.*

"Now, some of you may have heard this rumor about my writing a book," Frank says. A ripple of laughter runs through the crowd. "In a few minutes, I'm going to be sitting down and talking to this young man about it," he gestures to Bembé, standing along the edge of the tent. "You're all invited to come and watch, or stay right here and enjoy the party. You've all earned it."

More laughter. Franks waves and steps down from the stage and he and Bembé make their way to the interview set.

Angela nudges me. "Showtime."

Chapter 18

"Hello, everybody!" Bembé says to the camera. "And by 'everybody,' I mean my wonderful viewers, as well as everyone here today for *100 Revolutions!*" Bembé pauses as the riders, volunteers, and other guests gather around the set cheer.

Frank is sitting opposite him, wearing a matching wireless microphone and grinning. I'm standing in the shadow of the tent, close enough to watch but – hopefully – far enough away to not be noticed by Lena.

Bembé spends a minute or so getting his viewers up to speed on the history and purpose of the event. Then he turns to Frank. "And I'm here today with the event creator. He's the founder and CEO of the New England-based Hudson Hotels, and a recent first-time author, Frank Hudson. Frank, thank you for coming onto the show."

"Thank you for having me," Frank says, still grinning. "And may I say from experience, you look remarkably fresh for someone who biked 100 miles today. Do I need to check the security footage at the rest stops?" They chuckle like longtime friends. My heart sinks. This is starting off well, which for me means it *isn't* going well.

233

"Frank, your story has been summed up as a rags-to-riches-to-Robin-Hood adventure," Bembé says. "Every single year for the last two decades, you've given away a sizable amount of your hotel profits to local charities. As someone who has spent a large portion of his life living from paycheck to paycheck, I have to ask: for God's sake, man, *why?*"

Frank guffaws, as do most of the onlookers. For the next 15 minutes, they discuss Frank's history as it's outlined in *Giving It Away*. Frank shares stories of his underprivileged upbringing, his first ventures into the world of business, how it felt to attain actual billionaire status, and his commitment to supporting local charities through *100 Revolutions*.

"So, Frank," Bembé says. "You've had brilliant success as both an entrepreneur and a philanthropist. You have dozens of hotels – and millions of past and current customers – to communicate with via your business channels. Why write a book?"

Frank pretends to consider the question. I know he's answered it at least 20 times in previous interviews, and probably a thousand more in his head.

Not that there's anything wrong with a robust internal monologue, Gilda reminds me.

"You know, I feel that there's a difference between sharing my story with people traveling on business or vacation, and sharing it with the next generation of business leaders," Frank begins. "There are hundreds – thousands, really – of books out there on how to succeed in business. But what I wanted to do was give future entrepreneurs a vision of what they could do *after* they've made it. Contrary to popular opinion in these tomes, it really isn't all about them. At the end of the day, what's really important is the mark you leave on the *community* where you do business, not the business itself. Or its creator, for that matter."

The event guests applaud. Bembé nods thoughtfully. I catch Angela's eye from a few feet away and turn up my palms in a *this isn't working* gesture. She presses one hand towards me. *Wait*, she tells me silently.

"Your book appears to be doing well," Bembé says. "There are hundreds of rave reviews online about it."

Frank bows his head in a practiced show of modesty. "That's very kind."

"Well, you certainly have a built-in fan base; many of them appear to be staff from the organizations that you support through your foundation," Bembé says. "Were you aware of that?"

Frank smiles. Only those who've worked closely with him, like me, can see the first stirrings of caution behind it. "I wasn't. I don't get to surf the web reading reviews as much as I'd like to," he says, offering a gentle chuckle.

"Don't you?" Bembé asks. "During the ride today, I chatted with a woman from a nonprofit that provides early intervention services to children with disabilities. According to her, she was told if she *didn't* post a positive review, her grant wouldn't be renewed. Is that true?"

Frank's smile is frozen. The crowd closest to the set quiets as their attention refocuses on the interview. I lean forward, holding my breath.

Frank forces a chuckle. "I'm sure that isn't the case. She must have been mistaken. The book and the foundation are two completely separate ventures."

Bembé smiles back. "I thought that might be the case," he says. Frank's smile relaxes. "But I talked to several other grantees today, and they all told me the same story: write a good review of Frank's book, or forfeit their grant. In the wake of your book release, has the Hudson Foundation become 'pay to play'?"

"No!" Frank says, curtly. He pauses, perhaps to gather himself, and continues. "I have no idea why they would say that. Those people must not understand how the grant process works."

Right. Those nonprofit executive directors are notoriously grant-stupid.

A low murmur reverberates through the crowd.

"Listen," Frank says earnestly. "The more books we sell, the more we can give back to the community. The bottom line is all about the communities we're here to support." He looks to the crowd for support. A handful begin to clap in solidarity.

"Of course," says Bembé. "And it must be selling well; I've heard your book praised as a 'bestseller' many times today. As a self-published author, that's rare."

Frank smiles. "Thank you, Bembé. It *is* an honor. It's humbling to know that people want to hear what an old hotel guy like me has to say."

Bembé, I can tell from where I stand, isn't fooled. *Oh, thank God!*

"So how many copies have you sold?" The Book Prophet asks.

Frank chuckles again, appearing not a bit perturbed. "Oh, I couldn't begin to say."

"But when you first learned that *Giving It Away* had reached bestseller status, your team must have told you which list, yes?" Bembé presses. "*The New York Times*? *USA Today*? Surely you must remember the moment. I think most authors do."

Frank lifts his hands, as if waving away the question. "I... I just don't know, Bembé." He looks beyond the camera to where, I presume, Lena is standing. "You'll get on that, won't you, Lena?" Frank says amicably. "Well, I can tell you that of all the books I've written, this is the one that's sold the most." He forces a laugh, and looks to the crowd once more, pleading.

Bembé pauses a beat, which only reinforces the ineptitude of Frank's response. For a moment, the Book Prophet looks up and locks eyes with me. He gives a nearly imperceptible nod.

It's coming, Gilda whispers.

Bembé clears his throat before continuing. "So tell me, what are your hopes for *Giving It Away?*"

Frank shifts in his chair, appearing on surer ground "Well, as I mentioned before, I wanted to offer a path for entrepreneurship *and* philanthropy," he begins. "But since you asked, I think that, at the end of the day, I wanted to inspire. I wanted to let people – or, at the very least, one person – know that it actually is possible to achieve your dreams. That if they worked hard, stayed focused, and just believed in themselves, they could achieve what they set out to do."

Bembé leans forward, appearing rapt. "Like Georgie Fischer?"

∞∞∞

I freeze in my spot under the tent. In all the times I played out this scene in my head, I didn't expect to feel this naked. Just off camera, Lena begins scanning the crowd. I shrink further inside the tent, out of her view.

Frank's smile appears ironed onto his face. "I'm sorry?"

237

Bembé leans back in his chair, having landed his bomb. "Georgie Fischer," he says, appearing to relish the moment of surprise. "An entrepreneur who worked for you. Surely you remember her."

Frank shakes his head, slowly. "A lot of people have worked for my hotels, Mr. Jean-Baptiste," he says. "If you've spoken to someone dissatisfied with their experience here, then you have me at a disadvantage. This wasn't the direction you led me to believe this discussion would take."

Poor you, Gilda whispers. *Buckle up, asshole.*

Bembé glances down at the notepad resting on his lap. "Nor is it the direction I had planned for it to go, Mr. Hudson," he says. "But in my line of work, one must follow the story, wouldn't you agree?"

Frank refolds his hands on his lap. "If the story is true, then yes, Mr. Jean-Baptiste. I agree wholeheartedly."

Bembé beams. "Excellent! So let me be perfectly clear in what I've been told in recent days: a former employee of yours, Georgie Fischer, submitted a proposal for a new business concept to a grant organization where you currently serve as a member of the selection committee. You, in direct conflict with your responsibilities as a committee member, told her to sign her concept over to you, or else you would ensure the failure of her proposal."

Gasps, murmurs, and low groans ripple through the onlookers surrounding the interview set. Amongst them is a reporter I recognize from a Boston paper. He is scribbling furiously in his notepad.

"Well," says Frank, drawing out the word to buy time to gather himself. "I'm sorry that this former employee has wasted your time with such fanciful tales. And again, thank you for having me on your show." He begins to rise from his chair.

"To be clear," Bembé says, holding his hand out to stay Frank. "You deny this took place?"

Frank shakes his head, as if in sympathy with Bembé for even entertaining such a notion. "Of course I do. Now, I really appreciate…"

"And if I told you there was video footage of such a conversation between you and Ms. Fischer? Would that change your response?"

Frank's frozen smile vanishes, his expression turning to stone. His eyes narrow. "I don't know whose side you're on, or what you're playing at, but you've entirely misrepresented yourself here, and this conversation is over."

Frank gets up from the chair, his face red with rage and – could it be? – embarrassment. He yanks off his microphone and points to Lena. "Shut that damn thing off," he barks, gesturing to the webcam, and stalks away, bumping and shoving his way through the crowd, many of whom are now capturing his exit on cell phones. The Boston reporter trails after him, shouting questions I can't hear. I can't catch Frank's response, either. But the angry snarl thrown over his shoulder at the advancing reporter tells me everything I need know. Frank retreats behind the velvet ropes of the VIP section, gesturing frantically for the waitstaff to stop the media from entering.

On set, Lena advances towards the camera. Bembé turns to her, keeping his microphone on for the now-gawking onlookers. "I'd like to remind Mr. Hudson and his team that the camera is the property of The Book Prophet Productions, Inc., and under no circumstances do I permit any member of his staff to operate it."

Lena pauses. Bembé's expression is both calm and deadly serious. After a few seconds of this staring contest, she relents, remaining in her spot.

Angela appears next to me. "I'm surprised she isn't running after Frank," she says, her voice low.

"She won't," I reply. "At least, not yet. Not until she sees what Bembé does next and knows exactly what kind of situation she's dealing with."

Bembé presses a few buttons on a handheld remote. The image on the flatscreen behind him vanishes and is replaced with a nighttime view of the yellow neon sign outside Dee's. It is the view I had framed with my camera just over a week ago before realizing that Frank was behind me across the street. It's the view I had just before his threats, and my rage and despair. And – thankfully – it's the view of just *after* I decided Frank's presence at Dee's couldn't possibly be good news for me, and started recording video.

Bembé turns to the camera. "I want to assure my viewers – and all of you here – that this is never my goal when I bring a writer to your attention. My intention, always, is to give the often-overlooked authors who choose to self-publish an opportunity to shine. But if, during that opportunity, they prove themselves to be – pardon my frankness – fake as plastic shit, then I consider it my duty to tell you." He presses play.

The footage is dark in some parts, and shaky in others. But Frank's voice is unmistakable, and I even managed to effectively capture his face, munching smugly on his cigar, in the beam of the streetlight he stood by.

It's all there. The threat, the demand for ownership of Book Club, and the "girl bar" comment. The entitlement, the condescension, and the pettiness. All caught on camera.

The crowd is silent for a few moments after the video ends. Then the murmuring starts again.

"Fraud."

"Bully."

"What a fake."

Lena's expression is one of sheer disbelief, the very one I had daydreamed of months ago when I imagined riding across the finish line.

Bembé turns back to the camera. "To be clear, there is a lot to admire about Mr. Hudson. He is without question a self-made man. And I genuinely applaud his decision to, year after year, send his profits to local charities instead of further lining his own pockets. Through his foundation's grant program, he has done long-term good in the communities that have welcomed his hotels.

"Using this goodwill as a means of promoting his book isn't in and of itself a bad thing. Indeed, I have spoken to several people today who were delighted to both read and review it.

But to make future funding conditional pending a public and positive review of Mr. Hudson's book cheapens the generosity of the grant program, and calls into question the authenticity of the reviews. That may not matter so much to Mr. Hudson, but it matters greatly to me. And it matters to every writer I have ever met. Until today."

Bembé glances back to the flatscreen, which has reset to the opening frame of the exterior of Dee's. "And the attempted hijacking of Ms. Fischer's future business – for the sin of pushing back on his unethical, and probably illegal, marketing choices – is the vindictive action of an insecure man."

He leans forward, resting his elbows on his knees. It's a

gesture I've come to recognize as his wrap up pose.

"It appears Mr. Hudson, and those who have enabled him," Bembé turns and gives Lena a meaningful look, "have turned the *Business of Giving it Away* into the business of feeding an ego. Good night, and thank you for joining me."

∞∞∞

Music suddenly blasts through the sound system again, louder than before. I suspect it's an attempt by Frank to drown out Bembé's commentary. If it is, it's too late. The Book Prophet is out of his seat and packing up his equipment. Some of the people gathered around the garden begin to drift back under the tent, whispering amongst themselves. Many are leaving.

I turn around, searching for Lena. She is striding purposefully toward the hotel entrance, her dress whirling around her and her cell phone pressed to her ear. Kyle is trailing a few steps behind. In the VIP section, Frank is sitting at a table with some of his guests, the same fake smile frozen on his face. When the person he is talking to turns away, he lapses into stony silence.

On the interview set, the Boston reporter I spotted earlier is now huddling with Bembé. He gestures to the flatscreen, and they appear to exchange contact information. The reporter walks away, leaving Bembé alone. I can't bring myself to approach him. I am beyond grateful for the risk he took in coming after Frank; it could impact his channel sponsors and the willingness of authors to agree to be interviewed by him. This interview was not something he took lightly, I'm sure. I know full well, however, that he didn't do it for me. He did it for the integrity of the craft that he loves.

"Come on," Angela says. "Let's get another beer and then get out of here."

I am suddenly and overwhelmingly tired. All I want to do right now is go home, take a long, hot shower, and fall into my bed. I glance at my watch. Dan should be here soon. Angela and I drift back to the beer table, where I grab an ice cold red ale, and return to our earlier table. We sit in silence for a few seconds, both of us still absorbing what just happened.

I'm about to speak when Dan appears in my peripheral vision, beaming at me. I jump out of my chair and run the handful of steps to close the gap and hug him, fiercely. I pull away and we kiss.

"You're salty," he says, smiling.

"You have no idea," I say.

"You did it," he says. "I'm so proud of you."

I beam back at him. "I couldn't have done it without you," I say. "Thank you." We hug again. "Come and sit down," I tell him, returning to the table.

He helps himself to a beer and joins us, giving Angela a one-armed hug before sitting down.

Dan takes a deep sip from his cup and looks around at the crowd. "Did I miss the interview? What happened?"

Angela and I fill him in, tag-teaming on a play-by-play of the scene.

"Wow," he says. "It sounds like it pretty much went as well as it possibly could have." He looks from me to Angela, gauging our mood. "Talk to me. How do you guys feel?"

I look over at Angela, at a loss for words. "You first," I say.

She smiles. "I love what just went down," she says. "I don't feel an ounce of guilt. This guy has been bathing in praise for years. A lot of it was earned, I'll admit, but he assumed he would cruise his way to bestseller status. When he didn't, he tried to extort it. That's just plain wrong, and I'm glad he got called on it." Angela looks over at me. "How are you feeling about it?"

I take a sip of my beer, buying some time. "Honestly? I don't know yet," I begin. "I mean, on the one hand I feel *great*. Bembé delivered everything that I could have asked of him. I think the full impact of what just happened hasn't hit yet, but I think – I *hope* – that Frank is in for a tough couple of days at least. In my ideal world, I want to make sure that he's never given the chance to lord his influence over another grantee again. *Then* I'll be satisfied."

Angela reaches over and squeezes my hand. "What are you going to do about Book Club?"

I smile and turn to Dan. "Despite getting a very generous offer from the Bank of Dan Fischer's Retirement Fund," I begin. Dan smiles back softly. "I'm following up on several leads for additional loans. Which I guess is a long way of saying 'I don't know yet.'"

We finish our drinks, and I turn to Dan. "I'm ready to go home and take a long, loooooong hot shower," I say. "Are the kids at my parents' house?"

"Where else?" Dan asks.

We rise to leave. And walk directly into Frank's path.

He glances dismissively at Angela first. "You are fired. Leave at once."

She doesn't flinch. "I resigned last week."

Frank turns away from her and towards me.

"You are not welcome here," he says, his voice low.

"That's funny," I say loudly. "I think that's a phrase *you're* going to start hearing an awful lot yourself soon." I turn my back on him and exit the tent with Dan and Angela.

The three of us begin walking toward the racks of parked bicycles. I link my arm through Dan's as we approach my bike.

"Georgie!" Someone is yelling. *Now what?* Next to me, I feel Dan stiffen, preparing for battle if needed.

I turn around cautiously. It's Kyle, his lanky frame trotting across the parking lot, his face red.

I smile uneasily. "Hi, Kyle." I glance over to Angela, eyebrows raised. *Did he know in advance?* I silently ask her.

She shakes her head. "Plausible denial."

He stops and surveys the three of us. "Hey Dan, howareya," he says breathlessly, reaching out to shake his hand. Then he turns to me. "So, Georgie."

I hold up my hand. "Look, Kyle, I'm really sorry for putting you in a bad position," I begin. "I gave Bembé the video-"

"No, *I* did," Angela corrects.

"OK, *we* did," I say. "And I'm sorry. But listen, we gave it to him to do with what he wanted. No one forced him. Unlike what's been happening around here." I want to say more; I want to say so much more, but I sense it's time for me to listen. It's time for me to hear from someone else about what I've done.

Kyle waves his hand, dismissing my apology. "And he deserved it. I'm not here to, like, interrogate you or anything. I just have two quick questions."

"OK."

"First," Kyle breaks into a grin. "How awesome did that feel?"

I laugh. "I'm not gonna lie, Kyle," I say. "It felt pretty damn good." Angela nods vigorously. "What's your second question?"

"Lena is asking me to dig up that crisis communications plan you made," he says. "Can you tell me where you saved it?"

Chapter 19

"Hi everyone, I'm Georgie Fischer," I say to my phone's camera. A feeling of *déja vu* surfaces, and I remember that it was less than two weeks ago that I had recorded the same opening at Dee's as a finalist for the B♀ss grant.

"If you've found your way to my feed, you're either already a friend – in which case you already know my story – or you've seen *The Book Prophet*'s episode with Frank Hudson and are trying to figure out my story. Yes, I worked at Hudson Hotels. Yes, I was 'laid off' for pushing back on some marketing tactics that I thought were unethical, including lying about book sales and pressuring our grantees to write glowing reviews of Frank Hudson's book. And yes, Frank Hudson served on the selection committee for a grant that I was a finalist for, and threatened to kill my chances if I didn't agree to hand over ownership of my prospective business to him.

"Here's something I want to make clear right now. I don't know if Frank actually made good on his threat. And I don't *want* to know. I didn't get the grant, but another woman *did*, and I applaud her and wish her success. I exposed Frank to *expose Frank*, not to disparage the efforts of a great organization and the entrepreneurs they support. I hope you're all with me on that. Thanks for watching."

Dan stops the camera. "Is it OK?" I ask him.

He hands my phone back and smiles. "Better than OK. Helmet hair and all."

I flash him a quick smile and begin posting the new video to my social media feeds. We're standing in our driveway. I'm still clad in my biking gear, still tired, still hungry, and still coated in a fine layer of road grit. But this is something that couldn't wait.

We were halfway home when it hit me that the winner of the B♀ss grant would get drawn into whatever backlash from Bembé's interview is coming.

"Oh my God," I moaned, cradling my head in my hands. "I can't believe I didn't think of this earlier. She could get blindsided."

Dan glanced at me. "What are you worried about? It's not like they're going to revoke her grant."

"That's not the point," I said. "She's probably on cloud nine right now, as well she should be. I do *not* want to be responsible for taking any of that away. This wasn't about her, or even about B♀ss. Whatever comeuppance Frank has coming – and for I all know it could be just a few mean tweets – I don't want any of it raining on this other woman's party."

I finish uploading my message when my phone rings. I glance at the screen as I pass through my front door; it's not a number I recognize.

"Hello?"

"Hi…is this Georgie Fischer speaking?"

"Yes, I'm Georgie."

"This is Albert Frechette from the *Boston Globe*," he says. "I was at Hudson Hotel's *100 Revolutions* event today, and I'd like to ask you a few questions."

I sit down on the stairs that lead to the second floor, where my bathroom – and long overdue shower – await.

"Of course," I say.

Thank goodness you posted that video message just now, offers Gilda. *It was good practice.*

"A spokesperson for Hudson Hotels tells me that you were fired a few months ago for poor work performance and the interview was – quote – 'an ambush in retaliation,'" Frechette began. "How do you respond to that?"

I roll my eyes. *How original, Lena.* "As I remember it, I was shown the door an hour after I refused to falsify book sales or pressure grantees to write reviews. If that's 'poor work performance' then I stand by it," I said. "But that doesn't make what came out today any less true. As for the Book Prophet interview, I shared what I knew and what I experienced – both during my time at Hudson and when Frank Hudson threatened me just recently – with Mr. Jean-Baptiste. What he did with that information was his decision, not mine."

"What do you hope will come of all this? Are you David taking down Goliath?"

I can't help but chuckle at the comparison. "No. I'm not. I exposed a serious flaw in a man at the helm of a company that has done much good. Frank Hudson has a lot to be proud of, but that doesn't give him the right to threaten me, his grantees, or anyone else."

"Would you like to see him step down as head of Hudson Hotels?"

"That's not for me to say," I reply. "I'd like him to stop using his grants as leverage to advance his future as an author. But listen, the real hero here is Bembé Jean-Baptiste. He risked his livelihood today: his sponsors, his followers, and the willingness of other authors to be interviewed by him. This interview was not something he took lightly, and my sincere hope is that he is not negatively impacted by this."

"What about this BOss grant?" Frechette asks. "Are you taking any action against them?"

"No. None," I say. "And I hope their grantee has tremendous success." I sense the reporter waiting for me to say more. I stay silent. He thanks me for my time and we hang up.

Ten minutes later, warm water is coursing down my body. It is probably my favorite shower in the history of showers; it feels that amazing. My phone is resting on the vanity, filling the room with music. I'm scrubbing at a stubborn patch of bike grease on the back of my right calf with a washcloth laden with soap bubbles and singing along with Alanis Morissette when the song pauses and the phone dings briefly. A text, probably.

Another ding comes a few seconds later. And another. Soon there are more dings than Alanis. Then it starts to ring.

"And so it begins," I murmur, rinsing the last of the conditioner out of my hair.

But which is it? Gilda wonders. *The lady or the tiger?*

I deliberately wait until I'm dry, combed out, and dressed. If I'm going to get smacked around online, I want to at least be comfortable. I pull on my softest t-shirt and yoga pants and sit down on the bed, one leg tucked underneath.

I have four new voicemails from local radio and television news producers. They're all planning to air footage from my video outside Dee's, and would I be willing to speak on the record?

Yes. Yes I would.

I jot down their numbers and then open my YouTube app to Bembé's channel. The recording of the live streamed interview is up, named "The Business of Feeding An Ego." I look at the stats. It's been viewed more than 47,000 times in the last hour.

I switch over to social media. Frank, Hudson Hotels, and The Book Prophet are all trending on Twitter. With some trepidation, I call up my recent post. It has thousands of likes already, and the comments are piling up. There are a few indignant *how dare you, young lady*, but most are supportive.

"Georgie?" Dan calls up the stairs. "You should come down and see this."

I join Dan in the family room, where he's tuned the TV to a local news station. The reporter is standing outside the Hudson Hotel, recapping the revelations in Bembé's interview with Frank. The station airs a snippet from a phone call with an anonymous Hudson Foundation grantee, who confirms the "no review, no grant" condition.

"Mr. Hudson has declined to comment," the reporter says. "The only communication thus far has been via his Twitter account, in which he claims that Bembé Jean-Baptiste, a popular vlogger known as The Book Prophet, demanded to write a new foreword for Mr. Hudson's book, and was turned down."

Dan snorts. I smack my palm against my forehead. "Idiot. Put a little gas on this fire, why don't you?"

"I guess they didn't read your crisis communications plan," Dan says gleefully.

"How could they?" I tell him, grinning. "I deleted it."

"We'll be staying with this developing story as it unfolds," the reporter assures us.

My phone starts ringing again.

I turn to Dan. "This could be a long night," I tell him. "A long *and wonderful* night."

He smiles and shrugs. "I'll get us a pizza. With extra karma."

∞∞∞

By lunchtime the following day, Bembé's episode featuring Frank was viewed nearly half a million times, and The Book Prophet's followers increased from just over a million to nearly 1.4 million overnight. The video of Frank's extortion attempt outside of Dee's started popping up on social media, and pieces of it aired on every local TV and radio station's morning news; the coverage included snappy headlines like "Hudson Holds Grants Hostage" and "Billionaire Book Bust." News trucks staked out the Hudson Hotel headquarters waiting for a glimpse of Frank. Over the course of the day reporters and their camera crew took turns filming live updates standing "at the scene of all the drama" (as one reporter put it) in the garden.

I did seven phone interviews the night before, and two more on-camera for the news crews in the trucks that pulled up to my house in the morning. I stuck to the handful of messages I had expressed in my social media post. Yes, I felt the need to expose Frank's way of doing business. No, I have no intention of laying any blame on the people at BQss. I received a brief and carefully worded email from BQss's executive director assuring me that no single person on their grant committees has the power to reject a proposal. But of course they'd say that. I showed Dan the email and shrugged. He gave my phone the finger.

By the afternoon, reporters had shifted their focus and were now seeking out new people – both within Hudson Hotels and the nonprofits supported by Hudson Foundation grants – willing to speak publicly. Area business leaders, one by one, issued short statements disavowing Frank's approach to pushing his book. A statement released by the Attorney General's Office indicated that the top lawyer for the Commonwealth would be looking into the "no review, no grant" claims.

On social media, the video of Frank's threat outside Dee's was picked apart more finely than a well-boiled lobster. Hundreds of thousands of people zeroed in on his condescension toward women. One enterprising artist began advertising bumper stickers and women's t-shirts with "proud Lady Boss" printed on them. The hashtag "read more girl books" – to my delight – began trending. On Instagram, travelers staying at Hudson properties began sharing photos that portrayed the food in the least favorable light, all vying for the best "cheap breakfast buffet" or "short-order room service" memes.

"Can you believe this? My head is spinning," I say to Dan. "It's barely been 24 hours."

We're sitting on our deck, glued to our phones. I'm scanning the news sites and reading any new tidbits aloud to Dan, while also screening the calls and texts that are still coming in. He's keeping an eye on social media.

"Oh, hey," I say, scrolling with my index finger. "The folks at BQss – as well as a few other foundations that award grants – just announced that they're all banning Frank from current and future grant selection committees."

"Well, that was a given," Dan says. "Look at this one."

He turns his phone towards me and I lean forward. On the

253

screen is a photo of a guy standing outside a Hudson Hotel, holding a cardboard sign with 'will write good reviews for cheap breakfast buffet' written on it in black magic marker. I chuckle.

"Anything new from the folks at Hudson?" Dan asks.

I shake my head. "Nothing since the statement about Hudson Hotels's ongoing commitment to giving back to the community, yada yada yada. But they're holding a press conference tomorrow." I give Dan a wry smile. "Frank's own social media has gone silent. I think Lena may have taken away his phone after last night's tweet."

Dan rests his phone on the wide arm of his Adirondack chair and interlaces his fingers, stretching his arms forward. "What'll happen to the Foundation, do you think?"

"They'll be OK," I say. "Until Frank's demand for good reviews, everything about the Hudson Foundation has been above-board. The selection committees are made of staff and volunteers, and they're switched up every year. Frank wasn't really involved in the day to day of it."

"Until he realized it could impact book sales," Dan offers.

"Well, there's that."

"Will they force him to resign, you think?" Dan asks.

"No one can force him," I say. "Frank's in charge. It's not like it's a publicly held company."

"Even with this thing with the Attorney General?"

I consider his question. "I don't know. I suppose if there's enough public pressure, and it starts impacting hotel revenue instead of just book sales, he might have to."

My phone buzzes in my hand. "It's Dee," I tell Dan, then pick up.

"Hello?"

254

"Misogynistic blowhard?" Dee's laughter rings through my phone's tiny speaker. "How long were you holding onto that one before you could say it out loud?"

"About a year, year and a half," I tell her. "Did it sound too rehearsed?"

She laughs again. "That part was beautiful, but the rest was just awful. I hate knowing that he was here the night we made that video. He was threatening you while I was right inside, oblivious. I'm so sorry, hon."

"Not your fault, Dee."

"I saw you on Channel 5 this morning. You were really good. Calm, cool, and professional. Like a 'Boss,'" her voice is warm.

"Ouch," I laugh. "Too soon, Dee, too soon."

"How are you really, hon?"

"I'm fine," I say. "This has taken off faster than I could have imagined, and it all feels a little surreal right now, to be honest. But, I'm going to be OK, really."

I sit up in my seat, worried. "How are you, Dee? This hasn't blown back on you at all, has it?"

"Not a bit," she says, gaily. "It actually brought in a handful of new customers today to check the place out, so thank you very much."

"Well, happy to be of service," I say. "Listen, Dee. I'm not giving up here. If you're still in, then I'm still in." I glance over at Dan, he nods. "I will figure it out, and soon. I promise you."

"Well, it's funny you should say that, because that's what I wanted to talk to you about," Dee says, her tone suddenly becoming serious. "Any chance you can swing by the bar? We need to talk, and I'd rather do it in person."

∞∞∞

I pull up to Dee's, deliberately parking in the same spot where I stood the night Frank threatened to steal Book Club.

"I'm reclaiming this space," I say out loud, and then climb out of the car.

As I walk across the street, summoned by Dee, I'm reminded of the final walk from my cubicle into Lena's office to be summarily dismissed. Why did Dee get so serious all of a sudden? Why does she need to see me in person? My stomach tightens a little, in response to the possibilities flitting through my head.

Frank was right; she couldn't wait forever. I'm too late and she's accepted another offer.

She's not moving anymore, and is taking the bar off the market. In fact, her sister is now moving here *and they're going to rebrand it as Book Club.*

She's giving me the bar for free because she likes me that much.

I pull the door open and step inside. There's a modest Sunday evening after-dinner crowd. I scan the room while making my way to the bar, and recognize a few of the Thursday Night Hockey Moms from the night I filmed my final pitch to B♀ss. One of them catches my eye and smiles.

Dee is at the far end of the bar, leaning against its interior island and chatting with a group of six or seven women filling the stools along the width. When she sees me, she straightens up, excuses herself and gestures for me to meet her at the opposite end. The *quieter* end, I note. She's wearing a small smile, but her eyes give nothing away. I sit down, my back to the rest of the room.

"Buy you one?" Dee asks me.

"Seltzer with lime, thanks," I tell her. "I'm still rehydrating."

"That's right," she says, pouring my drink. "In your sly

256

takedown of Goliath, I'd forgotten about the ride. How was it?"

"Kind of like childbirth," I say. "During the last hour of the ordeal, I swore up and down I'd never do it again."

"And it hurts to sit the next day," Dee points out.

"That too," I say.

We appraise each other in silence for a few seconds, then Dee speaks.

"Look, Georgie," Dee begins. "It's unfair as hell about the grant. I know this last week has been shit for you, and I'm sorry about that, but I need to take the next step in my own life, too. If I could knock down the price for you, I would. But I just can't. We need to have an honest conversation about how we're both going to move forward here. Can we do that? Right now?"

Nodding, I try to reassure her. "I'd never ask you to lower the price we agreed on, Dee. Like I said on the phone, I've got some backup plans that I'm working on. Dan and I–" Dee stops me.

"I didn't know you had a backup, so I went with my backup," she says. "I need to show you something. OK?"

I try to take a sip of my water, but my throat clicks shut. Dee is looking at me, expectantly. I nod.

She wipes down the bar top in front of me with a Red Sox bar towel and pulls a laptop from underneath the bar.

Wow, Gilda says. *Someone's ready to talk business.* The knot in my stomach cinches tighter.

Dee's face is bathed in the light of her screen, eyes downcast. *Reading her crystal ball to tell you your future.*

"The grant would have been 50K, right?" Dee asks me over the edge of her laptop.

"Yep," I reply, deciding not to add the bit about the extra fifteen thousand or so I'd be pulling from my own savings.

"Well," she says, turning the computer around to face me. "Would this help?"

I peer at the screen. At the top is an image of 30 or so people gathered around the bar, cheering. I'm in the middle, with Dee. It's a screenshot of the group shouting "WE WANT BOOK CLUB!" In fact, the phrase itself is the title of the page.

What is *this?*

It's a fundraising site, you idiot, Gilda says, not unkindly.

It *is* a fundraising site. Before I can take it all in, my eyes dart to the total.

$74,675.

I look up at Dee, my mouth open. She's smiling, this time with her eyes as well.

"What the– how?" I stammer.

I look back at the site. The whole story is there. The video pitch I submitted to BǪss, Frank's attempted sabotage, and his unmasking during Bembé's interview.

"Did you do this?" I ask. "When did you do this?"

Dee beckons to someone over my shoulder. I turn, and there they are. *My* book club. They rush in and take turns embracing me, all talking and laughing at once. I'm crying, leaking tears of disbelief and gratitude.

"I made most of the site the day before the ride," Tess says. "It went live last night as soon as I could get Bembé's piece of it."

"And I shared the crap out of it," adds Nora.

Natalie hugs me again. "We all did."

"How did I not hear about this?" I say. "I've been on my phone literally all day."

"That's the beauty of the internet, my dear," Jules says. "We can share amongst all kinds of private groups and you're none the wiser."

I place my palms on my flushed face. I can't stop smiling.

"And, G., love," Jules says. "I know your electrolytes are a little low, so I taught Dee here how to make you a Miranda."

"Hydration is overrated," Dee says, winking over the martini glass. Its filled to the brim with the gin, grapefruit juice and rosemary simple syrup concoction I tinkered with at bartending class

I accept it gratefully. We toast, and then I'm drawn back to the website.

"I can't believe this," I say, scrolling through the donations. "Who *are* all these people? How is this much money even possible in, like, a day?"

"Are you kidding?" Nora says. "There are millions of women out there, and they're all pissed off at Frank right now. It adds up."

"Actually, some of them are the new customers I mentioned on the phone earlier," Dee adds. "I may have offered a free round to people if they chipped in to the fundraiser and brought their donation receipt here." She turns to the group of women I saw her talking with when I first entered.

"Hey, friends," Dee calls to them. "Come here and introduce yourselves."

The women walk down, each of them shaking my hand. One is a designer, another an electrician. An athletic-looking brunette owns her own general contracting firm. A cheerful grandmotherly woman declares herself a freelance book-keeper. They are all women in business, here to support me. I decide then and there that I'll support *them.* My new venture

259

will need people with their skills.

"What else do you have in store for me tonight?" I ask Jules, after collecting the names and numbers of Dee's customers. "Is Dan coming, too?" I look over to the door, suddenly sure he's there.

"Nah," Jules says, raising her glass. "This is Book Club."

Chapter 20

The early November evening is fully dark, carrying a hint of autumnal warmth. I stand outside, clad in the green wrap dress that I've come to think of as lucky, and look up at the unlit sign. I take a deep breath, and glance inside the front door.

"OK, turn it on!"

Erin, Dee's former hostess and occasional backup bartender, gives me a thumbs up. With a glowing reference from Dee, and a recently completed associate degree in business management she earned between shifts, Erin was my first official hire – a promotion to manager. She flips a switch from inside, and the quartet of elegant gooseneck lamps illuminates the sign in a warm, soft glow.

Book Club is etched into the otherwise smooth expanse of polished wood. The letters are painted a shiny gold, perfectly bathed in the lamplight. I exhale and bring one hand to my mouth, lump forming in my throat.

Keep it together for the guests tonight, will you? Gilda chides gently.

Beside me, Dan reaches for my free hand and gives it a squeeze. I turn to face him, and catch him wiping at a tear leaking rebelliously from his left eye.

I laugh. "Oh my God, Dan."

"Shut up," he says, laughing gruffly in return. "I'm just really, really proud of you. And it's allergy season." We grin at each other.

"It looks really good, Mom," says Shannon from my other side. "I like the gold."

"Thank you, honey," I say. "You were a huge help in picking the color. You can take all the credit for it." She beams back at me.

I turn to Max, flanking Dan's left. "What do you think, Max? Max?"

He looks up from his phone, where he's been surreptitiously playing a Godzilla-themed trivia quiz. "What? Oh, it's great, Mom. Can I go back inside?"

I nod and he jogs through the door. Authentic, wonderful Max. I glance at my watch, ten minutes to go. "Let's go in with him; people will be arriving any minute."

Dan holds the door open for Shannon and me just as a car pulls up. I recognize Dee's red vintage VW Beetle and motion for them to go in without me. Dee climbs out of her car, looking smart in black velvet palazzo pants and a silvery, long sleeved v-neck top. Her long hair is free from its usual braid, flowing in waves down her back.

"You look gorgeous," I say, as the passenger door of Dee's car clicks open. Unfolding from the tiny interior is a near copy of Dee herself, dressed in identical black pants and a chiffon blouse in a deep, rich plum. Her own silver hair is layered and short, its light color showing off the sea of freckles on her tanned face.

The two women join me on the sidewalk, and Dee greets

me with a hug. "Georgie, this is Nicole, my sister."

I begin to extend my hand, but Nicole waves it away with a light laugh and embraces me as warmly as her sister just did. She pulls away after a few moments and pats my cheek with affection.

"It's lovely to meet the woman who's bringing my sister back to me," Nicole says, a southern lilt in her voice. "And I know you encouraged guests tonight to help stock your library," she adds, reaching into her shoulder bag and pulling out a paperback copy of *The Prince of Tides*. "I brought one to help you think of us in South Carolina."

I accept it with gratitude and turn back to Dee. "Let's walk in together. It would mean a lot to me." Linking arms, we enter.

The footprint of Dee's is the same, but the space itself has been transformed. The walls above the wood wainscoting are painted an iridescent pearl that subtly reflects the light. Framed posters of iconic chick flicks – from *Thelma and Louise* to *Bridget Jones' Diary* – hang throughout, along with photos of legendary women of literature, entertainment, journalism, politics, and yes, sports.

"Oh…" Dee breathes, a hand on her chest. "It's just beautiful, Georgie. It's…it's Book Club, isn't it? You *did* it."

For the next hour, I weave through the growing crowd of friends and family, accepting their praise, well wishes, and books. The shelves in the library alcove fill quickly. There are novels made famous through screen adaptations, guilty pleasure beach reads, decades-old classics, and everything in between. The waitstaff – some new, and some who have stayed on from Dee's – travel between the circles of guests, offering trays bearing bite-sized samples from Book Club's appetizer menu.

Dan taps my shoulder as I'm chatting with Angela, who's filling in my parents and me on her new, Frank-free job in Boston. "It's time," he says.

I walk over to the far side of the room and climb the three steps to the small stage, a wireless stick microphone in my hand. "Hello, everyone," I begin. One by one, the people I love pause their conversations and drift towards me. "I want to thank you all, so much, for coming to the opening night of Book Club."

Jules, front and center, hoots and starts clapping. The rest of the crowd joins in. The lump forms once again in my throat.

"Six months ago," I begin, and my voice hitches. I steady it with a deep breath and start again. "Six months ago, I was in a very, very different place from where I am now, both literally and figuratively. And I have to say, the vantage point now is *much* better than it was then."

More applause.

"I would never have made it here without the people in this room tonight; without the love and support of Dan, the always-wise counsel of my mom and dad, the immeasurable patience of Dee, or the loyalty and resourcefulness of my beloved book club – my *original* book club. You lifted me up, cheered me on, and best of all, *you let me be me*. And because of that, women have a place to go where they can be themselves. I love you all so much. From the bottom of my heart, thank you. Now, the Mirandas are on me!"

I descend the stage stairs to cheers and am circled by Jules, Nora, Natalie, and Tess. We come together in a group hug.

"I love you, Book Club," I tell them.

"We love you back, G, and then some," says Jules, kissing my cheek.

"Hey, I've been meaning to ask you tonight," Tess says. "Why did you put a picture of Gilda Radnor on the Women's Room door?"

∞∞∞

"See you at 11?" Dan asks, walking me to the front door.

"Yep," I say, shrugging on my down vest. I hate driving in a heavy coat. "Will you be up?"

"That depends," he replies, a familiar glint in his eyes. "Would *you* be up for me to be up?"

I kiss him and open the door. "I will most definitely see you at 11."

"Have fun at Book Club!" Dan calls when I'm a few steps away.

I turn back to him, smiling. "Never gets old."

The evening is beautiful. Cold, for sure. But considering it's December, I guess that's to be expected. The air is crisp and light on my skin. My breath is visible, creating small puffs during the short walk from the house to the car. Watching the exhalation, I'm suddenly reminded of Frank and his cigar.

I wonder if he's had any cause to celebrate with a stogie lately.

Frank hadn't pushed back when area bookstores stopped selling *Giving it Away*. The hotels quietly removed the posters touting the book from its lobbies and elevators, and toned down its presence on the Hudson website. He appeared on camera as grudgingly contrite when the Attorney General reprimanded the foundation, prompting Frank and Lena to publicly announce new guidelines that would sever any conditions between grant funding and his book.

But he held on bitterly to the helm of the company following *100 Revolutions.* According to Kyle, Frank was convinced it would all blow over. It became clear, however, that people weren't having it. Reservations took a nosedive. A prominent woman-owned company pulled out of the conference that had been booked at a Hudson Hotel, prompting a few other businesses and trade associations to follow suit. By Thanksgiving, after seeing the writing on the wall – and the shrinking revenue on the balance sheets – Frank "retired."

Retired, sure. And I was "laid off."

I pull into a free space on the street and step out of my car. In the month since Book Club's opening night, the walk to the door never fails to bring me a rush of joy. *This is my place,* I think as I reach for the handle. *Mine.* I pull open the door and pause, taking it all in.

The evening dinner crowd tonight is sizable but mellow, which was the vibe I was shooting for on Sundays. Some people are chatting quietly at their tables, others are focused on the flatscreen TVs – tuned in to the Hallmark Channel, as I had once promised Tess – and listening through the wireless speakers that have been incorporated into the table centerpieces.

I wave to individuals on my staff and have a brief check in with Erin before making my way behind the bar, where I stash my bag and turn to relieve one of my Sunday afternoon bartenders.

"How's it been today, Dad?"

He dries his hands on a towel and shakes his head. "These movies are killing me, Georgie," he says. "New rule: I don't tend bar in December."

"Oh, come on, Colin," says Natalie, who's sitting at the bar with Tess. "I was just about to confess to Tess that she was right about the Hallmark Christmas movies."

"Is this the one where a big city executive gets stuck in a small town and falls for a local craftsman," I ask, refilling the glasses of cabernet in front of them. "Or is it the one where a big city executive gets stuck in a small town and falls for a local youth group director?"

"That's my cue," says my dad, waving. "Good night."

I spent the next few minutes fulfilling orders for drinks, then return to my friends.

"How was the weekend?" Natalie asks. Tess is glued to the movie.

"It was so great," I say. "Busy, but great. Those hockey moms can *dance*. And I confirmed with the author of that new mystery; she's doing a reading here in a few weeks. We'll have book club at Book Club." I glance at my Fitbit, which is no longer a toy for Shannon while on the trampoline. "I swear I don't think I've covered fewer than 15,000 steps a day since I signed the papers."

"Oh hey, I wanted to ask you something," Natalie says. "The other vets had a blast at the Trivia Night last week. We were thinking of organizing one as a fundraiser for the animal shelter we volunteer at. Could we have it here sometime in January?"

"Of course," I say. "Let's talk about this coming week, OK? January's starting to look pretty full for events, but there's definitely room. Speaking of January, are you coming with Tess and Nora to New Year's in London? We're almost sold out."

Hearing her name, Tess shifts her focus from the movie to

267

us. "I hadn't told her yet, but yes, Nat, come with us."

"What's New Year's in London?"

I smile. "It's our New Year's Eve party for parents. We start at five, toast the New Year at seven – when it's midnight in London – and then they can go celebrate the actual new year at home without feeling lame or spending $200 on a sitter."

"That is *brilliant*," Natalie shakes her head. "You're so good at this, Georgie."

I mock curtsy and move a few places down to take a drink order from two women returning from the restroom.

One of them looks at me. "I have never seen a women's bathroom so huge in my entire life," she says, approvingly.

"It has to be, doesn't it?" I ask with a wink as I pull them each a pint of cider. "We all go together, anyway."

On the TV, a pretty blonde in a chic Burberry coat kisses a redheaded man with a flannel shirt and five o'clock shadow. In a light snow. The movie's end credits begin scrolling over the screen.

"OK," Tess sighs and stands up from her stool. "That's *my* cue to go. C'mon Nat."

Natalie blows me a kiss. "You might find us here next Sunday, too. They're showing a new movie featuring my high school Hollywood crush."

"You know he's probably playing the leading lady's dad, right?" I ask. She gives me her middle finger in response.

I'm laughing when the front door opens and a woman walks in.

It's Lena.

∞∞∞

Our eyes lock right away. She breaks contact first and turns her gaze around the room, lingering over the lending library's bookshelf.

Don't bother looking for Frank's book.

Lena waves the hostess away with a small smile and points to the bar. She approaches casually, taking off her coat and draping it over the back of an empty stool before sitting. Just another woman out for a peaceful drink.

"Hi, Lena," I say evenly. "What can I get you?"

Over Lena's shoulder, Natalie raises her eyebrows. *You OK?* She mouths. I smile at her and nod, giving them both a quick wave goodbye.

Lena skims the cocktail menu before choosing the vodka, coconut water, and pineapple juice concoction I made during my bartending course. I named it the "Sarah Marshall," a nod to Kristen Bell in Hawaii.

I set about making it, giving her another glance. She looks tired. Her chestnut bob isn't as shiny or sleek. Her face is pinched, her foundation a little too heavy under her eyes. There's something else about her that seems different that I can't place at first, then I realize it's her burnt orange sweater. I've only ever seen her in white or navy.

It's like seeing your teacher outside of school.

I pour the cocktail into a martini glass and place it in front of her. She takes a sip from her glass, sets it down daintily and looks around again. "The place looks nice, Georgie," she says.

"Thank you. I'm enjoying it."

"It must be hard work," Lena says. "A lot of places like this don't survive the first year."

I roll my eyes at my former boss. "Try not to live up to all my expectations, Lena. What do you want?" I ask. "This can't be a social call."

Her fingers play with the stem of the glass. "I wanted to let you know that I had nothing to do with your grant. Or the threat."

"*Frank's* threat, you mean," I state.

She sips again and nods.

I lean against the island behind the bar and fold my arms. "I never thought you did."

"I was just as surprised as you were," she adds.

"Well, that can't be true," I say. "You know Frank. The *real* Frank. I can buy that you didn't know he came here that night to blackmail me, but don't tell me you were surprised. For Christ's sake, Lena, you're the one who told him about my idea. You've spent your entire career enabling him, all while making sure he never listened to anyone but you."

Her eyes flick away briefly, then her shoulders sag just a little. The change is nearly imperceptible, but in other ways, it's huge.

"It's not that simple," she says.

"Explain it to me, then," I say.

She shrugs slightly. "At first the things he was asking were small, like rounding up the revenue a little too much in a press release. By the time it occurred to me to start saying no, I had been saying yes for so long that it was too late to change."

"So 'if you can't beat 'em, join 'em,' is that it?" I ask. "Because from where I stood, Lena, you were squarely in his corner. When you weren't in your own, that is."

She looks back up at me. "Well, I saw what happened to the people who pushed back too strongly. You weren't the first."

I smile. "But I *was* the last."

She smiles back, weakly. A concession, perhaps. I feel myself soften a little.

"How are things at the hotel now, Lena?"

"Great," she says, a little too quickly. She fidgets in her seat for a few seconds. "It's better, at least. There's a new chairman in place. And she's bringing in a Vice President for Communications, so I'm getting a new boss. If they decide to keep me on, that is." She swirls a piece of skewered pineapple around in the liquid and pops it into her mouth neatly. "Things have slowed down, finally. It was really rough there for a while. I wasn't sure if the place was going to make it." She looks at me, presumably for my reaction.

I consider what I think she wants to hear. That I'm sorry she's had to scramble for the last few months? That I regret my role in exposing the shit that Frank pulled and she allowed?

Dream on, Sweetheart.

"I'm not going to apologize, Lena, if that's what you're after," I say finally. "Frank did what he did, and you stood by and watched. Actually, no," I correct myself. "You stood by and made lists of who complied with his order to write a book review and who didn't. And then you dangled their grant under a guillotine if they didn't give in."

"And then *you* gave at least one of those lists to The Book Prophet," she says, eyes flaring. "Tell me, have you talked to Bembé since the two of you took Frank down?"

I had, in fact, seen Bembé recently. He showed up to Book Club's first Trivia Night, taking selfies with me and a few other guests and sharing them on his social media feed.

"Thank you, Bembé," I told him that night. "Thank you for coming, and for *everything*. I wouldn't be here, right now, if it wasn't for you."

He clinked his glass against mine in a private toast. "You

would have found a way, Georgie," he said. Then he flashed me a conspiratorial grin. "But the route we took was much more satisfying."

Now, I look at Lena steadily. "Frank took himself down."

She glances away, muttering something under her breath. I don't know what it was, and I don't care. She isn't here to make amends with me; she came to spit shine her conscience by swearing ignorance of Frank's threat, and perhaps try to drag some kind of pity-apology out of me by playing the victim.

You don't get to bully me. Not anymore. And definitely *not in my own place.*

"I've got customers to attend to, Lena," I say. "Is there anything else? Want to reserve a spot for the Girls' Night Out we're hosting here on Valentine's Day?"

She shakes her head and slides off her stool. "I think we're done," she says, slinging her purse over her shoulder and picking up her coat.

I chuckle quietly. "I don't think so," I say.

She places a hand on her hip, annoyed. "What, then?"

I print out her tab and slide it over to her. "For the drink. Have to make sure I survive the year after all."

She stuffs some bills into the small leather folder and stalks out. I remove her glass and wipe the bar clean, grinning. On the TVs, a new Christmas romance is playing. A member of my waitstaff requests four cosmopolitans. As I pour the liquid – the perfect shade of deep pink – into the glasses, a group of five women in their early 30s enter. They're laughing conspiratorially in the wholly comfortable way of longtime friends.

"Good evening," I call to them, my voice silky with contentment. "Welcome to Book Club."

∞∞∞

Epilogue

Six weeks later

"Max," I gently shake my almost-teenaged son, who's currently buried under his thick forest green comforter. "Time to get up."

He stretches sleepily before sitting up. The room is still bathed in December darkness.

"Cover your eyes," I tell him. "I'm turning on the light."

Now that I can see, I place his prescription pill and a small glass of orange juice on his dresser, just in front of the newest addition to Max's Godzilla collection.

"It looks like Gigan is about to attack the glass," Max says, his voice light with amusement.

"If he does, he pays for it," I say. "Get dressed and come downstairs for pancakes. Want plain or blueberry?"

"Plain."

"OK. And long sleeves this time, please. Maybe even a sweater. It's cold."

"NO SWEATER," Max calls as I descend the stairs.

Downstairs, the smell of pancakes wafts from the kitchen. Shannon is sitting at the breakfast bar drizzling maple syrup in a chevron pattern over her stack. Her hair is tied back in a neat half-up, half-down. It is, she informed me importantly, the preferred style of the older dancers at her studio. Her other hand is splayed over an open copy of Misty Copeland's memoir.

"The king is awake," I announce to Dan, who's standing

at the stove, his hair still damp from the shower. "And has requested plain pancakes." He gives me a mock salute and puts a fresh pat of butter on the hot pan.

I retrieve my still-full coffee cup from the counter, sit down on the stool opposite Shannon and catch her eye. "How many days until Christmas vacation?" I ask her, warming my hands on the mug.

She smiles. "Five. Well, technically four and a half, but getting up is the hardest part so I'm counting it as one."

"Are you excited for Christmas?" I say.

She nods, and then looks at me. "Are we still going shopping when I get home from school? I need a present for Max and dad."

"You're getting one present for the both of us?" Dan asks, feigning disbelief.

"I wasn't, but that's a good idea," she shoots back. "Thanks."

Dan shakes Max's pancakes from the spatula to the plate and gives Shannon an appraising look. "That was funny," he says, pointing the spatula at her. "And quick. I'm impressed." She looks down, hiding her smile.

Dan and I exchange a look; it's our *she's growing up* look.

Max rounds the corner and enters the kitchen, clad in long sleeves, thank goodness. "Who's buying presents?"

I yield my stool to Max and stand, leaning against the sink. "Me and Shannon. Christmas shopping."

"Can I come?"

"Not if we're buying presents for *you*," I say, tousling his hair. "You and I are going tomorrow."

"Hey mom, if we won the lottery, could we go skiing over Christmas?" Max asks, taking a huge bite of his food.

"Yes," I say definitively. "We'd have a limo drive us to New

Hampshire, and stay in the largest, nicest room in the Mount Washington Hotel."

"Two rooms," Shannon insists. "With connecting doors."

"Done. And we'd have the limo drop us off and pick us up at the ski slope," I add.

"Ski slope?" Dan asks me incredulously. "No. We're going cross country skiing."

"Booo-riiiiing," Max drawls. Shannon makes gagging sounds in her throat.

Dan looks at me solemnly. "I've failed as a father."

"At least you're not being too hard on yourself," I say. I think about our current lottery fantasy for a few seconds. "But, it kinda sounds like fun, doesn't it?"

"What does?" Dan asks. "Skiing over Christmas?"

I shake my head. "During February break. Nothing major, just a couple of days. If we rent a condo we could eat in and not blow a ton of money on restaurants."

He makes a show of giving me the same approving look he gave Shannon a few minutes earlier. "That's a good idea," he says, once again pointing with the spatula. "I'm impressed."

"I'll just have to see if my boss will give me the time off," I begin. "Oh, wait! I don't *have* a boss anymore!" We high-five, smiling, then I glance at the stovetop's clock.

"OK, family," I say, clapping my hands twice. "Daddy, you finish getting dressed. Max and Shannon, eat up and then get your shoes and coats. You're out the door in ten minutes."

Within a few minutes they scatter, leaving me alone in the kitchen. I set about making their lunches, laying the bread, cold cuts, fruit, and juice boxes on the counter. Turkey and cheese for Shannon and Max, a glass container filled with leftover beef stroganoff for Dan. I slip the kids' lunches into their backpacks and place their hats and gloves neatly on top. I double-check the seal on Dan's lunch and slide it into his messenger bag.

I walk Dan and the kids to the front door. Now that Mondays are one of my regular days at home, Dan has started heading to the office early, and riding an earlier train home. The three of them step outside into the brightening winter morning and head down the hill to the school bus stop. From there, Dan will walk another half mile to the train. The holly bush is awash in bright red berries. The air is crisp with the promise of future snow. Something to look forward to; shoveling counts as exercise, doesn't it?

I close the door and pause, enjoying the quiet. It's nearly seven-thirty; I'm still in my fleece pajama bottoms and my tattered Provincetown sweatshirt, and there's no reason to change for at least another hour. Maybe two. It's nearly Christmas, after all.

Pouring myself a second cup of coffee, I pad into the family room and curl up on the sofa with my laptop. The screen flickers to life. I spend the next hour working, responding to a few emails from staff about shifts and inventory, answering questions posted to Book Club's social media pages, and replying with thanks to the people who have posted online reviews – voluntarily, of course. I accept a request to be interviewed by a lifestyle magazine in Boston, thrilled by its potential to spotlight Book Club to hundreds of thousands of women readers.

Finally, I approve a proposal from Erin to open early on a Saturday next spring and serve a champagne breakfast while diners watch a royal wedding live, and then shift my focus from work to family. I begin searching for available condo rentals near ski slopes in February. We won't be driven there in a limo, and we won't be staying in the largest and nicest connecting rooms in the Mount Washington Hotel.

But then again, it won't be a fantasy, either.

Perfect.

About the Author

Kerry Crisley is a nonprofit communications industry professional, including a combined 18 years at with The Nature Conservancy, Boston Bar Association and Acera: The
Massachusetts School of Science, Creativity and Leadership.
Fiction, however, is her first love; she wrote and directed an
original play performed by her second grade classmates, and
has been writing ever since. She lives in Massachusetts with
her husband, children, and (very spoiled) rescue dog. When
not at work, Kerry can usually be found reading, hiking, or
getting into a wide variety of shenanigans with her book club.
Summer of Georgie is her first novel.

You can connect with me on:

🐦 https://twitter.com/ KerryCrisley

lazysundaybooks.com

Made in the USA
Monee, IL
12 May 2023